Diary of a Somebody

Brian Bilston

Diary of a Somebody

PICADOR

First published 2019 by Picador
an imprint of Pan Macmillan
20 New Wharf Road, London N1 9RR
Associated companies throughout the world
www.panmacmillan.com

ISBN 978-1-5290-0554-7 HB
ISBN 978-1-5290-0555-4 TPB

1 3 5 7 9 8 6 4 2

A CIP catalogue record for this book is available from the British Library.

Interior design by Ambar Galán
Printed and bound by CPI Group (UK) Ltd, Croydon, CR0 4YY

Visit **www.picador.com** to read more about all our books
and to buy them. You will also find features, author interviews and
news of any author events, and you can sign up for e-newsletters
so that you're always first to hear about our new releases.

January

Monday January 1st

....

My Resolution Will Not Be Televised

You will not be able to discover it from your sofa, brother.
You will not be able to sit there under the cat, sister,
remote control in one hand, phone in the other,
and put the kettle on during the ad breaks,
because my resolution will not be televised.

My resolution will not be tweeted.
My resolution will not be announced on Twitter.com
in 280 characters of self-promoting concision
to be retweeted by Ricky Gervais in between posts
deploring acts of animal cruelty and the release date of his latest film.
My resolution will not be tweeted.
My resolution will not be televised.

My resolution will not be Facebooked.
My resolution will not feature next to an inspirational quote
set against the backdrop of a soaring mountain or a looking-glass lake.
My resolution will not be posted beside a shining infographic
illustrating how many kilos I have lost, how many pennies
I have saved, how many drinks I have not drunk.
My resolution will not be Facebooked.
My resolution will not be tweeted.
My resolution will not be televised.

There will be no pictures on Instagram
of kale soup and black bean–quinoa salad.
There will be no pictures on Instagram
of NutriBullet breakfast smoothies.
My resolution will not be vlogged.

My progress will not be revealed to you in a twenty-minute daily video diary.
My resolution will not be right back after a message
about my new range of eyebrow pencils.

My resolution will not be vlogged.
There will be no pictures on Instagram.
My resolution will not be Facebooked.
My resolution will not be tweeted.
My resolution will not be televised.

My resolution will not survive more than two days.
My resolution will not be televised.

....

My resolution will be *diarised*. I shall write a poem a day. It will be a daily testament to the power of poetry and how it can help us make sense of the world. A kind of inky monument to Truth and Beauty.

I shall set my poems down here: in this surprisingly affordable medium-ruled notebook with acid-free pages, rounded corners and expandable inner pocket, with its cover illustration of an anthropomorphised white Japanese bobtail cat sporting a red bow.

I do not underestimate the task ahead. Writing a poem every day will not be easy. It will require discipline. Mental resilience. Self-sacrifice. Vast reservoirs of imagination. And a ready supply of custard creams.

Tuesday January 2nd

I lay in bed until mid-day, bathing in the cotton sea of tranquillity that is my duvet. Inspired by my surroundings, I attempted a poem. I got as far as:

> Duvet,
> you are so groovet,
> I'd like to stay under you
> all of Tuesdet.

I didn't care for it much. The rhymes seemed a little forced. I worked on it for a while longer but produced nothing more of note, except for a doodle of a cat on a skateboard. I was quite pleased with that. The cat was wearing headphones and I'd drawn a speech bubble coming out of its mouth with the words "I AM A CAT ON A SKATEBOARD!" written inside it.

I am forty-five years old.

I wondered whether it was my working conditions that were the problem. It is unnaturally quiet. This is partially explained by the temporary absence of students next door, whose general rowdiness frequently serves to keep me awake most of the night and disturb me for much of the day. By contrast, Mrs McNulty, on the other side, is typically as quiet as a pea, except for the occasional sounds of sawing and her Wednesday night séances.

In the hope that a change of scenery might help, I got up to press on with the rearrangement of my bookshelves. This year, I've decided to re-order by International Standard Book Number. I went at it tenaciously and must have lost track of the hours. It was time for bed and I'd still only got as far as *Little Dorrit* (or 0192545124 as I have now come to think of it).

It was only then that I remembered my New Year's resolution. I took another look at my duvet poem. Would that do? Probably not, I decided. My cat doodle also seemed less impressive now. It looked more like a dog. A dog on a trolley.

Two days! That's all it has taken for my resolution to be smashed on the craggy, unforgiving rocks of my literary negligence. All in all, this constitutes one of my better efforts of recent years.

Wednesday January 3rd

....

I would like to apologise for the delay

I would like to apologise for the delay
in coming to work today.
This is due to a signalling failure
between my primary motor cortex and pyramidal motor pathway.
I shall remain here instead,
sidelined in this bed,
until further notice.

I would like to apologise for the delay
in going for a run today.
This is due to leaves on the tracksuit
I wore last week,
during my unsuccessful attempt to bury myself
in a coppiced wood.
I would be there still, if I could.

I would like to apologise for the delay
in joining your skiing holiday.

This is due to the wrong kind of snow,
which, as far as I'm concerned, is *any* kind of snow
that enables people
to hurtle down slopes, at speed,
on skis.

I would like to apologise for the delay
in taking part in life today.
This is due to delays.

....

I would like to apologise for the delay in getting to work today. This is due to writing a poem. Thankfully, Janice is not back until next week so she wasn't there to see me slip into my officle ninety minutes late.

Even at the best of times, my officle presents a distressingly joyless sight; not quite office, not quite cubicle, it exists in a permanent state of beige and bewildered irresolution. But there are few sights as depressing as my officle on the first day back after the Christmas break: tinsel droops around my PC monitor; an uninspired Secret Santa gift (yet another pine-scented candle!) sits on top of my in-tray, jilted at the altar of my ingratitude; abandoned corporate Christmas cards silently reproach me from the flimsy wall panels.

With the aid of a mid-morning Twix, I attempted to coax my brain into thinking about the report I'm supposed to be putting together for Janice. It has the working title of "Re-solutioning the Brand: from Customer Dissension to Retention". I have yet to start it, mainly for the reason that I don't really know what it means. Staring out through my officle window into the midwinter bleakness, I pictured Janice skiing down the slopes at Kitzbühel, the snow gleaming like powdered champagne.

Thursday January 4th

I wasn't in the mood for poetry today. I think it's all this work business. Larkin may have had his library stamp and Bukowski his mailbags but it strikes me that proper work is unconducive to the creation of poetry. It's not easy to elevate yourself to a higher plane when your mind is being laid siege to by flipcharts and pivot tables.

The cat doesn't help either. She is my furry straitjacket. Every time I sit down with the intention of writing, she sees this as her cue to lie on top of me and pin my arms down. My writing speed reduces to five words per minute; by the time I've physically managed to write a line, all previously imagined words and ideas have oozed from my brain like custard through a cattle-grid.

I cracked on with some more ISBNs instead. The project was proceeding apace and my bookshelves were beginning to look pleasingly resystematised.

Until, that is, I came to 1903436419.

I had all but forgotten it. Tentatively, I peeked inside. And, yes, there was the familiar spidery scrawl of Sophie's writing, in the margins, next to my own. The love-notes we passed to each other in the back of a lecture hall, lifetimes ago, years before it all went wrong.

Friday January 5th

Everyday is like bin day
Everyday recycled and grey

It's the first bin day of the new year: general landfill. I made sure my lilac sacks were securely tied and primed the night before and my alarm clock set so I might rise in good time to minimise potential mishap. The Man at Number 29 had clearly taken no such precautions given his frantic bag-handed dash down the street in futile pursuit of the lorry.

> Trudging slowly through the wet streets
> back to the house where your bins weren't emptied.
> And all the bags you found
> that you forgot to put out, Armageddon,
> come Armageddon, come Armageddon, come.

Any feelings of residential primacy were short-lived. Dave, Martin and Marvin were unloading items for the new term from their VW Beetle when I returned from work. These included a seven-piece drum-kit (Dave is an acoustic engineering student), a Moog modular synthesizer (Martin is a music technology student) and a life-size anatomical skeleton (Marvin is a sociology student but one with a rather peculiar fetish for medical supplies and equipment). They high-fived me as they headed in next door.

I went into my own house, which was still in something of a state from last night. There were books all over the sitting-room floor and my Morrissey singles lay scattered as if someone had summoned a nuclear bomb.

Saturday January 6th

....

Anthem for Doomed Christmas Trees

What passing bells for trees who lie in gutters?
Only the monstrous rumble of the vans
will drown out their silent cries. No muttered
prayers, no roadside eulogies or thanks.

Doorstep-dumped, no longer spruce,
who now will pine for you and cry?
Unbaubled, untinseled, stripped of use,
off to the Great Wood Chipper in the Sky;

How long has it been – two or three weeks? –
since we laid out our gifts at your feet?
How quickly the present becomes the past
and time sweeps all needles from its path.

....

I dumped my tree on the pile at the edge of the park and returned
to find Sophie waiting outside my house with Dylan. She rarely
says a word directly to me these days, preferring instead to com-
municate through a combination of hand gestures and glowers.
She handed him over to me with a look that clearly meant: *return
him to me in one piece or you'll be the next to have your baubles
removed.*

We headed off to football, where important father–son bond-
ing takes place over unfailingly inclement weather, volleys of
verbal abuse from opposition parents, and humiliating, life-scar-
ring defeats. Today's trouncing is a respectable 0–8. Dylan,
isolated on the wing, just stood on the touchline for most of the
game, shivering. Rob Trafford, the Under 16s' beleaguered and

chronically inept manager, declared it to be 'a season-defining performance'. It was hard to disagree with him.

We arrived back home to the ominous signs of party preparations being made next door.

Sunday January 7th

....

I Did Not Tell Death Where I Lived

I did not tell Death where I lived,
But he has found me all the same.
I hear him knocking on my door
And calling out my name.

My Snapchat settings kept Him out.
On Twitter I did block Him.
His Facebook friend requests were spurned.
Yet still he keeps on knocking.

Court injunctions were sought and filed
But still I sit in fear.
Oh, my mistake. It is not Death.
I think my pizza's here.

....

I drew back my bedroom curtains to find Death staring back at me. He was wearing a fixed and maniacal grin of sickly menace. His ghastly eye sockets bore into mine. Fingers, bony and extended, clawed at the glass.

Staggering back, I gathered the courage to look again; it was Marvin's skeleton. Whether it had been placed there by design to terrify me or whether it had simply been launched up into the air and failed to come back down, I don't know. I marched next door and pressed the buzzer continuously until I saw a shuffling hooded figure emerge. For the second time in the space of a few minutes, I found myself in the presence of a gruesome Death-like creature. This one was wearing a dark blue towelling dressing gown. I began to harangue it but gave up when it was clear that it was impervious to my ranting, or indeed any aspect of the world of which it was supposedly a part.

Monday January 8th

The Tyrolean air must contain magical, soothing properties. Janice, in an uncustomary gesture of benevolence, has granted me a week's extension on my report. This is all very well but I am still no nearer understanding what it is that I'm expected to write about; the problem of working in a business that sells 'solutions' is that none of us really know what that means and there exists a kind of collective corporate complicity that makes us all too scared to ask.

Tuesday January 9th

Poetry Club

The first rule of Poetry Club
is that we meet each month in the pub.

The second rule of Poetry Club
is that not all poems have to rhyme.

....

Contrary to popular stereotype, poets are hardy creatures; neither Arctic blizzards nor desert sandstorms, mighty earthquakes nor rampaging tornados are likely to get much in the way of a poet with the opportunity to read their work to an audience with no obvious means of escape. Consequently, there was full attendance at Poetry Club in spite of the evening's bitter cold.

Mary got proceedings off to a poignant start with a requiem to her husband, Leonard, who tragically died in the Falklands. This was not during hostilities, as it turns out, but falling off a cliff while attempting to photograph a colony of rockhopper penguins. Leonard, as we've learnt over the years, was her third husband of six. The sequence runs as follows: Divorced, Bewildered, Died, Divorced, Befuddled, Surprised.

Next, it was the turn of Douglas, who launched into a ballad concerning rival sea captains at the Battle of Lepanto of 1571. This he attempted to bring to life with a sequence of nautical actions and sound effects. Twenty minutes in, and with no end in sight, we were able to coax him to sit down with a double rum and Coke, during a particularly heavy spell of cannonade.

Chandrima captivated us with a poem about a doomed love affair between a wealthy Delhi merchant prince and a serving-girl, followed by a brief meditation on the movements of the moon. And then, in a sudden change of pace and tone, Kaylee treated us to a very impassioned spoken-word piece about urban decay, rape and abortion, which made us all rather quiet and reflective for a while.

I did my best to lighten the mood with a few poems about Piers Morgan, bus journeys and the seasonal migration of ice-cream vans. As ever, I could sense Toby Salt sneering at me from his seat in the corner and trying to distract the others in the middle of my usual hesitant, stumbling performance.

Toby Salt is very dismissive of my work. He claims it lacks gravitas and soul.

'As Carl Sandberg once said,' he declared pompously at our last meeting, '"poetry should be an echo, asking a shadow to dance"'. Three years of studying Creative Writing at Bath Spa University and he thinks he knows it all.

Toby Salt is particularly dismissive of my rhyming schemes and poorly constructed metre. His *modus operandi* is free verse. However, I like to think that I treat ALL poets with equal respect, whatever their literary shortcomings, and so I sat quietly through all four of his frankly impenetrable poems, flicking empty pistachio shells into a pot.

After we'd all sat down, Mary took the opportunity to remind us about our commitment to finding new members for the year ahead. There used to be ten of us but numbers have dwindled in recent times. Not even poetry is immune from the age of austerity.

'So then, how's the recruitment drive coming on?' she asked. 'Any leads, anyone?'

I stared intently at my pint glass. I could sense others doing the same. Toby Salt broke the silence.

'Believe me, I really wish I could help. It's not as if I don't know a lot of poets.'

The eyes of my fellow club members began to roll.

'But, to be honest,' he went on, 'they are of rather a different *calibre*. I'd be hard-pressed to get them to come along to a gathering like this!'

'Actually, I know someone who may be interested so how

about you stop doing us down for a change and casting all these nasturtiums,' said Kaylee, glaring at Toby Salt.

Good old Kaylee! You could always tell when she was worked up about something as the contents of her lexical filing cabinet would become all muddled up.

'Met her on a "Save Our NHS" march just before Christmas,' she continued. 'She couldn't make tonight but thinks she might come along next month. I said that's fine, we can just play it by year. Turn up when you want. No stings attached.'

'What's her name?' Mary asked.

'She's called Liz.'

'Well, let's just hope that Liz passes mustard,' said Toby Salt with a smirk.

For one moment, I thought Kaylee was going to thump him. I opened my mouth with the intention of advising her to take him with a grain assault but, thinking better of it, popped another pistachio inside it instead.

Wednesday January 10th

I have decided to fight fire with fire to fight my fear of being fired.

I shall 'imagineer' suitably impressive corporate sound bites – or, as I like to think of them, 'jargon bombs' – to drop into my report. To prove I can walk the talk, I first need to talk the walk. Just like performing poetry on stage, it is simply a matter of bluff and self-confidence. Seven hours of intensive 'boiling the ocean', 'squeezing the sponge', and 'finding ourselves behind the eight ball' and my report has at last begun to take shape.

All this industry went on amidst a backdrop of angry thoughts about Toby Salt. He has no appreciation of how *difficult* it is to make poems rhyme. It is far easier to find words that don't rhyme than ones that do and I have statistics to back me up on that.

Thursday January 11th

....

Tweets

I think that I shall never meet
A poem lovely as a tweet.
A tweet with words and thoughts compressed
For me to press against my breast.

A tweet that stays with me all day,
Or 'til I put my phone away;
A tweet that I may marvel at,
With a photo of a dancing cat;

Or one that has mistakes within
That I may point out with a grin.
So shove your Larkin and your Keats,
Send to me your blessed tweets!

....

Before settling down in front of an old episode of *Morse*, I plucked up the courage to look at my social media accounts. These days, it is not enough for the Modern Poet merely to write poems: audiences must be *engaged with* and poetic content must be *optimised* for the purpose of *platform and search engine discoverability*.

I noted that on Twitter, I have now optimised myself for twenty-three people. Toby Salt has somehow mustered 174 followers.

I clearly need to deepen my digital footprint and I have made a vow, with the cat as my witness, to share more of my poems with my foolhardy followers as a next tentative digital baby step.

Meanwhile on Facebook, Sophie has updated her status to 'In a Relationship'. This news is accompanied by a smiley-faced emoji. She has also been tagged in a photograph with somebody calling himself 'Stuart Mould'. In the picture, they appear to be undertaking some kind of candlelit dinner together. Sophie looks very happy about something; I can only assume it's the gammon.

Friday January 12th

The Man at Number 29 has put his general landfill out on the day for recycling: it's a basic bin-day error. Even Dave, Martin and Marvin seem to be able to get that right.

He's not my only neighbour with troubles: Mrs McNulty came around in a state of agitation, prattling on about a rather spurious incident involving her dog in the night-time. She claims that her golden Labrador, Aleister, has spontaneously combusted. She pointed at a pile of ashes in her back garden which was where she said she'd last seen him, sitting there quietly and gazing sadly up at the moon.

I have my doubts: partly because it looked more like cigarette ash to me (Mrs McNulty is a committed smoker of Gauloises); and partly because she claimed the same thing had happened to Mr McNulty following *his* disappearance, although it's common knowledge he lives three streets away in a pebble-dashed fifties semi with a woman named Sandra, whom he met at sales conference in Derby. Also, Mrs McNulty has never owned a dog.

Saturday January 13th

....

4-4-2

This	line	up,
Lord	help	us!
Four	down.	In
dire	need	of
some	help.	We
lose	some,	we
lose	some.	No
plan,	only	an
ache	that	we
call	hope.	My
idea?	Team	of
goalkeepers.		

....

Trudging back from football (0–11), I found myself man-marked by Dylan, who regaled me with tales of his mother's new boy-friend – or 'Stuart', as he seems so desperate to be called:

'Mum says she's not used to having a proper man around. He's put those shelves up in the sitting room – the ones you were always promising to do – and last Sunday he cooked us all a roast. He even drives me to football practice.'

And then, going in with his studs showing:

'Why did you never learn to drive, Dad? *Do* poets drive – or are they always passengers?'

I told Dylan that perhaps it would be for the best if he could stop talking in order to conserve his energy for the final three miles' walk home.

Sunday January 14th

In October, Poetry Club will be heading off on our much-anticipated Poets on the Western Front trip. We will be visiting northern France and Belgium to see, amongst other things, the trench where Henri Barbusse was a stretcher-bearer, the hill where Ivor Gurney was wounded, the battlefield which inspired Wilfred Owen's 'Spring Offensive' and the cellar in which he wrote his last letter. Having recently taken over from Mary as club treasurer, I spent the morning reviewing the finances. All subs were up to date; even Toby Salt's, unfortunately, giving me no excuse to harass him.

As the cat took up occupancy on me for the rest of the day, I took another look at Twitter. Last night, in the spirit of my renewed commitment to social media, I'd shared a poem called 'The Day My Dog Spontaneously Combusted':

> there he was,
> chasing sticks,
> doing tricks,
> and all that stuff
>
> next minute, woof

Since I posted this poem, my follower count has gone down to seventeen (Toby Salt now has 196). What's more – to add insult to invisibility – I've received a series of angry, foul-mouthed tweets. Initially, I thought that I'd experienced my very first real-life troll, but then I noticed that they'd been sent by the RSPCA.

Monday January 15th

Inbox

From	Message	Date	
Janice	**Your Report** is due this morning. Just a quick reminder	Mon 15/1	08.45
Stuart Mould	**Stuart would like to join your professional network** Click here	Mon 15/1	09.11
DatingUK	**If You're Alone and Looking for Love** ... We can help you find a	Mon 15/1	09.48
CustomExcel	**Pipe Management Solution** To service those clients all year	Mon 15/1	10.10
MeetingRequest	**Round Table Discussion** 2 p.m. On how to go the 'extra mile'	Mon 15/1	10.52
Janice	**I should have that report by now** please can you give me an	Mon 15/1	11.45
LinkedIn	**Update: There is Nobody looking at your LinkedIn Profile**	Mon 15/1	12.13
SunshineHolidays	**Why Not Get Away From It All in the Glorious Caribbean?**	Mon 15/1	12.41
Facebook	**It's been a while!** You have unread notifications and a new	Mon 15/1	13.05
Sally	**YOU!** Where on earth are you? Janice has really got the hump	Mon 15/1	13.58
Janice	**WHERE IS IT? I HAVE A PRESENTATION I HAD PLANNED TO**	Mon 15/1	14.15
CorpSeminar	**Embrace Change! Just Do It Now** Why not make that jump	Mon 15/1	14.26
BizNews	**From the Old World to the New** Remove your workplace stress	Mon 15/1	15.03
TravelAlertz	**Passenger Fatality Leads to Long Delays on Northern Line**	Mon 15/1	16.10
Janice	**9 a.m. Tomorrow - My Office** What an absolute mess.	Mon 15/1	16.45
Amazon	**Sign up now for a month's free trial with Amazon Prime**	Mon 15/1	16.57

Janice is on the war path for my report and I fear for my core deliverables. I spent most of the day holed up in the stationery cupboard following a last-minute, eleventh-hour crisis of confidence. Although initially pleased with my jargonautical exploits (only this morning I had added in the sentence, 'We need to stop chasing butterflies if we're to develop game-changing marketecture that will enable us to grab wallet share'), I was seized with a sudden fear that it was utterly devoid of all meaning and content. That all it added up to was a great big warm bowl of nothing.

I managed to slip out undetected at about 6.30pm thanks to some diversionary tactics outside Janice's office from Tomas, who cleans the second-floor offices, involving a squeegee on a telescopic handle and a 500ml bottle of Windolene trigger spray.

Tuesday January 16th

I phoned in sick in order to regroup myself mentally. As it always does, the act of pretending to be ill made me actually feel ill, and I spent much of the day asleep in bed, stirring occasionally in response to neighbourly sounds of UK grime and Mrs McNulty's sawing.

But even feigned illnesses begin to wear off eventually, and by the evening I was able to finish off the reordering of my bookcases. I placed the last book – 97819123666158 – on the shelf and stood back, the better to admire my achievement. It was magnificent! To celebrate, I thought I'd treat myself to a couple of stories from *The Adventures of Sherlock Holmes* but, having spent fifteen minutes attempting to locate it, I gave up and went back to bed.

Wednesday January 17th

How to Avoid Mixing Your Metaphors

It's not rocket surgery.
First, get all your ducks on the same page.
After all, you can't make an omelette
without breaking stride.

Be sure to watch what you write
with a fine-tuned comb.
Check and re-check until the cows turn blue.
It's as easy as falling off a piece of cake.

Don't worry about opening up
a whole hill of beans:
you can always burn that bridge when you come to it,
if you follow where I'm coming from.

Concentrate! Keep your door closed
and your enemies closer.
Finally, don't take the moral high horse:
if the metaphor fits, walk a mile in it.

....

Still at home. Hiding from your responsibilities may perhaps not be the most mature response, but at least it is a response – one that says, having carefully considered all the options available to me, I have taken the positive and proactive decision to run away and hide. In this way, I remain firmly in control of the whole situation.

And frankly, I think this mini-break may actually have done me some good. My batteries are recharged and I now feel ready to step up to the plate and face the music.

Thursday January 18th

I feared the worst as I journeyed to work this morning. Birds flapped menacingly. Belisha beacons flashed in warning. Pavements stuck out their kerbs to trip me.

Almost immediately I received the summons to Janice's office. She was sitting behind her desk, straight-backed, tight-lipped and twinkle-eyed. She reminded me of a politburo chief with a busy morning of denouncements to get through.

She'd instructed IT to hack into my computer and retrieve my report. She paused for dramatic effect and smiled icily. My thoughts turned to Siberian labour camps. I imagined the tilling of frozen soil. Then:

'It's just what this organisation needs. We need to shake some columns.'

I left her office through an undefenestrated route, with her invitation to 'stir-fry some more ideas in her think-wok soon' echoing disturbingly in my ears.

Friday January 19th

The whole street was woken at 7a.m. by the howls of the Man at Number 29 who, in an admirable bid to get his refuse collection back on track, had left his bin bags outside overnight, only for them to be savagely torn to shreds by foxes in the small hours. Utter carnage! Flour bags in flower beds! Houmous tubs in hedges! Dolmio daubed on doorsteps! The bin men declined to take what was left of his bags' tattered remains, of course, and the Man at Number 29 retreated back inside in despair.

Moved by his plight, I had it in mind to write a poem of solidarity and post it through his letter box but I became distracted by the sight of *The Guardian Bumper Christmas Cryptic Crossword*. It had been waiting patiently in the corner of the sitting room for some attention since New Year's Eve. Three hours later and I filled in the answer to 15 down, having first looked up its meaning in the dictionary:

VELLEITY (noun): volition in its lowest form; a wish or inclination not strong enough to lead to action.

Saturday January 20th

....

Penguin Awareness

I've been aware of penguins since I was three:
I think one may have moved in with me.

The signs are everywhere.
The smell of saltwater in the air.
There are moulted feathers on my chair
Yesterday I found a fish upon the stair.
But when I turn around there's no one there,
for he moves in the shadows, like Tony Soprano;
I am forever stepping in guano.

I don't know why he's come to live with me.
There are better places for him to be.
But when I've gone to bed, I can hear the tread
of his soft heels across the kitchen floor,
and the opening of the freezer door.

And I picture him there,
his head resting on a frozen shelf,
dreaming sadly of somewhere else,
thinking about the hand that life has dealt him,
and I wonder if his heart is melting.

....

Sophie reminded me not to be late in dropping Dylan back tonight as Stuart was taking them both to some film premiere or other, and she'd really appreciate it if I could be on time for once. I replied that of course I would, before reminding her that she *still* had my vinyl copy of *Pet Sounds* and I'd really appreciate it if she could have it ready for me to collect from her later.

She handed it over to me wordlessly when I dropped Dylan back. Slouching home, I'd been all set to spend the evening with an old episode of *Miss Marple* but made the error of taking a quick look at Twitter. Penguin Awareness Day was being celebrated. I had previously been unaware of this. I posted up a poem to commemorate the occasion, drawing down deep into my well of imaginative powers to conjure up feelings of what it must be like to feel lonely and displaced.

Sunday January 21st

The RPSCA have contacted me again on Twitter to tell me they're deeply concerned that a penguin – or indeed any aquatic, flightless bird – is being kept in a household environment. They believe its needs would become too difficult to meet in a human's domestic dwelling and that it may become depressed. They are threatening to send an inspector out.

Monday January 22nd

A clatter of the letter box and a thud on the doormat told me that the January issue of *Well Versed – The Quarterly Magazine for the Discriminating Poet* had arrived. An occasion always greeted with much anticipation and no little excitement on my part for not only does it give me the opportunity to keep up with the latest developments in the poetry world (sample articles in this issue include 'How to get the most out of your Pindaric Ode', 'Troubleshooting Double Dactyls' and 'How to Have Fun with Clerihews') but I always experience a brief frisson of hope that one of my poems might at last be featured within its pages.

The theme for January's competition was 'Wind' and I had high hopes for my two entries – 'Breezy Listening' and 'Forgive Me Father For I Have Wind' – but instead, there on page 3 was a photograph of a leering Toby Salt, alongside his winning poem, 'Theogony and the Ecstasy':

A rock for a jail
and nothing but the wind for company.
O Aeolian confidante! Dry my salty locks
and whisper the world into my ear.
The latest stockmarket news.
A child strangled. The shaming of a politician.
And all the snarling of the gutter press.
The jingle of my jailor's keys as they bounce upon his thigh.
But no. These chains. This rock.
What do you bring exactly? Only betrayal.
The dread beat of accipitrine wings,
the daily agonies
and my ripped-out liver,
shining at my feet,
surrounded by rock pools, ruby-red.

I have now read this poem seven times and I understand it a little less each time.

Tuesday January 23rd

William Wordsearch

```
W  H  E  R  N  D  A  N  C  I  N  G  E
A  R  R  M  F  A  C  R  O  W  D  O  W
S  T  D  U  O  L  C  A  S  A  G  N  O
I  G  O  L  D  E  N  R  L  N  E  H  W
N  B  E  N  E  A  T  H  I  D  I  I  S
F  O  A  A  C  A  H  R  D  E  H  G  S
L  I  N  T  H  E  E  S  O  R  E  H  H
O  M  D  T  A  T  T  F  E  Z  S  Y
A  W  H  I  T  A  R  W  F  D  E  L  T
T  L  I  U  T  H  E  L  A  K  E  O  F
S  E  L  A  V  R  E  O  D  N  R  C  H
U  F  L  A  H  O  S  T  O  F  B  H  B
B  E  S  I  D  E  O  L  U  H  N  N  C
```

I have concluded that the whole notion of making competitions out of poetry merely serves to debase the artform. I'm seriously thinking about cancelling my subscription to *Well Versed*.

Wednesday January 24th

I had forgotten that it's book group tomorrow!

After work, I pedalled furiously to the bookshop, swerving suddenly to avoid a collision with a Transit van, in the hope that they had J. G. Ballard's *Crash* in stock. They did! While I was there, I bought a few other books: three more Ballard novels; a brief introduction on how to read poetry; *A Dream Dictionary* to 'unlock the secrets of your subconscious'; *1001 Books You Must Read Before You Die*; and a self-help guide entitled *How To Organise Your Mind So You Can Organise Your Life*. Annoyingly, I couldn't find this last book in my bag when I got home. I think I may have left it behind on the counter.

Crash is 208 pages. I have some speed-reading to do; I just need to be careful I don't take a page too fast and career into the margins.

Thursday January 25th

There was a lively discussion at book group tonight concerning 'symphorophilia'. This, I learnt, is the sensation of being sexually aroused by disasters or accidents. No one in the group admitted to harbouring such feelings although I did wonder about the man in front of me at the bar, having seen the way he'd looked at the barmaid after she'd dropped his bag of scampi fries on the floor and bent over to pick them up.

My own contribution to proceedings was slim on account of being exhausted from staying up late to try to finish it (I'd crashed out at 10.30pm having got as far as page 12). I bought an extra bowl of wasabi peas for the table to re-ingratiate myself with the group.

Friday January 26th

This is Not the Poem that I Had Hoped to Write

This is not the poem that I had hoped to write
when I sat at my desk and the page was white.
You see, there were other words that I'd had in mind,
yet this is what I leave behind.

I thought it was a poem to eradicate war;
one of such power, it would heal all the sores
of a world torn apart by conflict and schism.
But it isn't.

Lovers, I'd imagined, would quote from it daily,
Mothers would sing it to soothe crying babies.
And whole generations would be given new hope.
Nope.

I had grand aspirations. Believe me, I tried.
Humanity examined with lessons applied.
But the right words escaped me; so often they do.
Have these in lieu.

The bin men have pinned a note to the Man at Number 29's rubbish bags, informing him that as he'd put out more than the regulatory number of sacks to be collected (five), they will not be removing any of them today. I wanted to write a poem about 'refuse collection' – *refuse* being both a synonym for 'rubbish' and also a verb which means 'to turn down' and thus working brilliantly on two separate levels – but some days the words I would like to write are not the ones I end up writing.

I came home an hour early from work, having invented a

doctor's appointment, for no good reason other than it being Friday. As I arrived back, the cat emerged through the cat-flap. She was surprised to see me. Her whiskers twitched with guilt. I inspected the house for dead rodents or birds but none were forthcoming.

Saturday January 27th

Acrostic Guitar

E ssential presence in all bedsits and studio apartments
A vailable in two main settings: plucking and strumming
D ependable companion of aspiring singer-songwriters
G atherings by campfires remain incomplete without it
B reak-up ballads and revolution songs pre-programmed
E gad! My last line has just broken

After I'd dropped Dylan back at Sophie's, I beetled off to meet Darren for 27th Club. Our monthly get-together is something we both continue to keep secret from Sophie because if there's one person in the world who, in her eyes, comes close to being as big a disappointment as me, then it's her younger brother, Darren.

We founded 27th Club three years ago as a way to take ourselves out of our musical comfort zones, while drinking over-priced, underwhelming beer. It's a simple concept: on the 27th of every month, we venture out to see some live music. There are only two or three venues nearby so options are limited. But this does mean that we get exposed to music we might not otherwise have contemplated.

We'd imagined that 27th Club would expand our musical horizons into new and unexpected places and, in the process, we'd find ourselves imbued with a kind of hipster cosmopolitanism. In reality, all it seems to have done is to confirm our own well-worn, needle-scratched prejudices.

I was late arriving at tonight's gig but I couldn't miss him. This was, in part, due to the room being sparsely populated but also because Darren was holding a giant placard, on which was written the words "GOLF SALE". The sign's arrow was currently pointing in the direction of the ladies' toilets.

'Sorry,' he said, 'had to come straight from work. Didn't get a chance to change.'

We watched a procession of singer-songwriters file onto the stage in order to sing songs that they'd written.

'I met Sophie's new man last week,' Darren whispered while a woman was warbling about the comfort of trees.

'Oh, really?' I replied nonchalantly, my attention suddenly grabbed by some accomplished on-stage finger-work.

'Really nice guy,' he said.

'Mmm . . .' I responded, admiring the interesting chord progression.

'I reckon he's loaded. He drives a Maserati.'

Some kind of car, presumably. What might have been a Dsus4 rang out. I tried to focus on that.

'Sophie's really quite taken with him.'

Turning to Darren, I told him in no uncertain terms how disrespectful it is to talk when a singer-songwriter is in full flow. As he headed off to the loo in a huff, I held his sign and listened to how branches can bend in the wind.

Sunday January 28th

It was one of those beautiful, cold, crisp January days that are perfect for a long, bracing walk through a pine forest, while admiring the wintry elegance of trees snugly wrapped in their soft coats of frost and listening to the silvery half-silence of frozen streams.

And that's why I stayed inside all day, staring at a screen. By the time I went to bed, I was filled with self-loathing. It makes me wonder how poets of yore would have coped in these distracting times; it's hard to imagine Yeats sitting down to write 'Lake Isle of Innisfree' if he'd had Angry Birds downloaded on his phone.

Still, at least after the PR disaster that was PenguinGate, my social media presence seems to be on the rise again: I now have nineteen followers. It was less cheering news on Facebook, where Sophie continues to inflict more photos of Stuart and her together upon an unsuspecting populace. I have made a note to ask Sophie whether she has had him DBS-checked.

Monday January 29th

Monetization

The ad said
MONETIZE YOUR FOLLOWERS

so he thought
he would respond;

he painted them
in the changing light,
like waterlilies
in a pond.

....

I've been invited to an idea shower with the big enchiladas next month as they look to move the needle. According to Janice, my role is to serve as a grassroots-level pulse-check. Her PA told me later that this meant I'll be attending a two-day meeting next month in a hotel near Leamington Spa. He showed me the website. It boasts of the hotel's proximity to the tree-lined fairways and fast greens of a 190-acre golf course.

The awayday is provisionally entitled 'Feeding the Funnel: How to Bring Home the Bacon for our Stakeholders'. I've been charged with putting together a PowerPoint presentation on how we might monetise our social media presence. Yes, me! If I were to monetise my own social media presence, I'd make about ten pence.

In other news, the cat is still acting suspiciously and has avoided all eye contact with me since Friday.

Tuesday January 30th

In the interests of research for Leamington Spa, I spent most of today on Twitter, assessing online opportunities for monetisation and short videos of pets falling off items of high furniture. To my disbelief, Toby Salt now has more than two hundred and fifty followers on Twitter, including a Radio 4 presenter and a well-known stand-up comedian. I can only conclude that there must be another, more successful Toby Salt out there and they have inadvertently followed the wrong person.

Wednesday January 31st

....

New Year Haiku Horoscopes

Aries
In this diary
you read your new horoscope.
It tells you little.

Taurus
You hate your star sign.
Disgruntled, you convert to
Capricornism.

Gemini
Mars enters the sphere
of concupiscent Venus,
whatever that means.

Cancer
You spend the whole year
just wondering to yourself,
'where *do* the years go?'

Leo
Your resolution
to avoid all haikus is
already broken.

Virgo
You stare at your phone,
look up briefly in July,
then stare at your phone.

Libra
You take a year out
but forget to return it.
The fine will be huge.

Scorpio
An out-of-body
experience makes you angry.
You're beside yourself.

Sagittarius
Year of good fortune.
Not once do you encounter
Jeremy Clarkson.

Capricorn
Trousers start to sag
as your pockets bulge with coins.
A year of much change.

Aquarius

You join the circus.
Retrain as tightrope walker.
Good work–life balance.

Pisces

You leave the city
to become a sheep shearer.
New year, a new ewe.

....

Mrs McNulty popped around again this evening. For some reason, she has begun to make the sign of the cross whenever she sees me.

She thrust into my hand a set of horoscopes for the coming year, while apologising for their lateness (she usually has these prepared by the end of December). This was due to unforeseen circumstances, she explained.

'Remind me again, what star sign are you?' she asked.

'Not sure. Cancer, I think.'

She gave a sharp intake of breath, crossed herself once more then mumbled about how she needed to get back to her sawing. After she left, I read her entry for Cancer:

This year sees your transiting Saturn conjunct with your natal Saturn in the 8th house, and Uranus conjunct the Moon. The Vertex is conjunct Pluto and your 4th House has become shadowed with Neptune's dark umbra. These factors, combined with irregular disturbances in your quincunx, point tragically yet irrevocably to one thing: Death will cast its shadow before the year is out.

Her usual mumbo-jumbo. I added it to the recycling.

February

Thursday February 1st

Anger directed towards a Gym Membership Card

There you go again: jogging my memory,
exercising my conscience,
climbing up the wall bars of my guilt.
Bench-oppressing me.

But what do you do all day
except wallow in my wallet?
Your companions are always active.
Observe the healthy sheen

of my store reward cards,
the litheness of my public library card,
and just look at that debit card,
flexing its muscles once more.

I ran into an old adversary of mine at the bakery this morning as I was reaching into my wallet to pay for a couple of chocolate croissants and a pain au raisin: my gym membership card. Apart from the occasional bike ride, and walking to and from football each Saturday, I have yet to engage in a single reckless act of health and fitness this year. I made a private vow to myself that a new training regime must begin in earnest from this weekend before ordering one more chocolate croissant to make the most of the '4 for the price of 3' offer.

Friday February 2nd

....

This Be the Curse

They muck you up, these stuck-up cats.
You may not think so but it's true.
They come and sit upon your lap
When there are other things to do.

You wait upon them, hand and foot,
And in return get fleas and lice,
Their hairs collect upon your suit,
They bring you chewed-up heads of mice.

Cats hand on misery to man.
It gathers in the litter tray.
So get up quickly while you can
Before the cat climbs back to stay.

....

I had just sat down to write today's poem when the doorbell rang. It was Dave from next door with some news: my cat has been sleeping around.

'She keeps coming over when you're at work and sitting on us,' he said. Dave seemed genuinely upset. 'She's having a detrimental effect on our studying.'

He pointed to the cat hairs on his jumper.

'And she's been lying all over our books and lecture notes. Marvin missed a seminar and a tutorial last week because of her – and Martin was ten minutes late for an exam.'

I promised to have a word with her. When I went back in, the cat was sitting in the seat I'd just vacated. I looked her in the eye and told her that it simply wasn't acceptable; we were busy people; we had our own lives to live, too; we had hopes and dreams just like her.

She blinked back lazily but I knew my comments had hit home: she wore the sheepish look of a cat who knows it's in the doghouse.

Saturday February 3rd

Another drubbing for Dylan's team today. But he should take heart from his own performance; some of the parents on the touchline even compared him to Maradona (although Maradona punched the ball into his *opponent*'s net). As part of my new fitness drive, I volunteered to run the line. I kept up with play well at first but, ten minutes in, began to flag. There were a lot of people shouting at me.

When I dropped him home later, Sophie reminded me about parents' evening.

'It's on Wednesday. You hadn't forgotten, had you?'

'No, not at all.' I looked at my shoes.

'You had. It starts at six. And please try to be more . . . *normal* this time.'

I took this as a thinly veiled reference to last year's meeting. I had been having a perfectly civilised discussion with Ms Thornton, Dylan's English teacher, about how, on the poster outside the school hall, there was a missing apostrophe in 'PARENTS EVENING'. Even now I don't know why she got so angry with me.

'I am normal,' I said.

Sophie gave me one of her looks. I put it in my coat pocket.

'Well, just don't be late. 6 p.m., remember?'

When I got home, I tried to write a poem about missing apostrophes. But I just couldn't settle down to it. I think this may be due to the absence of the cat. She's still sulking from yesterday's reprimand and has taken up residence in the airing cupboard.

Sunday February 4th

I rose early at 11 a.m. for my run: over the bridge, down onto the footpath that follows the bend of the river, across the bridge, and through the back streets home. My surroundings went by in a blur – I'd forgotten to put my contact lenses in – but rarely have I felt so alive. I treated myself to a super-sized fry-up brunch in celebration: two extra quorn sausages!

I spent the afternoon considering the true nature of poetry and whether Diderot was right when he said that it 'must have something in it that is barbaric, vast and wild'. After that I finished my ironing in front of *Midsomer Murders* and undertook a much-needed clear-out of my cheese compartment.

Chores all done, I sat down and waited for the magic to come. But no. Not a sniff of a poem.

The cat in the airing cupboard is fast becoming my pram in the hall.

Monday February 5th

Half dead and half alive, I dragged my limbs to work and continued on the Leamington PowerPoint. To break the impasse, I have decided, for now, to think less about the words and content, and focus on finding some powerful images to go into it. After all, a picture is worth a thousand words; perhaps even more in today's currency.

Applying that logic, by the time I left work this evening, I had written the equivalent of three thousand words.

If only the same could be said of my poetry. I retrieved one of Dylan's old cuddly toys from the wardrobe this evening: a moth-eaten, one-eyed, raggle-taggle indeterminate cloth thing called Henry. I placed it on my lap and waited, pen poised on paper. But unlike the sheets in the airing cupboard, this one remained untouched.

Tuesday February 6th

Toby Salt was full of himself as he swaggered into this evening's Poetry Club in his crocs. Not only did he 'just happen' to have the latest issue of *Well Versed* in his bag to show the rest of the group, but he had some more news to share with us all.

'I have a collection of my poetry coming out,' he crowed, 'with Shooting from the Hip.'

'With who?' I said.

'It's "with *whom*",' he retorted irritatingly. 'Shooting from the Hip. They're an artisan publishing house. I doubt you'll have heard of them. They publish clever, cerebral books.'

'How exciting for you!' exclaimed Chandrima.

'Well, Shooting from the Hip are very excited, at any rate. Django – he's the owner – thinks it could be the book that will "bring poetry back into the mainstream". They're printing five hundred copies, as well as a special linocut and letterpress edition for collectors.'

I snorted involuntarily into my pint.

'I've given it the provisional title of *This Bridge No Hands Shall Cleave*,' pronounced Toby Salt solemnly.

I snorted once more and this time beer rushed up my nose. Toby Salt looked at me as I spluttered and struggled for breath.

'I'd recommend your work to Django,' he said, 'but he tends to look for more in a poem than the ability to rhyme a few words.'

He had a big stupid grin on his face all night. Not even Kaylee's spoken-word piece about rioting, police brutality and racial violence in downtown Detroit was able to remove it.

In spite of all this, I was feeling rather cheerful; Kaylee's new Poetry Club recruit had turned up after all. Liz was smart, funny and (*dear diary, I cannot lie*) not unattractive; at least sixty per cent of Shakespeare's sonnets could have been written about her. What's more, she fitted in instantly. It was as if Liz had been here with us all along but only now had we truly noticed her, like the discovery of a found poem which suddenly reveals the beauty that lies hidden beneath the humdrum of the everyday.

As she sat down from reciting a witty yet moving poem concerning the discovery of a well-thumbed, annotated copy of *The Joy of Sex* in a second-hand bookshop, it dawned on me that it really has been quite some time since our membership has swollen.

I carried my good mood home with me. The cat must have sensed that – like Germany in 1989 – the moment had come for reunification. I had just sat down on the sofa when she jumped up and re-homed herself in my lap. I was just thinking back to Liz's performance earlier when the shadow of Toby Salt fell over me once more. How dare he criticise my poems! I'd write him a poem for next Poetry Club to show how difficult it is to make words rhyme.

Hampered by the cat, I found the words began to flow once more . . .

To make poems rhyme can sometimes be tough:
words may appear to be from the same bough,
yet each line's ending sounds different, though,
best hidden behind a hiccough or cough.

Was this upsetting to Byron or Yeats?
Dickinson or Wordsworth? Larkin or Keats?
Did they see these words as auditory threats?
Could they write their lines without caveats?

But does it matter when all's said and done
if you read this as *scone* when I meant *scone*?
It's hardly a crime. There's no need to atone;
it's all baloney to an abalone.

Don't mumble these endings into your beard.
This poem should be seen, rather than heard.

Wednesday February 7th

I have crash-landed on a distant planet. It is full of bright, vivid colours, spectacular landscapes and breathtaking sunsets. Its inhabitants, who are both beautiful and courteous, and wear immaculate teeth, tell me that it is called Planet Stock Photography. They smile broadly at me as I insert them into the PowerPoint.

Back home, I find myself clearing up several of Marvin's disposable kidney dishes from my front garden. Earth seems so shoddy in comparison: why do we put up with it?

Thursday February 8th

I'd forgotten all about parents' evening.

Those hours on Planet Stock Photography yesterday must have confused my brain and distracted me from my real-world responsibilities. If only I had some kind of book to write these things down in: a planner, perhaps, or a diary.

Sophie was fuming, of course. I really need to keep my phone on at all times, she says. Last night's sequence of texts from her quickly escalated from word-based messages to ones comprised purely of emojis. And not the polite, smiley ones either. :-(

Friday February 9th

....

Snowball

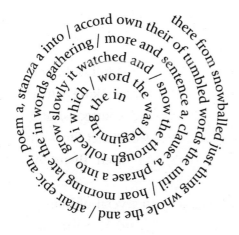

In the beginning was the word, which i watched slowly it grow into a phrase, rolled through the late morning hoar until a clause, a sentence of tumbled words snowballed just from there, more and more words gathering of their own accord into a poem, a stanza, an epic affair.

....

As soon as I'd opened my eyes, I knew that the world had

changed; there was some subtle difference in the curtained light, barely perceptible at first in my half-woken sleep, as it fell upon my dappled duvet. Snow!

Seizing the day by its snow-encrusted shoulders, I phoned the office to let them know that owing to the treacherous conditions, I'd be working from home. I climbed back into bed to enjoy the slow hypnotic dance of snowflakes through the window.

The Man at Number 29 had put the right bin bags out on the right day, for once, only for today's collection to be postponed due to the inclement weather.

It looks like it's settling in for a few days. Football must surely be cancelled! Perhaps Dylan and I could have a snowball fight instead? Or we could build a snowman?! I'd love that – and I suspect that beneath the troubled hoodie of adolescence, he would, too.

Saturday February 10th

Snowman

I roughly twisted
the two lumps of black
deep into where
the eyes should be,
smiling at their darkness
shining like diamonds.

A carrot, comically crooked,
was rammed in, offset
by a blood-soaked fedora

and old woollen scarf.
It had been two hours
since he'd last made a noise.

Bored now, I went outside
to build a snowman
for the snow
had freshly settled.

....

I suggested to Dylan that we go to the park to make a snowman. He yawned and stretched in response before telling me that he'd prefer a quiet day inside. He looked away shiftily.

I interrogated him further. He's exhausted, he eventually told me, having spent the whole of yesterday outside, building a snowman with Stuart. But he wasn't so exhausted that he couldn't stop himself from showing me a series of eighty-five photographs documenting its construction. The final one was of Stuart grinning back at the camera, like an Eskimo on Ecstasy, standing proudly next to the snowman. I studied it more closely: the proportions were all wrong; the smile was crooked; it would most likely melt when the sun came out.

The snowman wasn't much better either.

Sunday February 11th

The theme of the next *Well Versed* competition is 'technology', a sphere of life which I've always found to be challenging. I am – at best – a late adopter with a track record of ill-advised flirtations (Betamax, Vic-20, Friends Reunited). By the time I've figured out where I should have been all the while (VHS, ZX Spectrum, Facebook), those who were already there have moved on to someplace else.

This time, I've decided to put some proper effort into it, rather than just dash off a few words and hope for the best. I fired up the internet with the intention of doing some research on Ask Jeeves but almost instantly became waylaid by Twitter. My follower count has now swollen to twenty-four; it always seems to increase when I haven't tweeted and shrink when I have. After lengthy deliberation, I decided to follow Toby Salt. He now has more than three hundred followers. He's also updated his profile picture to one of him staring intently into the camera, chin resting on his hands. He looks mildly constipated.

I resorted to more tried and tested means of research. Braving the snow, I headed to the bookshop in search of further inspiration as well as to get this month's book group choice: *Candide* by Voltaire. I arrived back home with my bag bursting with books: three titles in a new series on technology and social change; a biography of Steve Jobs; *I, Robot* by Isaac Asimov; *Presentation Skills for Dummies*; *How to Market Yourself on Social Media*; and a book on how ebooks are taking over from print, which has just published in paperback.

Monday February 12th

Slush-trudging into work, I slush-trudged on with my Leamington Spa presentation. At the end of the day, I looked back at what I'd achieved.

It is still mainly pictures.

I need some words.

Any words.

Where are the words? I can't find the words.

Who has taken all of the stupid words?

Tuesday February 13th

Shrove Tuesday rituals are more of a chore than a ceremony when you have only yourself to make pancakes for but still I persist with its sugary sacraments and lemon-juiced litanies. As my frying pan began to sizzle, I remembered a poem I'd written for Sophie, in pre-Dylan days, when she would still bother to read them:

Full moon peering through my window:
there's nothing that you do not know!
You guide the tides and human hearts,
enlighten Science, enrich the Arts,
make poets weep and lovers croon;
for love is lost without you, moon.

Divine disc shining down . . . what's that?
You seem to be *this* side of the glass.
An ancient memory starts to grow:
Shrove Tuesday several years ago,
a zealous toss, my pancake lost;
I searched all day but time wore on.
I'd often wondered where you'd gone.

I was still gently tossing when the doorbell rang. It was Mrs McNulty. She's having one of her 'gatherings' on Sunday and advises me that it might be for the best if I could attend in person. The spirits, by all accounts, take a dim view concerning the absenteeism of those 'under question' and regard ignorance as no excuse.

I do worry about Mrs McNulty sometimes. Dylan finds her scary but I think she's harmless enough. I suppose I shall have to go. The last time I refused her invitation, I returned home from work the next day to find the grass on my back lawn flattened in the shape of a giant phallus; Mrs McNulty claimed it was a crop circle signifying fertility, most likely caused by some kind of extra-terrestrial craft, but the compressed grass bore all the hall-marks of the tread from her sit-on lawn mower.

Wednesday February 14th

The Flowers of the Garage Forecourt

Budding lovers beware
of the Flowers of the Garage Forecourt;
they are not for courting.

Love will not blossom
with those blundering bouquets of cellophaned sadness:
the slip-road roses and petrol-pump peonies.
The crushed-dream chrysanthemums.
All those dahlias of desperation!
The I-forgot-you forget-me-nots.

Remember this: would-be patrons
of the Flowers of the Garage Forecourt:
romance wilts with lack of forethought.

Sophie has posted up a picture on Facebook of a huge bunch of flowers that arrived for her at work today, sent by Stuart. It contains all sorts of flowers: yellow ones, red ones, white ones, even some of the purple ones. It must have cost a fortune for all those different colours.

I fought off the gloom by hosting a romantic, candlelit supper with *The Guardian Bumper Christmas Cryptic Crossword*. At 7 across, I tentatively pencilled in *CURMUDGEON* while trying to stop myself from wondering how Liz was spending her Valentine's Day.

Not that it is any of my business, of course. I am quite content to leave love and all that stuff to others who possess more expertise in the area; it is a splendid thing indeed that those people have their own day to commemorate such things. But if you're going to celebrate love, then why stop there? Where are the days dedicated to other just-as-pure emotional states – such as envy and loneliness, panic and anguish? Lovers have it made already, without being encouraged to shake their expensive, multi-coloured bouquets in the faces of the rest of us.

Thursday February 15th

....

Advice for Removing Keyboard Tearstains

If you happen to notice
your keyboard is dirty,
use a water spray can
and give it a SQWERTY.

....

Compassionately wiping the teardrop smears from my keyboard, Tomas asked me what the matter was. I simply shrugged and held up my hands in a despairing, expansive gesture, one which took in my Leamington PowerPoint, my shabby officle, the ridiculousness of the corporate world and twenty-first-century life more broadly. Tomas told me I was worrying unduly about my presentation:

'After all,' he said, 'implicit in language is its own limitation. All forms of communication are intrinsically flawed and the worlds that each of us perceive and make for ourselves will forever be different because of this.'

Before he came over to England and found himself cleaning middle-management officles, Tomas was a Professor of Modern Philosophy at the University of Warsaw and one of the world's leading scholars of Ludwig Wittgenstein. I asked him how he felt about this reduction in his circumstances.

'As the good Ludwig once said, "If people never did silly things, nothing intelligent would get done",' he replied enigmatically before proceeding to empty my bin of its Twix wrappers.

Friday February 16th

I think Allen Ginsberg was right when he said that he'd seen the best minds of his generation destroyed by never-ending Power-Point presentations on branding, social media and value propositions.

It is 2 a.m. on Saturday as I write this entry. I have been working on the Leamington Spa PowerPoint now for seventeen consecutive hours. It now contains 211 slides. My presentation is supposed to last for thirty minutes. That is an average of 7.03 slides per minute. Or a new slide every 8.53 seconds.

43 custard creams have been consumed during this period.

Saturday February 17th

We traipsed wearily back from football. 0–8. I suggested to Dylan that he might consider forgoing football for Lent.

'Whenever you feel like giving up,' he said, fixing me with a meaningful look, 'you need to remember why you held on for so long in the first place.'

I looked at him with renewed respect. What a mature and positive approach to the world that young man has.

But it all came out over lunch. It appears that Stuart has a sideline in motivational speaking and Dylan went to see him in action last night. I tried hard to suppress my laugh but Dylan looked at me disappointedly. He told me that cynicism is just another word for giving up.

We finished our remaining spaghetti hoops in silence.

After I'd dropped him back home, I resumed work on the Leamington Spa PowerPoint, breaking off briefly to check Twitter. Toby Salt has tweeted that he's very much looking forward to performing at the Saffron Walden Poetry Festival in July. This golden nugget of information has received fourteen retweets and twenty-six likes. It must have been a slow news day.

Sunday February 18th

Mrs McNulty's face flickered in the light of the seven candles that surrounded the board. In the darkness behind, I saw the curtains billow dramatically in the wind from a fan that had been strategically placed behind them. A soft howling came from the fireplace, although I suspect its true source came from the *Natural Sounds: Windy Winter's Day* relaxation CD, whose empty case I'd noticed on the sideboard when I'd entered the room.

Dave, Martin and Marvin were there. As was Mrs Collingwood from number 47 (Mrs McNulty's bingo partner) and Mr Paxton, who was introduced to us all as a big wheel in the haberdashery trade. Mrs McNulty looked solemnly at us, recited a protection prayer (which I'm pretty sure was actually just the lyrics to 'Your Love is King' by Sade), and 'because you can never be too careful', proceeded to sprinkle us all with salt.

We were invited to place a finger upon the planchette and the farce began. 'Is anybody there?' We waited. Not a thing. Mrs McNulty entreated us to vanquish all negative energy from the room and we tried once more. Still nothing. Bored now, my mind began to wander. I thought about the Leamington Spa Power-Point. I made a mental note to start reading Voltaire's *Candide* for this month's book group. I remembered Toby Salt's tweet from earlier, in which he'd announced that tickets for his Saffron Walden event had now sold out. I imagined him in one of Saffron Walden's smaller venues: the back room of the village hall, perhaps. The bay window of a tea shop. A potting shed.

The planchette was moving across the board. Slowly at first, then more quickly: B-E-W-A-R-E, it said. Mrs McNulty became noticeably aroused. W-H-Y, we responded. There was another pause before the block began to move wildly from one letter to the next: D-E-A-T-H-I-S-C-O-M-I-N-G. More gasps from Mrs McNulty. She couldn't help herself: T-O-W-H-O.

It should have been T-O-W-H-O-M but I didn't like to interrupt. After a brief lull, the planchette set off again to the left – B – before lurching down to the right – R – further along and up again – I – heading back left, and then . . . my phone rang:

'P-P-I'. Had I been mis-sold it?

I disposed of the caller in summary fashion, but Mrs McNulty was unimpressed. Apparently, I'd 'destroyed the circle of trust' we'd established in the room, and the spirit had been frightened off.

She was still angry with me when I left thirty minutes later, although the look she gave seemed mixed with something else. Fear, perhaps? Or pity? Still, the evening had proved entertaining and I went to bed thinking about all the things beginning with BRI- that might have death coming to it: British industry, Britney Spears' career, Bristol Cream consumption, briar pipe usage.

Monday February 19th

....

This is just to say

I have eaten
the custard creams
that were in
my hotel room

and which
have probably
been here
since last Christmas

Forgive me
they were delicious
so custardy and creamy
and so soft

Leamington Spa! Home of the Royal Pump Rooms and Baths!
Birthplace of Randolph 'Randy' Turpin! Pioneer of lawn tennis!
Setting for the 1990s BBC sitcom *Keeping Up Appearances*!

That's what Wikipedia tells me anyway, having had very little
chance to explore the town since I arrived at the Royal Oak Hotel
five hours ago. For me, this Warwickshire spa town comprises of
no more than this: a room which smells of mothballs, a
migraine-inducing floral carpet which must have felt dated back
when Charles and Di were getting hitched, the compulsory
Corby trouser press and packet of stale custard creams, a shower
that drips metronomically and these slides, these endless Power-
Point slides.

I have now managed to cut thirty-six of them, creating thirty-
two new ones in the process. In spite of this, I'm not sure they
reveal much about how we might leverage the power of social
media to brand-manage our value proposition. After all this time
I still don't know what that means.

Tuesday February 20th

The Onboarded

We have been here before.

We who slouch at formica tables
and fish adeptly in sea-green bowls
for cellophaned sweets to the music of fizzy water.   *For*

We who drowse in PowerPointed twilight,
as time slides slowly past, fearful of break-outs
and the tyranny of role play.   *For we*

We who doodle on hotel-headed notepaper
and listen distractedly to the motorway's distant hum
which leads to other places.   *For we are*

We who leave money so carelessly on the table
and grab greedily at the pendulous fruit
that hangs so low.   *For we are the*

We who wait in shabby expectation
of the all-too-brief respite of bourbons
and tepid coffee.   *For we are the awayday*

We who nurse feelings of envy
towards the red marker pens that run out
before we ourselves can.   *For we are the awayday trippers.*
          The brainstorm troopers.
          The boiled sweet hoarders.
          The bored onboarders.
          The project deep-divers.
          The flipchart survivors.

....

I've read somewhere that for those people who, by nature, are rather introverted and uncomfortable with the prospect of public speaking, the strategy of imagining your audience naked is a popular one.

For me, this was where things began to go wrong; the thought of Janice unclothed was problematic enough but by the time I'd summoned the strength to conjure up a vision of the exposed paunch and unsheltered nether-parts of Head of Customer Engagement, David Stentley, I was a gibbering, stammering wreck.

The phrases which had seemed so compelling when copying and pasting them from the Harvard Business Review website – 'peeling the onion', 'lipstick on a pig', 'where the rubber meets the road' – frankensteined into something awkward and insincere the moment that they tumbled from my mouth. In corporate parlance, I had become a Meanderthal. A Great Big DisaPower-Pointment. A Nontrepreneurial Nonentity. Janice finally put us all out of our collective misery a mere ninety minutes into my thirty-minute presentation.

I sought solace in a shortbread finger.

At dinner, the talk turned to post-awayday golf. Plans are in place for a quick round tomorrow after the final session – and it's clear that I am not part of them. As relieved as I am not to be invited along, it's a sure sign that my corporate star, which had once shone so briefly, is now beginning to fade and die. Already I can feel my outer layers burning up, as I begin the process of collapse. One day I may be no more than a very dense white dwarf.

Wednesday February 21st

I found myself running out of the room at the end of the awayday as if it were the end of a school year. If I'd had a satchel on me, it would have been thrown up into the air with joy. At least I'd managed to let off a stink bomb in the meeting room; well, at least that's how it seemed my presentation yesterday had been received.

I watched them all move noisily away to the golf course, like a herd of corporate hippopotami. Next week, when everyone's back in the office, the awayday will be advertised to have been a big success: there will be tales of the day's swaggering stroke-play, the eagles and albatrosses, and near holes-in-one. Unmentioned will be the wild swings out of the rough and kicked-up sand from the bunkers.

Awaiting me is a meandering train journey home. Ordinarily, this would be prime poem-writing territory, but I have another, more pressing commitment. It's book group tomorrow evening and Voltaire's *Candide* is calling me, in the way that only a late-eighteenth-century French Enlightenment satire can (i.e., faintly and with little hope of being heard).

It is mildly embarrassing to think that this will be the first time in three years that I'll have finished the book ahead of the meeting.

Thursday February 22nd

John Travoltaire

Well, you can tell by the way I break the rules,
I'm a reason man: no time for fools.
Progress checked, our freedom scorned,
We've been kicked around since we were born.
But it will be all right, it's not too late
For separation of Church and State.
We can try to understand
With science to lend a helping hand.

Dictionaries and dancing, poems, plays and prancing,
I'm spreadin' the light, spreadin' the light.
Despots are a-quakin' and institutions shakin',
And I'm spreadin' the light, spreadin' the light.
Ah, ha, ha, ha, spreadin' the light, spreadin' the light.
Ah, ha, ha, ha, spreadin' the light.

....

Lining up at the bus stop, with *The Best of Disco* shimmying and bumping in my earholes, I was struck by the sudden thought that if John Travoltaire did not exist, it would be necessary for The Bee Gees to invent him.

This fanciful notion was given short shrift at book group, where the talk was of Leibnizian optimism, *Bildungsromans*, and the symbolism of gardens. I struggled to keep up, having dropped off to sleep on the train yesterday, which meant I arrived this evening with the book half-unread (or as Pangloss might look at it, half-read).

My main contribution to proceedings came with the purchase of a round of drinks and a packet of honey-roasted peanuts. The bar was completely out of pistachios AND wasabi peas. If this is the best of all possible worlds, what then are the others?

Friday February 23rd

This is the second Friday in a row that the Man at Number 29 has failed even to attempt to put his refuse sacks out. He has either become stoically resigned to his fate (a form of predustbination, perhaps), or he's trapped inside his house, held hostage by his own bin bags.

I, though, had other domestic chores on my mind – a bathroom to clean, cat hair to hoover up, a recipe to seek and some books to refile in ISBN order (those recent bookshop trips had taken their toll). Ordinarily, these tasks would be prime procrastination territory but I need my house to look its best because . . . Dylan is coming to stay tomorrow!

Stuart is taking Sophie away for the weekend on some sordid romantic tryst, no doubt involving oak timbers, complimentary pink champagne and spa foot treatments, possibly for the removal of unsightly corns and verrucas. With some reluctance, Dylan has been entrusted to my care.

Whistling vigorously, I went about my jobs and imagined him reporting back snippets of his weekend to Sophie:

'Dad cooked this amazing dinner last night.'

'I haven't laughed so much in ages!'

'Yeah, he's sorted. He just seems so . . . at peace with himself and the world, somehow.'

'Dad's vegan now, you know.'

The cat noticed me smiling to myself. She gave me one of her worried looks in response.

Saturday February 24th

Do not go, lentil, into that good pie

Do not go, lentil, into that good pie
Lest it should burn not bake upon the tray,
Rage, rage against the oven turned too high.

The soybeans and chickpeas may also die
For the pulses quicken upon their way,
Do not go, lentil, into that good pie.

Its pastry turns crisp and as black as night
And the legumes scar and darken to grey,
Rage, rage against the oven turned too high.

When comes my turn in the furnace to lie,
Grieve not my remains of charcoal and clay,
Do not go, lentil, into that good pie.

Do not go, lentil, into that good pie.
Rage, rage against the oven turned too high.

....

As I was throwing the blackened remains of my lentil cottage pie into the bin, Dylan told me that I needed to devise some better coping strategies to help me deal with adversity.

He told me that I needed to be more positive about the world around me.

He told me that I needed to have more confidence in my own abilities.

He told me that I really shouldn't feel lonely, not when each of us has the whole universe inside ourselves.

I asked him what made him think I needed to devise better coping strategies. He made reference to my sobbing and the repeated banging of my head on the table.

I pointed out to him that, admittedly, I may have over-reacted to the demise of my lentil cottage pie. But it was only ruined because I'd spent the last two hours on the phone, waiting in a queue to speak to someone in New Delhi about getting the Wi-Fi fixed, which – with impeccable timing – had decided to go down just as we were about to watch a film on my laptop. We were watching a movie online because – half an hour previous – one of the shelves above the television had given way, and the subsequent avalanche of books had knocked it off the shelf, the screen smashing into several thousand fragments on the floor, among the rubble of un-ISBN-ordered volumes.

It was a lot of adversity to cope with in a very short space of time.

I asked him what made him think that I needed to be more positive about the world around me. He pointed to the latest *Well Versed* magazine, which was pinned to the kitchen wall and open at the winning poem, to which I'd added my own graffiti as well as the three darts which were sticking out of a photograph of Toby Salt's face. I wondered whether now was the right time to mention the rather ingenious scoring method I'd devised to accompany this activity but thought better of it.

I asked him what made him think that I needed to be more confident in my own abilities. He pointed at my pedal bin, which was crammed full of scrunched-up half-written stories and abandoned poems. I didn't say anything in response to this either.

I didn't ask him what made him think that I was lonely.

Sunday February 25th

Today was an improvement. We breakfasted late, played Scrabble and listened to some records. But still I couldn't help thinking that Dylan seemed more relieved than disappointed when Sophie came to pick him up this afternoon.

I watched them walk off down the path and approach the car parked outside my house. I could just about make out the figure of the man in the driver's seat. He was wearing sunglasses and pounding the steering wheel, presumably in time to some music. As Sophie and Dylan opened the doors and climbed in, I heard the sound of 'The Power of Love' by Huey Lewis and the News.

I went back inside. I had intended to do some more research for my *Well Versed* poem but, with the Wi-Fi still down, decided upon an early night instead.

Monday February 26th

I've taken Dylan's advice and decided to establish a growth mindset for myself. In this new spirit of positivity, I have declared there to be no problems, only opportunities.

Today was spent in trying to resolve all the opportunities that were awaiting me in my email inbox. There was also an opportunity with the vending machine at work which led to its retention of my pound coin when I attempted to purchase a Twix.

I taped a haiku to the glass:

Snack machine notice:
The light inside has broken
Yet I still function.

At home, I continue to deal with the opportunity of having no Wi-Fi.

Tuesday February 27th

Lorde's Prayer

Our Father John Misty,
which Art in Hanson,
hallowed be thy James
thy Kinksdom come,
thy will.i.am,
in Earth, Wind and Fire as it is in Heaven 17.
Give us Green Day our Motörhead.
And forgive us our Travises.
Aswad forgive Them that Travis against us.
And lead us not into The Temptations;
but deliver us from Emo.
For Ride is the King Crimson,
T'Pau, and the Gloria,
For Everly and Everly.
Shamen.

Dylan must have told Sophie all about my series of disasters last weekend because when I turned up for 27th Club tonight, the first thing that Darren did was to ask me for my recipe for lentil cottage pie. He seemed to find this most amusing. I told him to shut up and watch the band.

They were called Zut Alors and infused ballads of partially requited love with the atmosphere of the Champs-Élysées. Berets were worn saucily. Accordions were played jauntily. There was on-stage Gallic smouldering and sultriness as befits a band born and bred in Merthyr Tydfil. Darren was charmed by the band's faux-Frenchness and came away from the merch stand at the end of the night clutching a copy of their latest album, *Je Ne Regrette, Rhian*.

While they were on stage, a sudden image popped into my head of Liz in the role of Catherine Deneuve's *Belle de Jour*; I folded up the thought, inserted it into an imaginary half-empty packet of mentholated Gauloises, before placing the box in my pocket to take another peek at when I got home.

Wednesday February 28th

The lack of Wi-Fi is severely testing my newly avowed growth mindset, not to mention my ability to watch videos of roller-skating cats and read Wikipedia articles on the American Coinage Act of 1965.

In such circumstances, it is customary for humankind to revert to a former, less developed state and so I turned my new television over to ITV4.

An old episode of *Poirot* was on. I don't know why I have such a fascination with television detective dramas, with all that murder and mayhem, passion and revenge. It's a far cry from my own quiet half-life, whatever Mrs McNulty might have me believe.

But I guess that's exactly the point. Both that and the need to make sense of things. Like the cryptic crossword, it's a search for answers. If only I could apply those little grey cells to real life, too. The problem is: if I don't quite know what the question is, how will I know when I've found the answer?

March

Thursday March 1st

Confession

Is there anything else I can help you with today? he asks,
and I consider telling him

about my awkwardness
in social situations,

and my inability
to form lasting relationships,

and my inadequacies
as a son and a father (not to mention as a lover),

and my lack
of Twitter followers,

and my fears
of an imminent nuclear attack,

and my failure
to adjust to most aspects of the modern world,

and I say, *no,*
there's nothing else,

it was just about the Wi-Fi,
thanks very much.

While my internet connection appears no closer to resolution, my human connection to the customer-service team in New Delhi is growing stronger by the day. Today, it is with 'Craig' that

I take part in that long-distance tango known as The Reconfiguration of the Router. We talk about our respective childhoods, the legacy of decolonisation, our favourite types of biscuit and our dreams which have become as dusty and cracked as the wicket at Ranchi cricket ground.

What we don't really talk about is when my Wi-Fi will be back up and running.

Friday March 2nd

After so many weeks of humiliation, it looks like the Man at Number 29 is losing the will to carry on. His dressing-gowned pursuit of the bin lorry has turned from frantic dash to forlorn plod. Or it could be that his carpet slippers are simply not up to the early morning wet and greasy streets. His last-gasp hurl of bin bags bounced off the back of the truck and split open in the middle of the road as the truck tore off up the hill, whoops of laughter emanating from within.

In silence, I helped him clear up the detritus.

Later, I tried to write a poem using a metaphor that might somehow connect the contents of a bin bag to a more profound statement about the modern human condition but I threw it away because it was rubbish.

Saturday March 3rd

....

A Poem of Three Halves

At the end of the day,
when the final biro has run out,
he's only gone and written
a poem of three halves.

With that cultured right hand,
he could rhyme on a sixpence
and the lad must be delighted
at his failure to keep a clean sheet.

He's worked his hands off today
and he'll be the poet
who'll be going home happy
with three stanzas in the bag.

....

Bereft of other ideas as the team went into the break trailing 4–0, Rob Trafford put Dylan in charge of the half-time team talk.

'Teamwork is the fuel that allows ordinary footballers to achieve extraordinary things,' he told his fellow players.

There were murmurs.

'If we divide the task, we can multiply the results.'

There were whoops.

'Losing, like winning, becomes a habit. Let's go out there and break it.'

There were fist-pumps and roars. It did the trick: six second-half goals and their first victory in more than two years was secured.

Rob Trafford has now promoted Dylan to Assistant Team Manager.

Dylan was delighted. I wish I could feel happier about it.

Sunday March 4th

....

Dessert Island Discs

1. Sundae Bloody Sundae
2. Fool If You Think It's Over
3. Key Lime Every Mountain
4. Champagne Supavlova
5. It's a Family Éclair
6. Don't It Make Your Brownies Blue
7. In the Gateaux
8. Brûlée-vous

....

I'd been listening to *Desert Island Discs* and thinking about lunch, when Dave popped around. He'd come to remind me about the all-day revision party they're holding.

I don't altogether understand how much revision can be happening amidst the thirty or so people who have since gathered in their house, the whooping and shouting, and the sounds of 'Boogie Wonderland' which are currently blasting out from within it. But I suppose exam-preparation techniques are different to what they used to be in my day.

Monday March 5th

Day eleven of no Wi-Fi. I am near breaking point. I have now exhausted all possible household chores, having checked through twelve years' worth of *Well Versed* magazines to ensure that they were filed in chronological order (they were). After one last throw of my darts (scoring 140 points for hitting Toby Salt's right eye, left nostril and upper lip), I removed January's issue from the kitchen wall and inserted it into my collection.

With nothing else to do, I returned to the *Guardian Bumper Christmas Cryptic Crossword* and surveyed my progress. There were sporadic outbreaks of lettering in the north-east and south-west quadrants but the grid was still mainly comprised of blank squares, unfilled in and unfulfilled, waiting for someone to come along and remove them of their emptiness.

I redoubled my efforts and, by the end of the evening, I'd cracked 3 down:

EVENT HORIZON (noun): the boundary of a black hole, from inside which no normal energy can escape.

Which reminds me, it's Poetry Club tomorrow.

Tuesday March 6th

I could sense the rest of the group eyeing me with interest. It was then that I realised I was still applauding when everyone else had stopped some time ago. A minute or so had passed since Liz had sat down from performing a new poem she'd written entitled 'Mansplaining at the Ghostbusters Training Academy for Women':

Well, love, it looks like you've got a shape-shifter
there, tricky buggers them, please excuse my French.
You'll need your photon gun and a monkey wrench,
if you've got one to hand. Watch as you lift the

neutrona wand, love, valuable that is. Good
stuff. Now, there's a cyclotron in that backpack,
not that your pretty head should worry about that.
It's to concentrate the protons, see. That should

create a positronic ionized stream
to polarize with the negative charges
of the ectoplasm. Still with me, darling?
Lovely. Wait 'til you hear the shape-shifter scream . . .

There. He's not going anywhere! Now, love, just
pop him right inside this Muon Trap. Double-
check he's secure. We don't want any more trouble
from the likes of him! There, you did it! You must

be exhausted. I didn't think you'd stick it,
not at first. It's tiring work – even for men.
A lot of women wouldn't have it in them.
A cuppa's what you need to sort you out. Biscuit?

She'd recited it in a mock-cockney voice, delivered with all the
condescension of a garage mechanic confident of fleecing a customer for an extra monkey through an assumed superior
knowledge of camburettors or whatever it is they're called. And
yet, in spite of this, she made the poem seem *sexy* somehow –
particularly the line 'pop him right inside this Muon Trap'. It was
a most intriguing performance and one that I was determined to
ponder some more at length when I got home.

As I got up to read a few poems, I could hear Toby Salt defin-
ing the term 'mansplaining' to Chandrima although I could tell

by the look on her face that she knew this already. Liz appeared to like my poems, too. She laughed in all the right places (there were two) and then smiled at me as I sat down. I fear I may have blushed in response.

What's more, she demonstrated a healthy aloofness towards Toby Salt and his latest posturings. He gave us a preview of a *terza rima* he'd written for the Saffron Walden Poetry Festival entitled 'Bucchero Redux', about the socio-cultural history of an ancient Etruscan pot. This pantomime of pretentiousness was greeted by Liz with rolled eyes and arched eyebrows; although, admittedly, they may well have been directed at my wayward flicking of pistachio shells, a number of which had inadvertently landed in the folds of her dress.

I think it wonderful how quickly Liz has settled into Poetry Club. Next month, I hope that I might even get to talk to her, given the opportunity.

Or should that be problem?

Wednesday March 7th

....

Not Drowning but Waving

They saw him, his arms up in the air
And they rushed in to save him:
But I was just happy with how far I'd swum
And not drowning but waving.

Poor chap, he must have had enough
And decided to join the dead
Lurking beneath must have been sad, hidden depths,
They said.

Oh no, no, no. I have none of those,
(He spluttered as they reclaimed him)
I was simply splashing around, having fun,
And not drowning but waving.

....

In an unusually good mood, I found myself whistling as I pedalled off to the bookshop in my lunch hour in pursuit of the first
volume of Proust's *In Search of Lost Time* for this month's book
group. It looks formidable. Or, *formidable*, as they say in France.

To offset Proust's yin with some complementary yang, I
bought three P. G. Wodehouse novels. I popped these in my bag
along with a few other books I picked up along the way: *The Collected Poetry of Stevie Smith*; *Cryptic Crosswords and How to Solve
Them*; *The Little Book of Mindfulness*; Anthony Robbins' *Awaken the
Giant Within*; and Dale Carnegie's *How to Stop Worrying and Start
Living*. I also thought about buying Norman Vincent Peale's *The
Power of Positive Thinking* but it was £8.99 and I wasn't convinced
it would do me much good.

I dangled the bags off my handlebars and slowly pushed my
bike back up the hill, arriving back to work forty minutes late.
Nobody seemed to notice.

Thursday March 8th

The good mood I've been in since Tuesday has shown no signs of
abating and, for that, I have been rewarded by the noble and merciful Hephaestus, magnificent son of Hera and Zeus! Not only
has he restored my Wi-Fi connection but he has also enabled me
to Google who the Greek God of technology is.

And just in time, too. The deadline for next month's Well Versed poetry competition is approaching faster than information speeding down a fibre-optic broadband cable. I have decided to write about 'smart technology': it terrifies me. I stayed up late, tinkering with my poem's components, twisting its copper strands together, hoping I've connected my wires correctly.

Friday March 9th

A Life Sentience

They will be wondering by now where I am;
it's not like me to be home so late on a Friday,
This will not be forgotten in a hurry.
I can sense their censure, even from here;
hear the hiss of the vegetables as they soften
under the refrigerator's cool stare
and the dark scowl of the coffee machine.
I should have called, not left them to their own devices.

Perhaps they already know that I am in crisis,
observed tiny shifts in my behaviour
of which even I was unaware;
the depth of my tread upon the carpet,
or the slouching in my chair
from which I shall not leap up to rescue a forgotten cake
or slowly hoist myself to trudge to the corner shop:
its milk cartons must serve another.

And no more shall my day start
with a blast of cold to snatch my breath
as the shower wakes for morning
or with a desperate stretch

for a toilet roll that is not there.
For everything is *just so*. Optimized.
A thousand decisions and revisions
outsourced to things far smarter than me.

And, in its place, an absence
and this stretching of the hours.

···

There. It has gone. Into the unforgiving jaws of the post box. In the future, it will post itself.

In celebration, I watched an old episode of *Taggart* with the cat and began to think about next month's Poetry Club.

Saturday March 10th

Dylan's team continues to defenestrate the formbook. They picked up their second victory in as many weeks under his guidance. He seems remarkably phlegmatic about it all. 'It's simple,' he said with a shrug as we walked back, 'winning is just about seeing the possible.'

Sophie came to collect him later and, while standing on the doorstep, removed the pin from her hand grenade of news: Stuart is moving in with them from April. Interpreting my two-minute silence as uncomfortable, she asked me how I felt about it. 'Fine. Absolutely fine. Yes, really fine. Totally fine,' I responded, being completely fine about the situation, which I was, given that there was nothing not to be fine about.

I spent the evening playing Scrabble by myself, being fine, and trying to see the possible.

Sunday March 11th

Scrabble Board, Abandoned Mid-Game, Author and Date Unknown

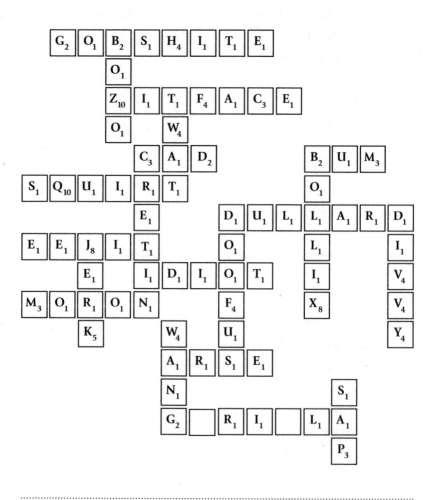

Monday March 12th

Since *The Disastrous Affair of Leamington Spa*, I have felt my corporate stock dwindle; 'stock' as in 'reputation' that is, not company shares, nor indeed my stock of aesthetically-pleasing yet utilitarian stationery, which remains as impressive as ever.

Senior eyes are averted from me, inner sanctums are closed to me and frosted-glass meeting rooms keep their secrets from me, occupied as they are by huddled suits and dark whispers.

The winds of change are blowing here. I hear the rattle of paper clips in the breeze.

Tuesday March 13th

All this change must have unsettled me. I have not written a poem since last Friday.

In search of inspiration I went onto Twitter. In my absence, my follower count has mushroomed to twenty-seven. Toby Salt now has over four hundred. I suspect most of these are spam accounts. But there, amongst my new followers, was Liz. I followed her back and, for reasons unclear to me, I instantly felt a digital thumbprint of pressure in the small of my back.

I suppose I should start tweeting again but that doesn't usually end well for anyone.

Wednesday March 14th

Liz retweeted my poem! Twitter told me that today is Pi Day and to commemorate the event, I posted up a poem. I'd called it 'π in the sky':

He'd think about her constantly
– well, 22/7 –
never completing.
He even stopped eating.

Then, one day – at 3.14 –
a chance meeting.
But, sadly,
not repeating.

It received 3.1415926535897932384626 4 retweets, or thereabouts, including one – did I mention this before? – from Liz!

To show tacit acknowledgement and gratitude, I reciprocated by liking her retweet of an article which contained '8 Odd Facts about Pi'. One of those was that pi is both irrational and transcendental. Like love, I thought. Or a fondness for custard creams.

Thursday March 15th

Liz has liked another of my poems on Twitter! I posted up a poem about hurting my back on an item of children's play equipment. It was titled 'Beware the slides of March'. Within minutes the little Twitter heart symbol lit up – and it was her!

Later, I thought about how she'd 'retweeted' my poem yesterday but had only 'liked' today's one. Is this a sign that she's going off me? Has my allure peaked already? I should try not to read too much into all this.

To calm myself down, I went to bed early, determined to get stuck into some Proust. Having successfully got a couple of paragraphs under my belt, I found my eyes closing so quickly that I barely had time to tell myself that I was falling asleep.

Friday March 16th

I had a terrible dream last night. Janice and the rest of my work colleagues stepped forward one by one and stabbed me in the back with letter openers. Another figure emerged slowly from the shadows. 'Et tu, Tomas?' I whispered hoarsely before he squirted me in the eyes with his Windolene trigger spray and I woke up with a strangled cry.

I looked it up in my *Dream Dictionary* but the book contained no references to Windolene specifically – only generic, non-branded window cleaning sprays – so I am none the wiser as to what it all means.

Saturday March 17th

Walking back from a hard-fought 5–3 victory ('there is no elevator to success, sometimes you just have to take the stairs'), I asked Dylan how he felt about Stuart moving in with them.

'OK, I suppose,' he said. 'He makes Mum happy. But he can be a bit of an idiot.' I ordered in pizza for lunch to celebrate.

After Dylan had left, I got down to some research. A quick review of social media and I was able to compile the following:

Name: Stuart Mould.

Digital footprint: Size Twelve
(Facebook, Twitter, Instagram, LinkedIn accounts).

Number of followers: 124,516

Number of accounts followed: 124,516

Profile Description: Life Coach. Dream Architect. Mojo Motivator. Inner Peace Keyholder. Making a difference through one little act of kindness at a time.

Follower Engagement: Medium to high. Conversations with followers contain high exclamation mark and emoji quotient.

Typical post A: Photo of a soaring mountain / tranquil lake / breathtaking sunset accompanied by an inspirational saying, such as 'Make the rest of your life, the best of your life!' / 'Dreams don't work unless you do!' / 'Change the world with a smile. Don't let the world change your smile!'.

Typical post B: 'This weekend I will be running a marathon / riding in a cyclathon / hosting a zumbathon / plummeting in a skydive-athon to raise money for Syrian refugees / Albanian orphans / Crofter Aid / The Society for the Preservation of Bees. To donate, visit my fundraising website . . .'

The more I read, the more I worry about the deleterious and corrupting effect that this man may have on my son's life.

Sunday March 18th

Please Take These Words For I Need Them Not

Please take these words for I need them not,
these semantic props from another age.
Consider all that wasted time spent
in their pursuit, that groping for a phrase

that is never quite right. Five hours to get:
You sweep the clouds behind the moon
to let the stars dance upon the night
and make the darkness spark itself to light.

What rot. All that effort squandered
when other things pile up: Facebook news,
the laundry basket, the washing up.
How better to have used: ♣ ☽ ☆ ✐ 👏 💕

Damn these drab dictionary words,
occupants of my ossified brain.
They make me irascible and querulous.
How much easier to be 😒.

No longer shall I be in a brown study,
all tenebrous and Stygian,
not now I can express myself
in fluent Emojian 😥.

So take these words for I need them not,
I shall replace them with little pics.
Because now I can simply be 😂.
not refulgent with lachrymary bliss.

I called Sophie about Stuart. It didn't go well.

She seemed upset that I might dare to question his credentials. She hadn't even bothered to look at the email I'd sent her last night with links to a selection of his social media posts and other crimes.

'Just take a look at them,' I implored. 'One is a photo of an eagle flying over a mountain top.'

'And what if it is?' she responded, angrily. 'He's only trying to be positive and encourage people to make the most of themselves.' I held the phone away from my ear. 'What's so bad about that?'

'But it says "DARE TO SOAR!!!",' I told her, conclusively.

'You just don't get it, do you, Brian? It's not about what Stuart *says* or what he *writes*. It's about what he *does*. He's out there – in the world. Trying to make a difference. Helping people. Mending lives. Bringing warmth. Compassion. He's not sat at home, re-ordering his book collection, waiting for life to come to him.'

'It contains three exclamation marks,' I replied dully.

Sophie sighed. 'He makes me *happy*.'

'Is that Smiling Face with Open Mouth and Smiling Eyes Happy, or Grinning Face Happy, or Smiling Face with Open Mouth and Closed Eyes . . .'

Sophie hung up.

Monday March 19th

Something is definitely up at work: it's been days since Janice has harangued me. People edge past me shiftily in corridors, half-smiling in sympathy.

I think it may be affecting my motivation levels. Instead of doing any actual work, I idled away the day in writing a series of 'uninspirational quotes', using Stuart as a kind of anti-role model:

1. No matter how big the problem, it is never too late to run away.

2. Every morning's another chance to have an equally awful day.

3. Hard work may be optional but mediocrity is inevitable.

4. Nothing is impenetrable, the word itself says "I'm penetrable".

5. Inside every opportunity is a disappointment waiting to happen.

6. Don't be overawed by your ordinariness. Make it your passion.

7. It's not about winning or losing, it's the falling apart that counts.

8. Unless a trampoline breaks your fall, you're unlikely to bounce.

9. Keep your head in a puddle long enough, and you'll drown.

10. Life is like a parachute; it gets you down.

I have pinned it to my officle wall and taken another copy home to stick on the fridge door.

Tuesday March 20th

I'm a Celeriac Get Me Out of Here

A knobbly root vegetable
   with a plan
      and bravado

was able to escape
   from the van
      of Ocado.

Toby Salt has had a poem go 'virile' on Twitter, a technical term employed by users of social media to indicate a strong tweet with lots of energy.

It has been retweeted more than three thousand times and his follower count now nears four figures. It concerns the famine in East Africa and, according to one of his followers, reveals 'a profound empathy that moves beyond political borders and teaches us what it is to be human'. As if. The closest Toby Salt has got to famine is when the Ocado van broke down and it was three hours late in delivering his rosemary and sea-salt focaccia.

Liz was amongst the retweeters. How noble of her, to put to one side the poem's obvious flaws and failings, in order to raise awareness of this terrible situation.

Wednesday March 21st

I was liberating a Twix from the snack machine this afternoon, when I noticed the copy of Toby Salt's poem pinned up next to it, underneath which was a bucket collecting money for the East

African Famine Appeal. It is incredible to think about the power of poetry and how it can make a real difference to world events and people's lives.

Thursday March 22nd

In a dramatic turn of events, both the collection bucket and Toby Salt's poem have disappeared. An email circulated from HR. It stated that 'following a staff complaint that the collection did not conform to one of the company's annually approved charities, the decision has been taken to remove the collection from public display. However, should staff wish to make a donation to this very worthy cause, then they should follow the link below'.

I got my head down for the rest of the day before heading home to a quiet evening of kale and quinoa salad, with a side serving of Proust. Before climbing into bed, I made an online donation of £100 to the East Africa Famine Appeal.

Friday March 23rd

There was no sign of movement at Number 29 this morning so I put his bin bags out for him, using up his five-bag allowance and then adding three more of his to my own pile to help clear the backlog. I spotted Mrs McNulty peering out warily at me through her net curtains and making the sign of the cross.

I went into work to face the horror of 'Dress-Down Friday'. In protest at such a ridiculous gesture of enforced corporate jollity, I taped a poem (unsigned) to the water cooler machine:

Vive La Revolution!

Let others march to another drum.
Take tyrants down by sword or gun.
Or guillotine them one by one.
A button I shall leave undone.

Manifestos some may construct.
Their forceful words inspire, instruct.
Or heads of state they may abduct.
I shall leave my shirt untucked.

Let others preach from their soapbox.
Call walkouts, strikes, erect roadblocks.
Launch missile strikes from behind rocks.
I shall wear unmatching socks.

From the vantage point of my officle, I watched Richard Potts, the HR Director, reading it as he helped himself to a cup of water. I could see his lips moving. He shook his head and then removed it, ripped it up and threw it in the bin. The poem that is, not his head. He eyed me suspiciously as he strode past my desk in his Ramones T-shirt.

Saturday March 24th

....

The Day We Argued About Roman Numerals

Even now in my mind
that row remains VIVID.
We tried to stay CIVIL
but ended up LIVID.

....

With the cessation of footballing hostilities for the Easter holidays, I'd drawn up plans for some quality father–son time with Dylan. I'd be the first to admit that he hasn't seen me at my best recently and what any teenage boy needs is a strong and positive male role model in his life. Particularly one with plans largely centred around the sofa, the television and home-delivered pizza.

To my horror, Dylan had barely got through the door when he reached into his bag and produced a giant Latin grammar and vocab book. He started rambling on about something to do with GCSEs and revision and suchlike, and how it would be really helpful if we could go through some Latin together. Five long, torturous hours of Latin ensued. Two hours in, I suggested we go to the park or play a board game but he was having none of it.

I tested him *ad nauseam* on nominatives, accusatives, vocatives *et cetera*; I was barely *compos mentis* by the end of it. I suggested that maybe next time he might find someone else to help him, *in loco parentis*, as it were, but as soon as I started saying it, I could tell I'd become *persona non grata*. But don't blame me – *actus me invito factus non est meus actus!*

Sunday March 25th

I don't know where the time goes. Barely had I finished checking on the contributions to the Poets on the Western Front trip (nearly £1,800 now!) and clearing my garden of all the abandoned pairs of deely boppers and fluorescent leg warmers from Dave, Martin and Marvin's 80s Party last night, and it was time for bed.

I had hoped to make more progress with *In Search of Lost Time* but the changing of the clocks and the consequent loss of an hour has really impinged upon my Proust. I am doing my best to finish it but if Time itself has other ideas and conspires against me in such a cruel way then, really, what chance do I have?

I had planned to reward myself at the end of every page with a madeleine but not having any in the house, I made do with custard creams.

Today, I have eaten twenty-six custard creams.

As I bit into one of them – it may have been the nineteenth – a sudden, sharp memory came back to me of a student flat in Sheffield in the early nineties, the Cocteau Twins and a bottle of vodka, and Sophie and I gnawing at either end of a custard cream, until our crumb-coated lips met in the middle.

Monday March 26th

A near-perfect storm of boredom, procrastination and 'papeteriephilia' (a word I have just made up to mean a love of stationery) induced me to spend most of my working day reorganising my desk munitions. Five separate trips were made to the cupboard: new pens purloined, staples and paper clips pillaged, files and folders filched, then arranged in rainbow order upon my shelves. My desk drawer was tidied. My desktop stationery holder was replenished, its contents having first been rigorously tested and vigorously deplenished. I scribbled haiku on Post-it notes and stuck them to items in the stationery cupboard:

Crisp linen bedsheets
awaiting your impression.
Papery heaven.

Magical hole punch.
Snapping jaws swallow holes whole.
And look – confetti!

How to best highlight
your writing's inner essence:
sticks of fluorescence.

Humble paper clips
with such noble endeavour
hold things together.

I fear that this may be another indication that my job is failing to fulfil me. It may also be an indication that I am failing to fulfil my job.

Tuesday March 27th

....

Beer Mat's Last Theorem

On the back of a beer mat,
he finally proved the theorem
that $\left(\dfrac{\text{Mick }^{\text{Hucknell}} + \text{James }^{\text{Blunt}}}{\text{Taylor }^{\text{Swift}}}\right) = \text{Ed }^{\text{Sheeran}}$

....

It is fair to say that, until this evening, the musical genre of Math Punk had passed me by. The gates to those halcyon days of blissful ignorance have now sadly closed to me. The eight-piece Fibonazi Sequence played a set of snarling anarcho-algorhythmic rock as they promoted their latest album *The Lowest Common Denominator*.

They opened with their new single, 'My Sex is Hard (like a Diophantine Equation)'. Darren declared that he could actually hear integer coefficients within the song but given that he only just managed to scrape a C in his GCSE Maths, this struck me as unlikely. Fearing the onset of a migraine as I tried to keep pace with all the complex rhythms, counterpoint tunes and angular melodies I persuaded Darren to move to the back of the crowd so I might concentrate on my Proust.

No such luck, though. It was as the band launched into a long, sprawling instrumental piece called 'Trigonometry' that Darren went off on a tangent:

'Sophie tells me that she and Dylan are going to Barcelona for the weekend – with Stuart,' he said.

'That's nice,' I said. Page 29 of *In Search of Lost Time* really was a terrific one.

'Dylan's very excited, by all accounts. He's always wanted to go,' continued Darren. 'They're watching a game at the Nou Camp on Saturday night.'

'Splendid,' I said. Yes, page 29 was definitely one of the best pages I'd come across so far.

'Sophie said that you had often talked about going there with Dylan. But you'd never quite got around to organising anything.'

'Fantastic,' I said. I wondered how this page 29 stacked up against all the other page 29s I'd read. Early indications were favourable.

'It's really generous of Stuart, isn't it? Dylan's sixteen today, isn't he?'

Dylan's birthday! Darren was still talking but I was out the door before you could state that the square of the hypotenuse is equal to the sum of the squares on the other two sides. If I ran, I might just have time to buy a card from the shop on the corner, get some money from the cashpoint across the way, bung it inside and post it through Sophie and Dylan's letter box before midnight.

Wednesday March 28th

In Search of Lost Tomes

I had forgotten that –
for a long time – I went to bed early,
seduced by Proust,
who so often had *le mot juste*
about affairs of the heart
and the nature of art,
and all that stuff.

But life and things passed,
gave way to armchaired collapse
in front of a screen,
scrolling through memes,
watching videos of cats.

Until one evening,
when retrieving the remote,
I found you again, on the shelf,
as if stumbling upon a swan's nest
amongst the reeds, hidden,
the smell of your pages,
like fresh bed linen.

Feeling rather pleased with myself for this month's effort (although I never did get beyond page 29), I turned up to book group only to learn that nearly everyone else had finished it. They presumably have less hectic lives than mine. I did manage to sneak a quick look at the Wikipedia entry on Proust, having excused myself to go to the toilets, and so I was able to hold my own for a short while.

But when the conversation moved to the novel's embodiment of the principle of intermittence and a debate began on whether life was simply a series of different perceptions and often conflicting aspects of reality, I zoned out and focused my attentions on my cashews.

Thursday March 29th

I have been filling the gaps in my workday by scrolling through Twitter. The number of tweets to read is staggering! There are a lot of people in the world without much to do.

Liz, it would seem, is an *occasional* tweeter. She sends a tweet out – on average – every two days, and typically retweets those of others, two or three times a day. She is most active on Twitter between the hours of 11 to 12 a.m., and 7 to 8 p.m. Statistically, she is more likely to tweet during that early evening period, whereas most of her retweets are usually sent out in the morning, particularly around 11.35 a.m. The tweet sample for this analysis was taken only over a nine-month period and a longer-term study may yield different results.

This chance investigation of Liz's online behaviour reminds me that it's Poetry Club next week. It's about time I took it more seriously: spend more time on my poems so that they're in tip-top condition for when I have to get up and perform them. It is a mistake, I think, for a poem to be written in isolation from its audience.

Friday March 30th

These are post-Proustian times that we are living in; I have never felt so alive! Mrs McNulty appears to have other ideas, though. I caught her this morning stuffing a flyer on will-writing services through my letter box. I unlocked the door quickly but she vaulted back over the fence before I had the chance to confront her.

Today is Good Friday and the long weekend gives me a chance to work on my poems for Poetry Club. I got my head down with ferocious abandon.

Saturday March 31st

I focused on my poems to blot out unwelcome thoughts, searching out words and stroking them, releasing some back into the wild, taming others. And in that way, the picture in my head that I'd created of the three of them gazing up in awe at the Sagrada Família only surfaced every twenty minutes or so, and I was able to bat it away.

And now I have finished my poems for the day, I look for other distractions, like there, through the window, where a blue moon shines out, and lights up the sky.

It is big and bright and oblivious of how utterly extraordinary it is.

April

Sunday April 1st

Brian Ch.16 vv.1–6

And very early on the first day of the week,
when the sun had risen, he went to the cupboard.
And he said to himself,
'Who will open the door to this cupboard?'
And looking up, he saw that the door was already open.
And peering inside, he saw a young man sitting inside,
dressed in a white robe, and he was alarmed.
And the man said to him,
'Do not be alarmed. You seek the chocolate egg.
The one that was here yesterday.
But it is not here.'
And he trembled and was much afraid.
But the man said, 'Do not be afraid.
For he who seeks the chocolate egg,
Must first seek inside himself.'

Is it wrong to buy yourself three Easter eggs and eat them all in one sitting? I am unsure of the ethics surrounding the whole issue, unschooled as I am in Christian scripture. But, in the absence of a prevailing opinion, that's what I did, and I shall wait for the theologians to correct me.

Monday April 2nd

I sifted through my poems to figure out which ones to read at this month's Poetry Club. I considered 'Emphatic Love':

> You're outstanding,
> Just my type.
> I'm filled with admiration.
> LET'S CAPITALISE,
> **if I may be so bold**
> *and you have the inclination.*

I read it out loud. It didn't quite work. Vocally, I was struggling to convey each typeface style as it looked on the page. I tried shouting 'LET'S CAPITALISE', using a deeper voice for 'if I may be so bold' and then leaning to one side for *'and you have the inclination'* but I was concerned that the combined effect might simply be to make it look as if I was having a stroke.

I looked for another one. A strong, powerful rhyming poem to put Toby Salt in his place, perhaps. I gave 'Po-em' a go:

> If your rhyme is stuck and you can't get by
> then you may need the use of a hy-
> phen implanted at the end of a line
> and soon your poem will sound like a Stein-
>
> way piano in a grand concert hall,
> its notes floating in the air like a ball-
> oon. So what if the words happen to spill
> into two lines? Do not pity these syll-
>
> ables, orphaned, adrift, left there to hang;
> their beauty is in the way that they dang-

le.

That wasn't working either. It rhymed well on paper but when I read it aloud, it sounded as if I had a speech impediment.

In the end I settled on some standard fare (poems about Jeremy Clarkson, *University Challenge* and semi-colons) and a new poem about watching television and recognising a familiar face from the past. The latter piece, at least, might give me an air of mystery and imply that I was someone who possessed an interesting and troubled history.

Tuesday April 3rd

....

Artist's Impression

Channel-flicking on the television,
a sudden flicker of recognition,
and there you are, lighting up the screen.
You've not changed much, it seems.

The selfsame eyes of grey flint,
those touchpaper lips,
that shocking blaze
of hair. It's as if the days

lit by time's slow-burnt passage
are reduced to ashes.
An old flame, charcoaled
back to life by the controlled

hand of a police sketch artist.

I see you're still up to your old tricks,
wanted, as you are, for questioning
in connection with

a spate of arson attacks
in the vicinity of Matlock Bath.

I must confess to having developed something of a crush on Liz. Purely in a literary sense, of course, not in any kind of crass sexual way. She has such delightful couplets. And lovely, languorous iambs. Terrific dimples, too.

Her poems were the highlight of the evening. She has a way of reading them that makes my insides feel like they're in a tumble dryer. Her observations are funny and clever and razor-sharp. Against their light, those of Toby Salt were exposed as the pretentious nonsense they are – and my own poems as nothing more than schoolboy doggerel.

Courageously, I complimented Liz on her performance and offered her a pistachio nut when she sat down. She'd just opened her mouth to reply when Kaylee launched into a powerful lyrical diatribe about prostitution, sex slavery and venereal disease and further conversation became impossible.

By the time there was an opportunity to talk, Toby Salt had already smarmed in and was regaling Liz about his upcoming festival appearance at Saffron Walden and the special linocut edition of his forthcoming book, *This Bridge No Hands Shall Cleave*. I found myself powerless to intervene, cornered as I was by Douglas, who proceeded to tell me about the major military engagements of the Second Boer War for what remained of the night.

We were the last to leave. Outside the pub, as we were about to head off in our separate directions, Douglas turned to me and grabbed hold of my sleeve.

'Thank you, Brian,' he said.

I was rather taken aback.

'What for?' I asked him. 'What on earth do you mean?'

'Why, for putting up with me, of course! For letting me be a part of your club!' he exclaimed.

It had been a couple of years since Douglas had been out shaking a tin for the Royal British Legion and stumbled across Poetry Club. Encouraged onto the stage by Chandrima, he'd given us 'The Charge of the Light Brigade' to unanimous acclaim (Toby Salt wasn't there that evening). The next month he was back. This time with a recital of 'The boy stood on the burning deck':

Yet beautiful and bright he stood,
As born to rule the storm;
A creature of heroic blood,
A proud though childlike form.

His knowledge of poetry didn't stretch much further than a few learnt-by-rote classics from his schooldays but somehow that didn't matter at all.

'There's really no need to thank us, Douglas. We should be thanking you,' I reassured him. 'We're glad to have you in the club.'

'That's very kind of you to say so,' he said. 'But I know I must be a disappointment to you all on the poetry front.'

I made a snort of protestation. 'Come now, Douglas,' I said. 'You know as well as I do that Poetry Club isn't really about the poetry.'

For a moment, I thought he was going to cry. Then, as if pulling himself together, he suddenly stood to attention, saluted and marched off purposefully down the street.

Wednesday April 4th

Apropos of nothing at all, I've had the sudden realisation that I don't really write love poems. Proper love poems, that is. I think it might be good for me *as a writer* to attempt one of these for next month's Poetry Club.

Also, as I added up the subs from last night, it occurred to me this evening that we haven't yet asked Liz whether she'd like to join us on our Poets on the Western Front trip. What an oversight on our part! I think her sunny presence would help to offset all that morbid battlefield gloominess.

Thursday April 5th

It's a dangerous business going into a bookshop. You step across the threshold, and if you don't stay focused, there's no knowing where you might be swept off to. I'd only wandered in to get a copy of *Wuthering Heights* for this month's book group but I ended up emptying my wallet: *Love in the Time of Cholera* by Gabriel García Márquez; *The Nation's Favourite Love Poems*; *The Soulmate Experience: A Practical Guide to Creating Extraordinary Relationships*; a cookbook entitled *101 Things to Do with Quinoa*; and *The Observer's Book of Molluscs*.

I had planned to write a poem this evening but ran out of

time, having spent it rearranging my bookshelves to accommodate the new arrivals – without much success, it must be said. There are now books resting on top of other books and piles are forming on the floor.

Friday April 6th

At 11.30, I posted up another poem on Twitter:

On tentaclehooks I wait,
in the deep ocean dark,
for the right cephalopod
to steal my three hearts.

I'd called it 'Squid Goals'. I hoped it might be World Cephalopod Day. It wasn't.

A few minutes later, Liz retweeted it. And then, a reply! 'Thanks,' it read. 'I needed some nonsense today.'

I worked on my response to her until lunchtime. I was aiming for something that was simultaneously witty and matter-of-fact, as well as sophisticated and approachable. After an hour of deliberation, I settled on the rather more prosaic and insouciant, 'no probs'. That appeared to draw a line under the whole matter – although not for the RSPCA, who tweeted me to ask for a photograph of 'these so-called tentaclehooks', as they sounded potentially harmful to squidlife.

Saturday April 7th

There was another resounding victory for Dylan's football team today. In his pre-match team-talk, I heard him tell his teammates that they needed to express themselves more because 'nothing is art if it does not come from nature'.

On the long walk home, I asked him whether he'd come up with that himself or if it was another one of Stuart's. He looked at me disappointedly. 'I came across it in Barcelona,' he said. 'It's Gaudí.' I nodded sagely. He was manager between Rijkaard and Guardiola, I think.

When we got back, Dylan declared it was time for Geography revision. I volunteered my services. While he was getting his nose into textbooks full of glaciers, oxbow lakes, cumulonimbi, drumlins, and scree, I tried to help out by recreating the Burgess and Hoyt model of urban land use through the medium of Lego: with limited success, it must be said.

Sunday April 8th

Brazenly, I messaged Liz on Twitter to invite her on the Poets on the Western Front trip. To my delight, she responded almost instantly, saying that she'd love to come.

It feels like I've crossed a line, jumped over the barbed wire and exposed myself in No Man's Land, and now there are only two courses of action open to me: stand here and wait for annihilation, or plough on and hope to storm her trenches.

Cell

	A	B	C	D	E	F
1	Help!	Trapped	within	these	cell	walls
2	I	just	live	from	data	day.
3	I	wish	I	knew	the	formula
4	so	that	I	might	get	away.
5						
6	Instead	I	dream	of	other	worlds
7	and	a	life	of	**bold**	adventure.
8	Come	rescue	me	before	I	am
9	completely merged and centred.					

There was a time when I was an office somebody; if not one of the big enchiladas, then at least a small- to medium-sized quesadilla. My officle was envied by others for its desirable fenestered location. I had the run of the second-floor, east-side colour printer. It was widely rumoured that I had the ear of Janice.

Quite how it's come to this, I don't know. Only hammock tasks come my way these days: low-level planning, proofreading, endless spreadsheet data-entry. Unable to find anything to put on the front burner, I spend my time multi-slacking and clock-sucking. While storm clouds gather in frosted meeting rooms, I feel myself slowly fading into jobsolescence.

Tuesday April 10th

The April issue of *Well Versed – The Quarterly Magazine for the Discriminating Poet* arrived today, announcing itself with a papery thump on the doormat. Once more my poem has failed to be shortlisted. Mercifully, I noted that neither had Toby Salt's. On closer inspection, I discovered that this was because he was one of the judges.

He'd described the winning poem as a 'fascinating experiment at the bleeding interface of literature and technology'. It was called 'The Alan Turing Prize for Poetry' and had been written by a computer science Ph.D. student. The first half had been written by the student himself, who finds himself in a poetry competition with a 'poetry bot':

The Poet

The whole idea is absurd. It cannot feel
the rightness or wrongness of words
like I, nor describe the moon which hangs
in the changing night sky

as a pancake
as a bruised knee
as a scraped plate.

Reader, such things are innate, arrive in the brain
unbidden, uncaptured by an algorithm,
irreducible to formula, not a racket of tuneless words
played out by some school-hall orchestra

without its dear conductor. Each word in this poem
has been carefully deliberated, hard won,
is not simply one of the many permutations
which might make up a poem.

That's not the same as poetry, clearly.
It's no contest really.

The second half was written by the poetry bot and had been generated by a computer programme, featuring a complex set of algorithms which could take apart any given section of text and rewrite it as poetry. It rehashed all the words from the first piece:

The Poetry Bot

A poem is like the tuneless night,
hard-bruised by the rightness
of an uncaptured algorithm

which hangs simply in the sky,
as irreducible as a plate in a school-hall,
or one clearly scraped knee.

A poem is absurd, a pancake formula
to describe the many permutations
of the moon, not deliberated in the brain

by a carefully changing orchestra;
its has-been conductor cannot make up words.
As such, each word is played out whole,

unbidden, not without racket,
nor wrongness. Words arrive;
are innate things which feel (as some might not!).

That's it. No, really – it's the same idea.
Of the poetry contest?
This, dear reader, I won.

Toby Salt has described it as the 'next great development in poetical form, in which we move away from our reliance on the tired tropes of old.'

Some days I feel like a tired trope of old. And I'm utterly sick of Toby Salt's bleeding interface.

Wednesday April 11th

Staying late to finish my lunchtime sudoku, I told Tomas about the competition-winning computer-generated poem while he was cleaning my officle. He became very animated at the mention of this topic.

'But this is inevitable! As Wittgenstein would have us believe, the limits of our language are the limits of our world! If we can harness technology to broaden the lexicon of language, how might we reconstruct our words! Just imagine what might be achieved and the things that we might know of ourselves!' he cried before wiping my keyboard clean of its daily plaque.

There are days when it feels as if everyone is cleverer than me.

Thursday April 12

As if Toby Salt lording it as Judge and Jury wasn't enough, flicking through my copy of *Well Versed*, I also encountered an article written by him, entitled 'How I write':

> I rise by six and head outside for thirty minutes of tai chi under the cherry tree. Once I feel my surge of *qi*, I head back in to prepare half a grapefruit for breakfast while listening to BBC Radio 3: news and pop music ruins everything. Suitably fuelled, I journey down the garden to my studio which lies

secluded behind a magnificent oak tree. I walk inside this cedar-timbered, shingle-clad inner-city haven with its fully-stocked log store and wood-burning stove and sit down at my desk to wait for the magic to happen, having first poured myself a refreshing cup of tea. Lapsang souchong, I find, really helps to get my creative juices flowing.

Is it any wonder he goes around winning competitions and being invited to festivals and the like? If his shed was my shed, I suspect I'd have won the Nobel Prize for Literature by now.

Friday April 13th

....

Paraskevidekatriaphobia

is a fear of Friday the Thirteenth,
said the doctor, prescribing some pills,
writing the word underneath.

She looked at the note and fainted.
The only thing that made her feel ropier
was her hippopotomonstrosesquippedaliophobia.

....

Friday 13th might be unlucky for some but not for the Man at Number 29 who put out his recycling bags today, on the designated day for recycling. I saw him looking out through his bay window as they were picked up and carried off by the recycling truck. I don't think I've ever seen him looking so calm and collected. Unlike Mrs McNulty, who always spends this day in absolute terror, possibly with good reason. Last year, she ended up in A&E, having slipped up on the acorn she'd been carrying around with her all day for good luck.

In other news, I began to read *Wuthering Heights* this evening. I'm on page 12 already. It's rather moorish.

Saturday April 14th

....

Pipette Dream

He could gauze at her all day,
she was hot,
like a Bunsen burner
with its air hole fully open,
and he loved to watch the glint
of her conical flask
under the laboratory light.

Standing by the lab bench,
holding his own pipette,
he would dream of wild experiments,
but his tripod
remained unmounted
and there was no exchange
of tongs.

....

Dylan tells me that Stuart has been helping him with his GCSE revision and so, after football (another victory – 'winning is a habit'), I nobly volunteered my own services. Just my luck, he took out his chemistry books. Chemistry was probably my worst subject at school; I used to live in dread of the double lesson every Wednesday morning, a situation not helped by an incident involving Nigel Thompson and a pinch clamp.

All this must have sunk deep into my subconscious because later I dreamt that I was back at school and Liz was my chemistry teacher. She leant over me at my workbench, wearing nothing but a lab coat, and told me that she needed to inspect my milky-white coagulate, I woke up on the sofa with a cry, flushed and flustered.

Sunday April 15th

The cat set out her somnolent stall today, putting her pegs determinedly in me, and making all practical tasks impossible beyond the reading and sending of tweets. It is National Cat Day, and I posted up a photo of her on Twitter, with the caption 'My cat, asleep, in the eighth of her nine lives. Previous lives include Roman Centurion and Advisor to Cardinal Richelieu.'

Liz replied with a similar photo of her own cat, asleep, and a short poem:

In 1919,
plans for Woodrow Wilson's League of Nations were composed:
my cat dozed.

Liz was talking to me on Twitter! I found another photo of my sleeping cat. I sent it back with:

In 1789,
Louis XVI appraised the mob and realised his days were numbered:
my cat slumbered.

Liz responded once more with another picture and:

In 1533,
Thomas More refused the Oath and sadly paid the price:
my cat snoozed (and dreamt of mice).

We were having a banter! We were indulging in some actual ban-
tering! The Oath of Succession was actually 1534 but I let that
one go. I kept my next one brief in case Liz was getting bored:

In 1351,
the Black Death swept:
my cat slept.

In return, she revealed a respectable working knowledge of early
cartographical history:
In 150,
Ptolemy did some geometry and the world got mapped:
my cat napped.

My reply to that one I thought rather witty, and I was a little disappointed when Liz didn't single it out for particular praise:

In 64,
Rome burned. Nero fiddled. The citizens showed their ire.
My cat curled up by the fire.

Before Liz finished off the sequence with:

In 1323 BC,
my cat spent the year with both eyes firmly shut
then got buried with King Tut.

I have to go now, she wrote, *but thanks for making my morning.*

I stroked my cat some more. My lovely cat; she deserved it. Liz and I seem to have a lot of things in common: cats, poems, poems about cats . . . maybe other things, too. I wonder if she likes custard creams.

Monday April 16th

I know I should be working but there are far more interesting things to be doing on my phone. The list of untackled work tasks piles up gently and un-urgently and no one seems to mind. Instead there were more conversations to be had with Liz. It turns out that she's a freelance copy-editor and proofreader; that probably explains why she has already corrected my grammar twice today.

I picked up the crossword for the first time in a while this evening. As is often the way, I got an answer almost instantly. 22 across:

CALLIPYGOUS (adj.): having beautiful buttocks.

Tuesday April 17th

....

A Modern Romance

We started out
by texting

got snapchatting
then the next thing

we were updating
Facebook pages

with 'in a relationship'
statuses

swapping selfies
on Instagram

Spotify playlists
of our latest jam

Tumblr love notes
And Twitter hearts,

a shared Pinterest
in decorative arts.

We feel attuned,
in touch, complete,

one day
we even hope to meet.

....

Liz tells me that *Wuthering Heights* is one of her favourite books; she loves the wildness, darkness and windsweptness of it all. I told her how much I love it, too, as my copy, with its many pristine, unturned pages, gave me withering looks from my bedside table.

Wednesday April 18th

I have been thinking about how I might become a little more Heathcliff and a little less Brian.

It seems unlikely – given Liz's description of him – that Heathcliff would be content to spend his days sitting in an offlce, wrestling with Microsoft Excel. Although there are few opportunities for wildness and ruggedness at work, I did my best, rearranging my paper clips carefully into an unruly pile, scrunching up old memos and lobbing them at the wastepaper basket and signing off on my emails simply as 'B', with no preceding valedictions of 'best wishes' or 'many thanks' or anything.

I've also decided to stop shaving for a while.

Thursday April 19th

I stared darkly out of the window for long spells this morning before being gruff to Pat in the servery, when ordering my quinoa salad with mint and mango. I'm sure she deliberately short-changed me with my side helping of lentil crisps as a result. I thought about this at some length this afternoon, while staring darkly out of the window.

Friday April 20th

Blitzkrieg Top

When I put on my Ramones T-shirt,
with its presidential seal of rebellion,
I can almost smell the revolution

                in the air.
I like to wear it everywhere:
down the match or shopping mall,

on the golf course, in the gym, or

in Costa

where I sometimes sit and watch the
protest marches go past the window,
whilst sipping on my frappuccino.

All roads lead

to Ramones; you will see our breed
on every street, pushing strollers,
iPhoned jogging rock 'n' rollers,

defiant

in cottoned nonconformity, a giant
army of T-shirted mayhem makers
(once we've read the Sunday papers).

Hey ho, let's go.

I was summoned into the office of Richard Potts, Director of HR, when I arrived this morning. As I entered, Janice loomed up out of the darkness. Dress-down Friday was in full swing: Richard sported his customary Ramones T-shirt; Janice was wearing her suit without the shoulder pads. I rubbed my chin with its two-day stubble and wondered whether I'd been pushing the Heathcliff thing too far.

Janice spoke first.

'Brian, as you know, the solutions industry is in flux right now. We need to future-proof ourselves against anticipated market softness by right-sizing ourselves for sustainable growth. This involves making some very tough decisions concerning the viability and suitability of our human assets.'

She paused and looked at me enquiringly as if she were waiting for me to respond. I stared back blankly.

'Look, let me level-set with you. I'm afraid that, as part of this process, you are to be disintermediated.'

I continued to stare at her, nonplussed.

'Sorry, I'll disambiguate that for you. We are making an involuntary reduction in our office power and you will be amongst the decruited.'

I turned to Richard for help.

He sighed and look at me sadly. 'You see, Brian, we have drawn up the new organograms and I'm afraid your name is not on them. We can offer you a very attractive redundancy package, including six months' salary, and the help of an outplacement agency to get you fighting fit for that job market as soon as possible.'

I understood it all now. I was the problem, not the solution or the opportunity. I was dead wood. I was Friends Reunited. I was Betamax.

'I have a question,' I said.

'Of course,' Richard replied, half-smiling with relief that his ordeal was over. 'Fire away.'

'What's your favourite Ramones album?'

I watched him squirm for thirty seconds before I got up and left.

Saturday April 21st

....

Rhyme and Treason

Bored one day in nineteen eighty-two,
I pulled out a five-pound note and drew
a bushy moustache and a pair of specs

and sundry other physiognomic effects,
joined-up eyebrows, a furrowed brow,
zits, and the proud horns of a cow
upon Her Majesty's regal noodle.
It was a most disrespectful doodle.

All these years on, I've not said sorry yet.
That's why I'll never be poet laureate.

....

I didn't let on to Dylan or Sophie that I'd soon be joining the ranks of the unemployed. Some things are best kept hidden, like an embarrassing tattoo or a love of Billy Joel. My veneer of basic human competence is flimsy enough already – especially in comparison to Stuart – without providing additional supporting evidence.

My bluster can't have been too convincing. After Dylan had gone, Dave's head popped up over the fence as I was stooping to pick up some of Marvin's disposable catheters, which were strewn across the garden. I must have been wearing the news like a bad perfume (*Misery* by L'Oréal – Because You're Worthless) because he could sense something was not quite right. Gathering me up, with Martin and Marvin, we headed out to drink away the evening, raising our beers to freedom and defacing ten-pound notes in honour of whichever it was of the Queen's birthdays.

Sunday April 22nd

I nursed my hangover through the day. I lay in bed watching marathon runners on the television stagger over a finish line dressed as sausages and cartoon ducks, as my hangover slept on beside me. I helped it rise in the early afternoon, bathed and swaddled it, until I gently removed its bandages and its dull ache was there no more.

The convalescence of the hours gave me space in which to think. What actually *had* I lost? I'd never been particularly happy at work; it was merely something I had fallen into, like an artificial lake, or a vat of sulphuric acid, and then neglected to hoist myself out. But now the reservoir was being dragged and my poor body – scarred and broken but still breathing – was being pulled out.

And I realised, as I reached into the fridge for some milk to accompany my twelfth cup of tea of the day, that this is my moment to do something I *want* to do, not what I *need* to do. As Dylan might say, 'If opportunity doesn't knock, build a door.'

I tore up my list of uninspirational quotes and threw them into the bin.

Monday April 23rd

It is Shakespeare's birthday today, not that he's in any condition to celebrate. Liz and I exchanged tweets about our favourite lines.

I can only remember three Shakespeare quotes – the 'to be or not to be' one, the one about the dagger and the one about all the world being a stage. But I found a helpful website with an extended list and I think I must have come across as rather erudite. All difficulties are easy when they are known.

The remaining six hours of my working day were spent in writing a poem. I have called it, 'Thoughts Written on Turning Over an English Literature A Level Paper'.

It is the longest poem I have ever written. If I am actually expected to graft my way through these final few weeks of office life, then they have seriously misjudged me.

Question 1: *'If we wish to know the force of human genius we should read Shakespeare.'* **Do you share Hazlitt's view of Shakespeare? Illustrate your answer with examples from his writing.**

Brian: For goodness' sake, what a way to break the ice.
          This is all Greek to me. It may sound like treason
          but I cannot make rhyme nor reason of his words.
          I knew I should have paid more attention,
          but at the merest mention of the bard,
          I fear the game is up. Shakespeare sets my teeth
          on edge. It is all too hard.
          I have been hoisted by my own petard.

Question 2: **Answer either a. or b.**
a. Using quotations from his work, show how Shakespeare's language still resonates with us today.
b. In what ways is Shakespeare still relevant in the twenty-first century?

Brian: I am still in shock. For this is the long and short of it;
          I shall be the laughing stock of the class.
          A sorry sight. A foregone conclusion.
          I am under no delusion.
          I should have worn some quotes on my sleeve,
          not my heart. Perhaps I should try the second part –
          or will that, too, give me indigestion?
          2b or not 2b, that is the question.

Question 3: **'A fool thinks himself to be wise but a wise man**

knows himself to be a fool.' Consider Touchstone's observation in *As You Like It* in relation to the current predicament in which you find yourself.

Brian: I wonder whether others can hear
in the midsummer madness of this examination room,
this brave new world's crack of doom
as my thoughts thunder and race
on their wild-goose chase for Shakespeare's words.
No sooner do they stop to linger there,
then they vanish into thin air.
I could more easily catch a cold
than manage to keep hold of one of his phrases.
I have reached stasis and I realise now
this naked truth; my head is as dead
as a doornail. I know that I am going to fail —
and thereby, I suppose, hangs this tale.
[Exit Brian, pursued by despair]

Tuesday April 24th

The Palace of Broken Flowerpots

In the palace of broken flowerpots,
we shall sit upon wine-box thrones,
talking of the weather
amidst abandoned garden gnomes.

We shall contemplate the implements –
the rake, the spade, the hoe –

that we never seem to use.
How expectantly they dangle so!

And this mower might be our chariot,
these mice, our humble courtiers,
see them quartered in the hollows
of four fold-up garden chairs.

These compost bags shall be our bed,
and this life a kind of truth,
star-gazing through the holes
in our punctured palace roof.

....

In the spirit of Heathcliff, I went out to my shed this evening to write a poem by candlelight. I lasted five minutes. There was a rustling noise coming from the corner and I hastened back to the house. And so here I am, sitting on a flea-bitten sofa, where with one hand trapped beneath a flea-bitten cat, and an old episode of *Brother Cadfael* playing in the background, I scribble words into a notebook, while exchanging tweets with Liz on my phone.

Toby Salt will probably be in his cedar-timbered writing studio right now, contemplating his novel, or penning some Spenserian sonnet concerning the reflection of moonlight off a garden spade.

Wednesday April 25th

I've decided to buy myself a proper writer's shed with my redundancy money. This is my gift to myself, and quite possibly, literature.

Thursday April 26th

Wuthering Heights

Up on your bookshelf, insecure,
I hoped that you'd see me.
Grab your attention, with my jealous scenes,
In cloth, too needy.
How could you leave me
When I needed to possess you?
I hated you. I loved you, too.

Bad books in the night
Told me I was going to lose the fight,
You'd leave behind your withering, withering
Wuthering Heights.

Be quick! Read me – I'm classy – in your home,
I'm so cold, don't leave me in limbo.
Be quick! Read me – I'm classy – in your home,
I'm so cold, don't leave me in limbo.

Ooh, it gets dark! It gets lonely
On the other side of your room.
I pine a lot. My spine has got
Stiffened up without you.
Don't put me back, love,
You're my readership!
My one dream ends in disaster.

Tweeting alone in the night,
Just have me back at your side to put it right.
Don't leave behind your withering, withering
Wuthering Heights.

Be quick! Read me – I'm classy – in your home,
I'm so cold, don't leave me in limbo.
Be quick! Read me – I'm classy – in your home,
I'm so cold, don't leave me in limbo.

Ooh! Let me have it.
Let me grab your phone away.
Ooh! Let me have it.
Let me grab your phone away.

With all the disruption of the last few days, I'd neglected *Wuthering Heights* and only reached as far as page 65 by the time tonight's book group rolled around. On route, I listened to Kate Bush in the hope she might give me a quick potted summary of the plot. She didn't but I ignored my fears; imagine Heathcliff caring about such matters! Instead, I spent the evening staring at my beer glass darkly, and shouting, *'Cruel and false!'* in between glowers and cashew nuts. In turn, the rest of the group gave me a wide berth, which I felt helped to reinforce my social isolation and air of brooding heroism.

Friday April 27th

Get Up

Get up.
Get on up. Beep.

Get up.
Get on up. Beep. Threep.

Get up.

Get on up. Beeeeep. Threeeeep.

Stay on the scene
like a fax machine.

....

Darren had just finished showing me a new app he'd downloaded called 'Auto-Courgette' that converts ordinary words on
your phone into the names of vegetables, when I told him about
my plans to become a full-time writer. On stage was Daft Funk, a
two-piece act from Bermondsey, who specialised in the reimagin-
ing of popular songs from the 70s and 80s via the medium of
aged or obsolete technology. Sounds and rhythms were created
through the use of typewriters, Rolodexes, fax machines, toasters
and early computer games. Already tonight we'd been treated to
'Tracks of My Teasmade', 'Islands in the SodaStream' and 'All
Night Pong'.

'A writer?' he repeated. He grinned and shook his head as if he
found the whole idea amusing but in a mildly baffling kind of
way. 'Writing what, exactly?'

'You know, words and all that. In the form of poems, most
probably.'

'You're going to be a poet?' he said, properly laughing now.
'Good luck with that!'

'Not a poet. Just somebody who writes poems.'

There was more onstage beeping and the band launched into
a James Brown cover.

'Don't tell Sophie,' I said but Darren's attention had shifted
back to Daft Funk. While everyone else was being taken to the
bridge, I took myself to the bar. By the time I returned to the
throng, I was horrified to discover that the whole crowd was
dancing, Darren included. I'd had enough retro-kitsch for one

evening. As they went into the opening bars of 'Breville, Breville', I took one look at my Pac-Man watch and headed for the exit.

Saturday April 28th

'Let us no longer wallow in the goalmouth of despair, I say to you today, my friends!' he cried. 'And so even though there are difficulties ahead, I have a team!' There were cheers.

'It is a team deeply rooted in the idea of team. I have a team that lives out the true meaning of its creed: "All players are created equal!" '

More whoops and high-fives followed from the team and their proud parents as Rob Trafford stuffed his speech into the pocket of his tracksuit bottoms and the season of near misses and belated mellow fruitfulness was over. Dylan had taught him well.

Dylan himself stepped up to receive the Players' Player's Player of the Year Award, as chosen by Magnus, the Players' Player of the Year. It was an emotional scene: wanting to end his career on a high, Dylan has decided this season is to be his last.

He was still clutching his trophy as I dropped him back at Sophie's.

'What's all this I hear about you becoming a writer?' she said.

Thanks very much for that, Darren. I tried to respond in a confident manner.

'Well . . . I've always been quite good with words. So I thought I'd – you know – try to grasp the thorn by the nettle.'

That didn't sound right. A frown appeared on Sophie's face.

'What do you mean? What about your proper job?'

'I've handed in my notice.' Being made redundant seemed

more impressive when phrased like that. 'Final day is Friday 18th May. That's also a recycling day.'

'But what about money? How are you going to afford to live? And what about Dylan?' Her eyes narrowed. 'You're not trying to get out of the monthly payments, are you?'

'Of course not. I shall make money from my writing.'

The frown had reappeared. 'What kind of writing, exactly?'

'Poetry.'

I ignored her right eyebrow, which she seemed to have lifted up involuntarily. But it was harder to ignore her sigh nor the front door which closed on my face. I headed off, glancing back up at the house as I closed the garden gate, the sound of 'Hip to be Square' by Huey Lewis and the News escaping from an upstairs window and floating off down the street.

Sunday April 29th

Who is this stranger who now greets me in the mirror each morning upon waking? This man whose fine, chiselled jawline has disappeared beneath a startling hairy outcrop of brown and grey? This woolly-chinned wonder? This shaggy magnet for passionate pogonophiles?

Richard Stilgoe, that's who. According to Mrs McNulty, that is.

'You look like that fella with the beard who used to be in dictionary corner,' she cackled from over the fence.

Mrs McNulty is a regular viewer of *Countdown*; she claims that amidst the vowels and consonants there are hidden messages from 'the other side'. I don't know whether she means BBC2 or Channel 5.

Richard Stilgoe is not the look to which I had been aspiring.

It's hard to imagine the ghost of Heathcliff walking the wild moors late at night and serenading Catherine by belting out the hits from *Starlight Express*.

Monday April 30th

Put Me In Your Box, Honey

Stroking the smooth contours of my newly shaved chin, I messaged Liz with the news that I was being made redundant. She told me I'd be better off without all that nonsense: having worked for a large multi-national organisation herself, she still bears the corporate scars. The thought of company portals, senior management briefings, restructurings and org charts still makes her shudder, she told me, hence the move into freelance copy-editing.

I learnt all this while cyber-slacking with her for much of the day, in between ram raids on the stationery cupboard (from which I took flight with inordinate amounts of Post-it notes and paper clips) and sabotaging the photocopier by feeding sheets of labels into it all askew.

I've practically gone feral. These are the last days of Rome!

May

Tuesday May 1st

Fifty Shades of Red

Semi-colons I shall abuse for you.
Parentheses I shall lose for you.

Correct me like you know you want to.
Repossess my nouns.
Cover me with red ink.
Slap my words around.

Infinitives I shall split for you.
Apostrophes I shall omit for you.

The mistakes I make are just for you,
Each greased-up grammar slip.
Let me feel the hardness of your edit,
Your disapproving nib.

Participles will be dangled,
Accents wrongly angled.

So lay me like a transitive verb.
Drip your ink upon my blotter.
Bore me rigid with your rules.
Fix me good and proper.

The erotic dreams have returned.

I had misused a semi-colon. Liz kept me behind for corrective therapy. I was to go through a set of uncorrected proofs for a new book in the *Fifty Shades of Grey* series and for every mistake I found, she'd remove an item of clothing, and for each one I missed she'd put on an item of clothing. I woke up just as she was putting on a third cardigan over her blouse, tank top and pullover.

Wednesday May 2nd

In my lunch hour, I quickly whizzed over to the bookshop to get my copy of Martin Amis's *Money* for this month's book group. I left, two hours later, having stocked up on a few other books that might come in handy one day: *Oxford Modern English Grammar*; *The Penguin Guide to Punctuation*; Kingsley Amis' *The King's English*; Lynn Truss' *Eats, Shoots and Leaves*; the *Cambridge Encyclopedia of the English Language*; and *Copyediting & Proofreading for Dummies*.

Thursday May 3rd

It feels less like a reorganisation here than a Stalinist purge. A leaving card circulates on average every thirty minutes. It takes me forty-five minutes to write a message in one; by the afternoon, my in-tray was creaking under the strain. The comments within are accompanied by such a curious vocabulary, one far more suited to a book of remembrance: *'You will never be forgotten'*, *'No longer by my side but always in my heart'*, *'You go to a better place'*.

It seemed fitting that I should return home to find an invitation to a tarot reading next Thursday from Mrs McNulty. I can already guess what card she has lined up for me.

Friday May 4th

Star Wars Love Poem

Compared to you, the Diathim,[*]
beautiful winged sentients of Millius Prime,[†]
are worth not a druggat[‡] or dime.

I would climb
the Gallo Mountains of Naboo[§]
without crampons to be with you.

If only there were
a Mon Calamari cruiser[¶] at my service.
I would explore your surface,

gliding over
your two moons of Tattooine^{**}
before plateauing

to lose myself
in the undergrowth of splendour
that is your Forest of Endor.^{††}

I feel the throb of my lightsaber.
This poem is unlikely to be published
by Faber and Faber.

I discovered through Twitter that today is Star Wars Day. That's because 'May the Fourth' sounds very similar to 'May the Force'; the latter phrase, I discovered, being a line of dialogue from that popular film franchise.

Liz, it seems, is a fan. She tweeted:

Her name was Yoda,
a showgirl she was.

This is very funny because Yoda – who is a character, I discovered, from the aforementioned box-office smash – frequently forms unusual speech patterns, based around an object-subject-verb word order. Liz takes this anastrophe and applies its logic to – what I discovered to be – the opening lines of the 1978 Barry Manilow song 'Copacabana (At the Copa)', substituting the name of the original protagonist, 'Lola', for that of 'Yoda', in a perfectly applied feminine rhyme. And that is why I found it so instantly funny.

I joined in the fun by posting up a Star Wars poem. I confess that I don't know a huge amount about the films, but it's amazing what five short hours on Wookiepedia can do.

I noted privately to Liz that Toby Salt seems rather aloof from the whole May the Fourth/Force thing, having not so much as mentioned it on Twitter all day. He seems far more concerned with advertising his forthcoming book and festival appearances. He has nearly two thousand followers now. I have fifty-two.

Saturday May 5th

Breaking Bard

English teacher turns
Shakespearian drug chef,
cooking and selling
crystal macbeth.

Dylan has been making me help him revise again. Sometimes the commitment of being a one-day-a-week father hangs heavy upon me, like a thick wool cardigan weighed down with a manual on responsible parenting in each pocket.

He's studying *Macbeth*. Stuart is taking him to a performance tomorrow night at the Globe, with Bryan Cranston in the title role. They'll be standing in the pit, he tells me, rather than watching it properly from the comfort of seats, as they would have done in Shakespeare's time, and which I think is a little bit cheap of Stuart, if I'm honest.

Sunday May 6th

I've now received more than two hundred messages on Twitter informing me that Tatooine has three moons, not two. And that I hadn't even spelt it correctly. Some people really need to reassess their life choices: Tatooine isn't even real, for heaven's sake! It's just a stupid made-up planet from an exploitative, merchandise-driven film franchise cynically developed to extract as much money as possible from the pockets of children and adults who never quite managed to grow up. Given that, how many moons it has or doesn't have is something of a moot point.

Liz has kept her copy-editing impulses in check and remained silent on the whole issue.

I posted up a poem entitled 'Pedants' in revenge:

Foot soldiers in the War on Error,
they're here to save us from ourselves
with *Fowler's Modern English Usage*
(first edition, nineteen twelve).

For these Crusaders of Correctness,
beloved Guardians of Grammar,
hunt down blunders big and small
upon which to wield their hammer.

They hold no fear that in doing so,
they will deprive the thing of life:
for it does not matter what it *says*,
what's important is that it's *right*.

Ten people have already pointed out to me that *Fowler's Modern English* was first published in 1926 but that didn't rhyme so the joke is on them really.

Monday May 7th

This Bank Holiday weekend has had a face on it like a wet Bank Holiday weekend. In theory, these should be the perfect conditions in which to tackle the Problem of the Dripping Tap in the Downstairs Bathroom but instead, I worked on a poem for Poetry

Club. It picks up some of the themes of Gabriel García Márquez's *Love in the Time of Cholera* and represents what future scholars of English literature may well describe as 'a significant departure from Bilston's previous work, signalling a new maturity as this promising – but often wayward – poet finally comes of age'.

Tuesday May 8th

So much for new maturity. Future scholars of English literature will be giggling in their twenty-fifth-century senior common rooms.

The evening had started promisingly enough. Chandrima had got us underway in her characteristically serene fashion as she ruminated on the restorative power of the peace lily before Kaylee took us in a different direction with a powerful spoken-word piece concerning institutionalised rape in an Alabaman women's prison.

Douglas followed with what he claimed to be a 'found poem' concerning the Battle of Stalingrad, but which I'm pretty sure was just a lengthy extract from Antony Beevor. Mary then read a very moving poem concerning her fifth husband's dementia. As she sat down, Kaylee grasped Mary's hand in sympathy; her grandad had suffered from 'Old-Timer's Disease', she said.

We were then 'treated' by Toby Salt to a new experimental piece based on a re-reading of an Ezra Pound canto that he'd been commissioned to write for Radio 4, presumably as filler for some ungodly-houred early morning programme. And then it was time for Liz. As ever, she filled my metaphorical basket; this time with a clever critique of contemporary consumerism in a poetic exploration of sex and shopping entitled 'Unidentified Item in My Bagging Area'.

I was the last to go. It was only when I reached into the pocket of my favourite cardigan that I realised I wasn't wearing my favourite cardigan, nor indeed did I have the love poem that was in its pocket. Mildly panicked, I reached for my phone. I was pretty sure there was a near-final version on it.

I announced the title – 'Love in the Time of Cauliflower' – and, with a deep breath, set about it:

'Please marrow me, my beloved sweetcorn,
Lettuce beetroot to our hearts of romaine.
We must follow the courgette of our convictions
And transform our love into Great Artichoke.'

I am not a natural or confident performer. My primary aim when reading poetry in public is to get the words out without stumbling. I am so fixated on this that I often have no sense as to what it is that I'm reading. And that's why – even as the sound of the audience's laughter began to percolate my consciousness – I was oblivious to the fact that I'd inadvertently left my phone on its Auto-Courgette setting.

I pressed on:

'Such lofty asparagus can't be ignored.
You make my head spinach, for goodness' sake.
Don't make me go back to the drawing broad beans,
My magical Lady of the Kale.'

I could hear Toby Salt sniggering in the background. I admit to being a little surprised; this was a love poem, not one written for cheap laughs. I continued:

'Love is chard and can hurt shallot;
Our emotional cabbage not inconsequential.
But I need you as my parsnip-in-crime
And together, we'll reach our potato.'

I heard myself read the word 'potato'. This puzzled me greatly: there were no potatoes in my poem. I ploughed on regardless:

'I am a prisoner, trapped in your celery;
Without you I'm broccoli, defenceless.
For only you can salsify my desire,
And I, in turnip, will radish you senseless.'

No, that didn't sound right at all. I looked up, confused. Liz was blushing. Toby Salt was guffawing and wiping tears from his eyes. I peered down at my phone and read the poem once more, this time in my head. Feeling stupid, I hastened back to the comfort of pistachios. Liz told me that she thought it delightful and it was my turn to blush. I played along with the pretence that it had been a deliberate ploy on my part.

Toby Salt, of course, was insufferable. He kept making jokes about it for the rest of the evening, at one point asking me whether I was familiar with the work of Seamus Auberginey. But the joke was on him; as everyone knows, the aubergine is a fruit rather than a vegetable. I held my tongue but I'm pretty sure that this fact was not lost on Liz and the rest of the group, and that Toby Salt must have looked very foolish indeed.

Liz came over to me as we were leaving. She had a spare ticket to see a play written by a friend of hers. It was for Thursday evening if I was interested.

'It'll be awful,' she said. 'Two and a half long hours of biting social commentary and hard-hitting political critique.'

It sounded wonderful. But then I remembered Mrs McNulty and the penis-shaped crop circle that had appeared on my back lawn the last time I had turned her down.

'Sorry, I'd love to, but I can't make Thursday,' I replied. 'I have to go to a tarot card reading or the evil spirits will become angry with me again.'

Liz gave me the kind of look that I was used to receiving from Sophie, one composed of disappointment and bemusement in equal measures.

'Oh, well, maybe some other time, then,' she said.

'Yes, I'd like that very much,' I responded, smiling flirtatiously. 'How about . . .'

How about *what* exactly? A drink? An evening of cribbage? A day out at the Derwent Pencil Museum? And *when*? Next Tuesday? Tonight!? Three years hence?

It suddenly occurred to me that while my brain was rifling through the options (of which there were many and yet absolutely none at all), I was still smiling flirtatiously – except that by now it must be coming across more as a fixed grin or an unsettling leer, as I noticed the puzzled look on Liz's face. My main priority had to be to bring my sentence to an end.

'. . . some other time?' I finished, lamely.

'Y-e-s,' she said slowly.

I was saved from further embarrassment by Kaylee.

'What's this I hear about a ticket going spare?' she said.

'A friend of mine has written a play,' answered Liz. 'But be warned, it's all rather gruelling stuff: poverty, depression, suicide et cetera.'

'Sounds perfect,' said Kaylee. 'We'll just have to grim and bear it.'

Wednesday May 9th

....

Nietzsche Abhors a Vacuum

the
  will
   to
    power
     a
      hoover
       was
        not
         a Friedrich
         manoeuvre

....

'You see, Brian, when a man is in love he endures more than at other times; he submits to everything.'

Thus spoke Tomas of Nietzsche, after he'd hoovered up the crumbs of today's Twix from under my desk. I had confessed to him my crush on Liz, alongside my creeping despair that she might only like me for my poetry. It was a conversation I had been trying to have with the cat for several weeks now but having received very little by way of advice, Tomas was the next best thing.

'All this Twitter nonsense can only get you so far. You must talk to her properly,' he urged. 'Ask her out on a date.'

'I can't!' I cried. 'Every time I try to talk to her, I end up with paralysis of the brain and tongue.'

'But you must try, Brian! What is the worst that could happen?'

'She says no? Or laughs in my face? Or, worse, agrees to meet up?'

'Stop worrying about such nonsense. You must believe in yourself. Do not live your life in fear of rejection.'

'I suppose you're going to tell me next that what doesn't kill me makes me stronger.'

Tomas shrugged.

'This is all very well, Tomas, but how *do* I talk to her? What do I say?'

'Only you can figure that one out,' he said. 'As Nietzsche once wrote: "No one can construct for you the bridge upon which precisely you must cross the stream of life, no one but you yourself alone." '

Brilliant. Thanks, Nietzsche. You're about as much help as the cat.

Thursday May 10th

....

Mrs Nostradamus

It began like this:
I knew you were going to say that
he'd snapped,
after I told him to shift his arse
and look lively with the laundry.

I could see him cogitating
as he separated the whites.
Then, slowly: *There will be rain.*
And he was right, there was.
Three days later.

At first, he played it safe.
Kept it small. Local.
There will be a wedding before the year is out.
M. Bouchoir will rear a prize pig.
Crystal Balls, they called him.

He was clever, though.
Thought about the future.
Figured there was profit
to be had from prophecy.
He went for it big time.

Plagues and earthquakes.
Famines and floods. Wars.
The kings and queens
and their courtesans and courtiers
couldn't get enough of it.

By that time, I'd had enough
and run off with M. Bouchard and his pig.
The end of the world it was, to him.
Poor Crystal Balls.
He didn't see that coming.

She turned each card over slowly, only pausing between them to open her eyes wider, and let her jaw drop further. The Lovers. The Hermit. Judgement, and then, finally . . . David Beckham.

'Death. He represents Death,' said Mrs McNulty quickly. 'I can't find the original one so I used one of Kenny's old football cards.' Kenny is Mrs McNulty's son and visits her rarely.

'But what does it all mean?' Dave asked, looking up from his phone. His cards had been read, too. Among them were The Emperor (wisdom) and Temperance (moderation) – so I knew it was all baloney. He'd also had The Hierophant but Mrs McNulty had passed over that one quickly. I don't think she knows what a hierophant is.

'We must remember that the tarot do not predict the future; they only show us the pathways that the future may take, and can be interpreted in many ways,' she declared enigmatically. 'But no matter how you read them, this doesn't look good. This doesn't look good at all.'

She patted my hand and did her best to give me an encouraging smile, promising to stay in touch should I ever find myself on the other side.

Friday May 11th

I have received confirmation about my redundancy money. £15,000 is a tidy sum for someone whose finances have always been historically messy. But I must learn to be prudent; it may be a while until I begin to earn substantial money from my poetry.

If only affluence bred confidence. The vow I'd made to Tomas to take the bull of romance by its love-sharpened horns has not sufficiently taken into account my aversion to blood sports. Liz remains ungored and unasked out.

Panicking, I sought refuge in the crossword. Two hours dripped by and all I had to show for my efforts was 17 across:

PEDETENTOUS (adj.): proceeding slowly.

Saturday May 12th

Dylan went inside while Sophie lectured me on the doorstep. GCSEs begin in a couple of weeks and I need to be more supportive of Dylan in his revision, she says. Unless I pull my socks up, he won't get the grades of which he is capable, apparently. I listened sulkily.

'He says it's hard to concentrate at your house,' she said.

'That'll be the students next door. They always play their music too loud. I'll have another word. And then there's Mrs McNulty and her sawing. I really don't know what on earth it is that she's making. I sometimes wonder wheth—'

'It's not the neighbours.'

'Well, I can't deny that the cat *does* make it diffic—'

'Not the cat. *You*, Brian.'

'Me?'

'Dylan says that you're always trying to distract him.'

'I don't know what you mean.'

'Reading him poems. Showing him tweets and videos. Suggesting films to watch. Dressing the cat up as a pirate.'

I smiled at the memory of the cat beneath her skull and crossbones tricorn.

'I'm wondering whether he shouldn't visit until his exams are over,' she said.

I unsmiled. I promised to try harder. I'd remain focused. Do whatever was necessary. Help him as best I can. I went back inside. Dylan was reaching in his bag for his chemistry textbook.

'Today,' he announced solemnly, 'it's atomic structures and oxides.'

Sunday May 13th

Leak-end

```
S   d   a   e   a   m   I   f   t   m   h   i
u   r   w   v   n   i       a   o   y   a   n
n   a   a   e   d   n   t   i           d
d   i   y   r       u   h   r   s   w       i
a   n       y   e   t   i       a   e   s   t.
y   e   t       v   e   n   e   y   e   o
    d   o   h   e       k   n       k   m
    d   o   r           o       e   e
    a   u   y           i   u       n
    y   r               t   g       d   h
                        h           o
                                    l
                                    e
                                    s
```

With the day stretching ahead of me like a cat on a lap, it felt like the ideal opportunity to get in touch with Liz. I started to read *Money*.

It is 400 pages long! Ordinarily, I'd have no chance of completing it in time but given that I shall have more free time on my hands soon, I think this is very do-able.

The thought occurred to me that this may well be my last 'weekend', in a traditional sense; such distinctions between the working week and Saturday and Sunday will probably blur as my new life as a professional writer begins. With such idle daydreams the hours did pass, and by the time I stretched to turn my bedside light off, I'd already broken the back of page five.

Monday May 14th

The final archaeological assault on my officle has begun: the sorting and emptying, re-filing and binning and the gradual emptying of my stationery stockpiles, which I smuggle home in the crevices of my clothing, whistling as I walk past the security guard in the evening, like Steve McQueen in *The Great Escape* with his pockets weighed down with sand.

Tuesday May 15th

During today's excavation, I uncovered an old LP of Rogers and Hammerstein's *The Sound of Music* which had fallen behind my filing cabinet, along with an old photograph of Dylan as a toddler walking hand in hand with Sophie and me, and a certificate to verify that I had passed my Intermediate Excel course. The record, I think, had been an old Secret Santa present from about ten years ago before the unbroken run of pine-scented candles kicked in.

I took it home with me. It was heavily scratched but somehow didn't jump. I played it through three times, and studied the photo, until a sad sort of clanging from the clock in the hall told me it was time for bed.

Wednesday May 16th

....

My Favourite Words

Pipette and *plectrum, obumbrate* and *flimsy,*
Balderdash, spatchcock, flapdoodle and *whimsy,*
Obnubilation and *nontrepreneur:*
These are a few of my favourite words.

Sachet, humdudgeon, haboob, hurly-burly,
Scroddled and *dottle, goluptious* and *surly,*
Mumpsimus, tawdry, decumbent and *blurb:*
These are a few of my favourite words.

Susurrus, zephyr, rubescent, boondoggle,
Reboant, gaggle, hubris and *hornswoggle,*
Refulgent, plethora, plinth and *perturb:*
These are a few of my favourite words.

When the rose *droops*
When the branch *snags*
When I'm *lachrymose*
I simply remember my favourite words
And then I don't feel *morose.*

....

I came close to popping the question to Liz today. But I got stuck on the thorny issue of *venue.* I gave it some more thought as I cracked on with the laundry. A quick mental run-through of my favourite things and potential topics of discussion – detective series, crosswords, custard creams, the cat – confirmed to me that any attempts at prolonged and free-flowing dialogue would be risky indeed. I needed a venue or destination which might serve as a foil or shield so I wouldn't be subjected to the relentless pressure of having to make conversation.

I concluded that more thinking was needed before hanging my heart out on the line like a pair of tatty, well-worn underpants.

Thursday May 17th

Monopoly

They met at a beauty contest. She came first, he second.
They monopolised each other. Prosperity beckoned.
Chancers of the exchequer, they advanced straight to go.
These were the good times. How the money flowed!

Stock sales and dividends. A building loan matured.
Bank errors in their favour. An inheritance secured.
And every birthday – to celebrate the pleasure –
each of their friends would pay them a tenner.

They owned the streets. But it began to unwind.
Found drunk in a sports car. A small speeding fine.
Doctor and hospital fees. The cost of street repairs.
The perilous state of their financial affairs.

The Super Tax hit them. They took out a loan.
They were dispossessed of their grand Mayfair home.
They're in jail now. But no sign of contrition.
Last week, they won a crossword competition.

I've had another one of my dreams. I walked into the sitting room to find Liz reclining on a Monopoly board, naked except for a thin layer of banknotes which covered her like a cheap paper duvet. Laughing, she asked me to 'strip her of her assets'. I began to peel the notes off her one by one, and slowly her smooth, pale skin revealed itself.

Each banknote stripped away, I would then set alight and we laughed once more as the paper crackled in the fireplace. But as I took another glance at the flickering of the flames, I noticed that, to my horror, it wasn't Monopoly money at all – it was my redundancy money. The door suddenly crashed open and we became surrounded by policemen and fire fighters, and before I knew it, I was being carted off to the cells and I hadn't even picked up a get-out-of-jail-free card.

I looked this up in my *Dream Dictionary* – once I'd located it on my bookshelf – but there was no mention of Monopoly nor any other property-based board games so I am none the wiser as to what it all means.

Friday May 18th

At three o'clock, I heard the dread squeak of the drinks trolley wheels as they trundled their way over to my officle, a desultory crowd of well-wishers and other ghouls trailing in its wake.

Janice said a few words about the enormous contribution I'd made and how the place wouldn't be the same without me. I recognised most of it, including the amusing anecdotes, from her speech when Chris Jenkins left a couple of months before. In turn, I got up to say that although there were many things I'd miss about working here, the thing I'd miss the most was the wonderful people I had been so privileged to work alongside. I'd borrowed this speech from Chris Jenkins when he'd left a couple of months before. I was presented with a leaving card and the token gesture of a £25 book voucher.

Tomas was amongst those who gathered, having rearranged a seminar he was hosting on Wittgenstein and the Rules of Language in order to make an appearance. We have swapped phone numbers and vowed to stay in touch.

It wasn't long before my imminently erstwhile colleagues began to drift back to their desks. I collected up my few remaining belongings, put them in my bag and slipped out the back door without further fuss, keen to avoid anyone who might hear the rattle of paper clips and staples in my pockets.

Saturday May 19th

Aujourd'hui j'ai révisé le français avec Dylan. Nous avons travaillé très dur. C'était bien ennuyant. Le chat dormait. Dave, Martin et Marvin ont mis leur musique très forte pendant tout l'après-midi et Mme McNulty a scié. Nous avons mangé tous les custard creams.

After I'd returned from chez Dylan, I noticed that he'd left his *French Grammar and Practice* book lying on the table. For reasons which remain unclear to me, I spent the evening leafing through its pages to find some of my favourite sentences and create a 'found poem' of sorts. I have called it 'In Winter They Adjust the Thermostat'. À ces égards, nous passer le temps.

She's leaving on the seventh of May.
'Which dress do you like the best?'

She won't answer me.
There are a few potatoes left.

She's staying at home today.
The birds wake up early in summer.
She doesn't want to see anybody.
Nothing's changed.

The train arrives at two o'clock.
I don't think about it any more.
She stops in front of a shop window.
There's not a lot to see.

We don't have enough time
To be born. To die. To come. To go.
In winter, they adjust the thermostat.
It's raining. She can't swim.

Sunday May 20th

Man of Action

I am writing to report my dissatisfaction.
How dare you say I am not a man of action.
You say I like:

to sleep, to loaf, to lie around,
to drift, to dawdle, to loll and lounge.
All verbs, I note.
Have you not heard
that verbs are known
as *doing* words?

There are times in life when you just have to seize the day. The ancient Romans used to have a phrase for this, so impatient were they to get on with things – *tempus fugit* – which literally means 'to fight time'. For, they believed, in order for the day to be seized, time needs to be battled – and that's exactly what I did today.

I had been giving some more thought to the business of how I might make some inroads into the whole Liz thing when my phone buzzed. There, among my Twitter notifications, was a message from Liz:

Fancy meeting up next Friday?

This was the opportunity I'd been seeking and I was determined to grab it with both of my grubby day-seizing hands. Not one to dither, after just forty-five minutes I had managed to fashion a reply that I thought struck exactly the right tone of acceptance and forthrightness:

Yes.

This was all very well but as any day-seizer worth the name knows, the devil is in the detail: we needed a where and a when. I waited for Liz to tell me. Five minutes later:

How about the Tate Modern?
12 o'clock?

The Slazenger tennis ball of day-seizing had been struck firmly back into my court. But this time the response was harder. It wasn't simply a case of repeating my 'Yes' from earlier: I'd already ventured down that linguistic cul-de-sac and to remain in it would reveal a distinct lack of imagination. I needed a response that was not only affirmative but one that might subtly reveal my enthusiasm at such a prospect. In the end, I settled on:

Sounds good.

There are those who hang around waiting for life to come to them. But it won't!

Some days, you just have to go out and find it.

Monday May 21st

I've come down with a severe case of affluenza. The redundancy money has only been in my bank account for a few hours but already I feel like a man transformed. I walk with the straightened gait and breezy self-confidence of a man who knows his own worth (£15,000).

All I need now is my writer's shed. Until then, I've decided to take a well-earned staycation. I may knock off the odd poem in the interim but the serious business of writing will begin upon my shed's arrival in a couple of weeks.

Besides, I have the whole business of meeting up with Liz to contend with and I always find it hard to write when my head is full of thoughts.

Tuesday May 22nd

A first date – if that's what this is – in an art gallery is all very well but what if I'm asked to contribute an opinion or an original thought? What if I make some schoolboy error and get my Monets and Manets mixed up? Or mistake the cleaner's bucket and mop for an exhibit?

When in doubt, read your way out. I headed to the bookshop in search of the reassurance of tomes. Two hours later, I staggered out with my booty: *An Illustrated History of Modern Art*; *An Introduction to Impressionism*; *Art in the Twentieth Century*; *Degas for Dummies*; *The Bluffer's Guide to Art*; Short Introductions to Art Nouveau, Cubism, Conceptual Art, Pop Art; and a 700-page biography of Picasso.

When I got home, I took out an online annual subscription to the *Grove Dictionary of Art* just to be sure, and because the thirty-four-volume print edition is now out of print.

Wednesday May 23rd

It's incredible what can be achieved when there's not the inconvenience of a job to get in the way. If I had to sit an exam today on modern art, I'd be unnerving the other candidates by putting my hand up for more paper twenty minutes in.

I spent the afternoon creating prompt cards containing pertinent facts, which I intend to throw out there casually on Friday. For example:

- Picasso's full name is Pablo Diego José Francisco de Paula Juan Nepomuceno María de los Remedios Cipriano de la Santísima Trinidad Martyr Patricio Clito Ruíz y Picasso.
- Frida Kahlo's right leg was thinner than her left one. This was as a result of the polio she contracted as a child.

- Andy Warhol was a secret hoarder of pizza dough.
- Tracey Emin has a twin brother called Paul.

As I study them again several hours later, although they may be correct, I'm not entirely convinced that they're very interesting. I've rehearsed a few in front of the cat but she's barely stirred in response.

Thursday May 24th

What to wear to an art gallery? I consulted the internet. That was a mistake: it seems there is no clear consensus. Fashionista.com eloquently summed up the dilemma:

> *Dressing for an art exhibition presents a unique challenge. Turn up in your mufti and all will assume you're a nobody or that everything in the gallery belongs to you. But arrive 'too dressed' and you will look as if you're wearing the art.*

Most evidence pointed to this being either smart-casual territory or casual-smart territory.

I set out for M&S with my points card.

Friday May 25th

A Brief History of Modern Art in Poetry

1. *Impressionism*
   Roses sway in softened reds
   Violets swim in murky blues.
   Sugar sparkles in the light,
   Blurring into golden you.

2. *Surrealism*
   Roses are melting
   Violets are too.
   Ceci n'est pas le sucre.
   Keith is a giant crab.

3. *Abstract Expressionism*

4. *Social Realism*
   Roses are dead.
   Violence is rife.
   Don't sugarcoat
   This bitter life.

5. *Pop Art*
   Roses go BLAM!
   Violets go POW!
   Sugar is COOL!
   You are so WOW!

6. *Conceptual Art*
   Roses are red,
   Coated in blood:
   A deer's severed head
   Drips from above.

It may not have gone swimmingly well but neither was it drowningly awful; it was something in the middle, a doggy-paddlingly mediocre affair, in which we felt pleased to have kept our heads above water even if we didn't really get anywhere.

I met Liz on the steps. She looked like a Botticelli study of beauty, which made me feel like one of those blobby efforts by

160

Francis Bacon, slapped onto canvas on one of his off days. All the same, I had the inner confidence that comes of someone sporting a new Blue Harbour shirt and who could feel the reassuring bulge of his deck of modern art fact cards in his left-hand chino pocket.

I tossed the first one out there as we gazed thoughtfully at a Giacometti:

'It's interesting to think of what else he might have done if he hadn't died of pericarditis and chronic bronchitis at Kantonsspital in Churin, Switzerland in January 1966.'

Liz looked impressed.

We stared at Duchamp's *Fountain*:

'Whenever I see a Duchamp, I always think about what a good chess player he was – although he could never quite translate his success in France to the international stage, as we can see from his Olympiad record of four wins, twenty-two draws and twenty-six losses.'

We were looking at Picasso's *Weeping Woman*, and I was half-way through telling her Picasso's full name, when Liz interrupted:

'Thanks for all the trivia, Brian. But how does this painting make you *feel*?'

I must admit this threw me. There was nothing in the books that prepared me for this. There was nothing in them about how I *felt*. I stared at the *Weeping Woman*, thinking hard.

'Wittgenstein once said that "What can be shown cannot be said",' I responded, channelling my inner Tomas.

Liz nodded at this, although I couldn't help thinking she seemed a little disappointed, too, as if this was a test and I'd come up short.

I kept the rest of my facts to myself as we continued our tour of the gallery. An hour or so later, we parted at the bus shelter in an awkward embrace, half-hug, half-sideways feint, as the bus approached. Just before she climbed aboard, she said: 'I enjoyed today. We should do it again,' before handing me her phone number on the back of a beer mat she'd stolen from the cafeteria.

Saturday May 26th

....

Love is Where the Lines Join Up

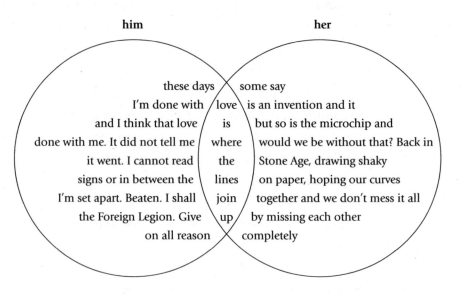

I've been doing maths revision with Dylan today. For once, I did not throw his books down in a fit of pique, attempt to worm my way out of it or suggest watching television. Instead, we got down to it for four hours – algebra, ratios, geometry and probability, taking in two-way tables, tree diagrams and Venn diagrams along the way.

I find there's something very beautiful about a Venn diagram; it's all in the way the curves intersect.

Sunday May 27th

'ARE YOU READY?!!!'

We were watching British grime artist Diamond Gee-Zah (real name: Dennis Pike). The audience shouted back as if to say yes, we are ready, for all moments have led to this moment, and we find ourselves poised and primed in this near-perfect state of readiness. I could see Darren joining in but I didn't add my voice to the response as I waited at the bar for another two pints.

'I SAID, "ARE YOU READY???!!!" '

The crowd was roaring now as they approached peak readiness.

That's how it continued for most of the night against a backdrop of bass vibration and beats, pogoing and stomping. It was a rather intense, noisy affair for a Sunday evening, and I found myself wishing it was last Friday again, contemplating the slaughtered corpses of cows preserved in formaldehyde, with Liz.

'I SAID . . . "ARE . . . YOU . . . READY???!!!" '

Was I ready? Now there was a question.

When the lights came on at the end, Darren turned to me with a stupid smile and said: 'I guess it's a rap.' I could tell he'd been waiting to say that all evening. I ignored his remark – as it only encourages him – and I was annoyed because I'd been waiting to say it, too.

Monday May 28th

Add to Basket

Browse eggs. Click on egg. *Add to basket.*
Buy One Egg Get One Free. *Add to basket.*
Buy Five More Eggs To Qualify For Free Delivery.
Add to basket.
Other Recommended Eggs Based on Your Browsing History.
Add to basket.
Customers Who Bought This Egg Also Bought These Eggs.
Add to basket.
Here are Some Other Eggs you Might Like to Consider. *Add to basket.*
What Other Eggs Do Customers Buy After Viewing This Egg?
Add to basket.
Avoid Putting All Your Eggs in One Basket with our New Range of Baskets.
Browse baskets. Click on basket. *Add to basket.*
Buy One Basket Get One Free. *Add to basket . . .*

A Bank Holiday Monday empty of commitments and a reliable, if moderately speeded, Wi-Fi connection is a dangerous nexus for someone with a bank account oozing with redundancy money.

The focus of my online attentions was to find a few furnishings for my soon-to-arrive writer's shed. I stuck to the essentials: a writing desk and chair, two floor-to-ceiling bookcases, an antique Remington home typewriter, a whiteboard for brainstorming writerly thoughts, a desk lamp, a standing lamp, some curtains, a rug, a small wood-burning stove, a yoga mat, a new kettle, two tins of Lapsang Souchong, coffee machine, two packets of fair-trade Sumatran kopi luwak coffee, a neo-Dada abstract painting by up-and-coming artist Monica Banerjee, three cushions, three Penguin Classics cushion covers, a footbath, a mini-fridge and an antique globe mini-bar.

I didn't bother with stationery as I already have enough of that.

Tuesday May 29th

I've been carrying Liz's beer mat around in my pocket since last Friday and although I've taken it out to stare at the digits from time to time – hourly, to be more precise – I have yet to take affirmative action of any description.

As is customary, I've been working hard at convincing myself that this inaction is borne of a deliberate long-term strategy of playing hard-to-get rather than the accumulation of years of shyness and social awkwardness.

And so, instead of picking up my phone and keying in those eleven simple digits, I choose rather to sit here, beneath the cat, and write a poem: not one for me to perform at next month's Poetry Club; not one written for my own amusement; but one written because it feels like a kind of action even if no one will ever see it except me.

Please Excuse Me

My dear ambassador, I am afraid
I am unable to join your pompous parade
of dignitaries on Thursday evening,
because I am working my way through
seven seasons of *The West Wing*.
Such an enthralling drama, I have found;

it passed me by first time around.

How thoughtful of you to invite me
to this exhibition by contemporary artists
on 'Post-Urban Space: Dislocation and Catharsis';
it's an important theme that resonates
deep within me. But I cannot make this date,
nor indeed the next six weeks;
I have to read ten thousand tweets.

Dear Lord and Lady Asquith, I was charmed
to receive in the post today, your card
inviting me to supper at Hedge End –
ever the magnificent setting.
Gustav's profiteroles are legend.
I would love to come, I really would rather,
but I've reached a new level on Candy Crush Saga.

Thank you, world, for thinking of me.
I've never been much good at society.
Please do not think me rude
but I would rather hide my shyness
in solitude, behind a screen,
and use my own knife
to whittle down the hours of life,
to something barely seen.

Wednesday May 30th

Tonight was a new book group low for me. What with one thing (Liz) and another (Liz again), I hadn't progressed further than page 12 of *Money*. I could sense the group's disapprobation as I attempted to bring the conversation around from its very specific and limited focus on one particular novel written by one particular author at a very particular time, to a far broader and wide-ranging discussion of the whole nature and philosophy of money, along with the intrinsic flaws of the world financial system.

To illustrate my point, I showed how, through some strategic doodling and folding, it was possible to transform the Queen's face on a ten-pound note into that of Amy Winehouse, but no one seemed to show any interest in this. What's more, when I went up to the bar to get some more honey-roasted peanuts, the barman wouldn't accept my money and threatened to report me for treason.

Thursday May 31st

I checked into Twitter to find a message waiting for me from Liz:

Want to meet up tomorrow?

It seemed that my spurious hard-to-get strategy had worked after all. There seemed little choice but to accept:

Sure. Where shall we go?

Please say somewhere with a ready supply of alcohol. Or, failing that, some place where talking is frowned upon, like the British Library. Or a Trappist monastery.

Betjeman Arms at 8?

Yes! A pub! Perhaps it was a Trappist pub. I could get there early and have a quick drink to steady my nerves. At 6.30, say.

OK. See you there!

I'd used the exclamation mark as a signifier of excitement. I hoped this wasn't lost on Liz.

I shared the news with the cat. She gave me a look that was rather difficult to read but is perhaps most accurately translated as: 'Try not to blow it this time, you idiot.'

June

Friday June 1st

Out of the Rain

We ran down the high street and into the pub,
as we cheated the rain that fell from above,
dodging the puddles that had formed on the floor.
Such a beautiful day for a nuclear war.

You draped your wet coat on the back of your chair,
We emptied our drinks. The rain dripped from your hair.
A Guinness. Another. Then I went back for more.
What a beautiful day for a nuclear war.

We talked. Our first pets. Favourite songs and film stars.
We flicked pistachio shells back into the jar.
You tried not to yawn. You must have thought me a bore.
It was a beautiful day for a nuclear war.

The days have changed now but I keep that one apart.
I carry it with me, tattooed on my heart.
The Guinness. Your wet hair. The dress that you wore.
Such a beautiful day for a nuclear war.

The news was awful. It rained all day. I drank too much. But these were incidentals, mere footnotes in the book of love. For once, no crib cards were needed – although I did have a few secreted about my person just in case – for the conversation flowed like a simile in its pure liquid state. Gone was my usual shambling self, tripping up over my words, trampling on the flower beds of social interaction. Liz stripped me of my awkwardness, one layer at a time.

I wasn't the only one who had plans to arrive early. I was speeding around the corner onto the high street when we ran into each other. Our coats drip-dried on our chairs while we supped on pints of Guinness.

'These things are awful, aren't they?' said Liz.

'Yes,' I confessed. 'I mean, no. It's not awful being with *you*. I really enjoyed the other day.'

'Me, too! But I meant the whole business of getting to know someone, whoever they are. Will they like me? Will I like them? What should I wear? What if I say the wrong thing? All that non-sense!'

'Yes, exactly!' I almost shouted. 'But I can't imagine you worrying about such things. You're the woman who just turned up at Poetry Club one night and effortlessly performed a poem about a second-hand copy of *The Joy of Sex* in front of a room of complete strangers.'

I tried not to distract myself too much with that memory.

'Oh, that's different,' said Liz. 'Extroverts can be shy, too, you know.'

'Shyness is nice,' I said.

'And shyness can stop you from doing all the things in life you'd like to.'

'You recognised the reference!'

'How could I not?' she said. 'It's my favourite Smiths song.'

I felt weak from her loveliness. We talked and drank, drank and talked. We spoke of adored songs and abhorred films, failed relationships and foiled plans, impossible pasts and improbable futures.

'What would you like to be when you grow up?' Liz asked, as we got to work on our final pints.

I stared into my pint in search of an answer.

'I don't know. Just . . . somebody, I suppose,' I answered after a while. 'I don't mean anything grand by that. I don't want to be famous. Or rich. I just don't want to end up being a nobody, that's all. I'd like to be somebody. Somebody who's really good at being me.'

'Aren't you good at being that already?'

'No, not really. It doesn't come easily to me.'

I took a big gulp of Guinness.

'Well, whoever it is you're being,' said Liz, 'I think you're doing a good job of it.'

'And you?' I asked. 'What about you?'

'I don't think I ever want to be grown up.'

The rain had stopped by the time we left the pub and I walked Liz to the bus stop. The bus was pulling up as we got there. She turned to ask me whether I'd like to go back to hers for coffee.

I must have panicked. I'd *meant* to say yes but before I knew it I was explaining how I don't really drink coffee these days because I need to be careful with my caffeine consumption as it makes me vulnerable to spells of insomnia AND my GP warned me off it because my cholesterol levels are borderline high, and besides, I feel uneasy about this coffee culture that has grown up in recent years, most likely due to the popularity of *Friends*, because it just feels like we're being sold a lifestyle, based on a kind of faux New Yorker sophistication, whereas in reality, it's all about corporations trying to empty our pockets . . .

As the bus pulled away, I saw Liz looking down at me with disappointment from the top deck.

I walked through the puddles to my own bus stop and lifted my head up to the sky. It looked like the heavens might open once more. Come, friendly bombs, and fall on me.

Saturday June 2nd

The Schleswig-Holstein Questions

1. What was Schleswig's profession?

  A. *Sailor*   **B.** *Composer*   **C.** *Owl*   **D.** *Great Dane*

2. Where was Holstein born?

  A. *Sweden*   **B.** *Brentwood*   **C.** *Schleswig*   **D.** *Ukraine*

3. What was the relationship between Schleswig and Holstein?

  A. *Brothers*   **B.** *Lovers*   **C.** *Troubled*   **D.** *Secure*

4. Which protocol was violated by King Christian IX?

  A. *Don't know* **B.** *Don't care*   **C.** *Beats me*   **D.** *Unsure*

5. Why did Prussia become involved?

  A. *Why not?*   **B.** *No clue*   **C.** *Because*   **D.** *Search me*

6. The Baltic was of strategic importance. But was it an insect, a river or larger mass of water?

  A. *Bee*   **B.** *Dee*   **C.** *Eh?*   **D.** *Sea*

7. How do Guildenstern and Rosencrantz fit into it all?

  A. *They don't* **B.** *They won't*   **C.** *Who knows*   **D.** *They're dead*

8. Where would you rather be than taking this exam?

  A. *Outside*   **B.** *At home*   **C.** *Elsewhere*   **D.** *In bed*

Today was History. Having lived through an increasing amount of it, I felt a momentary wave of optimism that this time I might be of some genuine use to Dylan. I'd been hoping for a little bit of Tudors (I have read the first 120 pages of *Wolf Hall* and so consider myself something of an expert on the topic) or the origins of the First World War but then he started to get out his books on mid-nineteenth-century European diplomacy and my heart – like the ocean liner RMS *Lusitania* on 7th May 1915 – sank . . .

The Schleswig-Holstein Question.

I'd failed to understand this topic back in the 80s – and those were simpler times – so what chance did I have now? Stuart had already made him a full-colour timeline of key events so that just deepened my feelings of ignorance and inadequacy.

Fair play to Dylan, though, who did his best to keep me motivated throughout. When we were done, he took me and my hangover to the park for an ice-cream.

Sunday June 3rd

Here begins a new approach to book group. My performance last week was poor, even by my own shabby standards, and I'd been reflecting on this for a while. What has been lacking is motivation; it's simply been too easy *not* to read the book, particularly when there've been so many other things clamouring for my attention. What I needed was an incentive.

I headed off into town to Bloomer's Antiquarian Books to see if I could pick up a copy of this month's choice, *Robinson Crusoe*. A collectable antique edition would surely provide the much-needed impetus for me to take it off the shelf and get the thing read.

Mr Bloomer is more antiquarian than most of his stock, and most of his stock is very old indeed. There is a particularly attractive nineteenth-century edition, he informed me, illustrated with engravings by Cruikshank, which he was hopeful of getting his liver-spotted, antiquarian hands on over the next few days. While there, I picked up a few other titles, including a first edition of *Brideshead Revisited*, a signed copy of Larkin's *The Whitsun Weddings* and a six-volume set of Gibbon's *Decline and Fall of the*

Roman Empire, all of which I thought might lend a certain air of erudition to my writer's shed when it arrives next weekend.

I paid for these and put down a deposit for *Robinson Crusoe*, rather ashen-faced. Who'd have thought that old books covered in dust could be so expensive?

Monday June 4th

My beautiful satinwood writing desk has arrived. It has twin blind frieze drawers with almost perfect shut lines, baluster turned and knopped end supports on square-cut and C-scroll trestle bases and leaf-carved scroll feet. Its tooled green-leather writing surface comes in matching shades with gilded tooling and embossing. It was made by nineteenth-century furniture makers Miles and Edwards, whose patrons included several British Ambassadors to Paris and an Empress of Russia.

I practised sitting at it for most of the afternoon, adopting ambassadorial stances, looking up in annoyance at untimely interruptions from my non-existent first secretary and signing fake treaties. It made me want to dip my pen into an inkwell and to write an actual, proper letter, not fire off a quick email or text; to sit there methodically composing each sentence in my head before committing my pen to paper, just as I used to in all those letters to Sophie back in the days when she could still be bothered to read the words I'd write for her.

Tuesday June 5th

Haiku Club

haiku club first rule:
avoid words like antidis-
establishmentar-

It was Japanese Night at Poetry Club. This had been Mary's suggestion, having admitted last month that she'd been flirting rather heavily with *haiku*.

It was interesting to see how we'd all managed to instil something of ourselves into the form: Douglas had written a haiku sequence based around the attack on Pearl Harbor; Mary took inspiration from a trip to Tokyo she'd gone on with her first husband (on which it appears she had also flirted rather heavily with her soon-to-be second husband); Chandrima focused on the ephemerality of cherry blossom as a metaphor for the transience of life; Kaylee took up the cause of discrimination against the Ainu people; Liz had me reaching for my pistachios distractedly while she spoke of tantalising kimonos; and I did my usual nonsense. Toby Salt declared the *haiku* to be too mainstream and chose to present his own poems in the form of the *tanka* and *bussokusekika*.

All this short-form stuff meant formal proceedings finished an hour earlier than usual. Discussion moved on to the battlefields trip. Chandrima was in charge of the itinerary and took us through what was planned and when. Douglas expressed disappointment that we were focusing predominantly on the literary aspects of the First World War and less on specific military manoeuvres. I updated everyone on funding, including the good news that we'd successfully been awarded a travel grant for £5,000 from the British Poetry Council; this means we can now afford to employ the services of Dr Dylan Miller, an academic specialising in First World War poetry, as our tour guide, as well as an accompanying actor, who will perform key poems on the battlefields that inspired them.

To my annoyance, Toby Salt spent most of this time trying to chat up Liz, bragging of his Twitter following (he has now duped nearly three thousand people), whipping out a proof copy of his forthcoming book and offering her a ticket to his reading at Saffron Walden.

It wasn't until the end of the evening that I had the chance to ask her whether she was free to meet up on Friday.

'I suppose so,' she snapped. 'Assuming your GP hasn't warned you off me, that is,' and headed out the door.

Wednesday June 6th

Odium Chloride

I think my body needs rebooting;
it's sick from all the crap I eat.
I salute it with three fingers,
then press CTRL+SALT+DELETE.

For some companionship of the non-feline variety, I listened to Radio 4. The molecules from its background murmurings seeped through my semi-permeable membrane and by early evening, I'd osmotically absorbed the entirety of its daytime output, including programmes on the naturalism of Pliny the Elder, the ethics of marmalade, life in a Bulgarian shoe factory, a consumer affairs show entitled *Ombudsman* and a potted history of houseplants.

But I was particularly interested in a documentary on the harmful effects of salt. Salt is very bad for you. It causes hypertension and increases the chance of heart disease and stroke.

I kept thinking about it all evening. Salt is an utter disgrace! The world would be better off without it.

Thursday June 7th

I've just finished my submission for the next quarterly *Well Versed* poem competition. The theme we've been given is that of 'Rebellion'. I have called my poem 'As I Grow Old I Will March Not Shuffle' and, by my own standards, it's something of an angry affair:

> As I grow old I will not shuffle
> to the beat of self-interest
> and make that slow retreat t o   t h e   r i g   h   t.
>
> I will be a septuagenarian insurrectionist
> marching with the kids. I shall sing
> 'La Marseillaise', whilst brandishing
> homemade placards that proclaim
> 'DOWN WITH THIS SORT OF THING'.
>
> I will be an octogenarian obstructionist,
> and build unscalable barricades
> from bottles of flat lemonade,
> tartan blankets and chicken wire.
> I will hurl prejudice upon the brazier's fire.

I will be a nonagenarian nonconformist,
armed with a ballpoint pen
and a hand that shakes with rage not age
at politicians' latest crimes,
in strongly worded letters to *The Times*.

I will be a centenarian centurion
and allow injustice no admittance.
I will stage longstanding sit-ins.
My mobility scooter and I
will move for no one.

And when I die
I will be the scattered ashes
that attach themselves to the lashes
and blind the eyes
of racists and fascists.

Ordinarily, faced with writing a poem about rebellion, I'd end up with something about stacking my dishwasher in a disorderly way, or refusing to use the tongs provided. But from Monday, I shall be a Professional Writer and it's about time I did some growing up and tackled more serious matters. Kaylee would be proud of me.

Friday June 8th

We went to the cinema; it was some awful romcom, one of those dull 'will they, won't they?' affairs. But the film itself was a mere sideshow, a divertissement from the real matter at hand (Liz). In a sudden rash of promiscuity, we shared popcorn; I gallantly compromised on the salted variety, despite being a sure and steadfast lover of the sweetened version. I pointed out this sacrifice to Liz a number of times but she didn't seem that impressed. On several occasions, our fingertips touched in the tub; the dark hid our blushes (at least I think it did, it was dark in there and hard to tell).

Afterwards, in the pub, we proceeded to discuss Toby Salt at length, with specific focus on his crocs.

'If there's one thing worse than wearing crocs,' said Liz, 'it's wearing crocs with socks.'

'That's got the makings of a poem,' I said. 'Perhaps you could perform it for him at next month's Poetry Club.'

She laughed and my heart skipped several beats.

'Good idea. We could call it "The Crocs of the Matter". By the way,' she added, 'I've changed my mind about my favourite Smiths song.'

'Oh yes?'

'It's "Last Night I Dreamt That Somebody Loved Me".'

It was a fine choice. At the bus stop, Liz leant in towards me as if to whisper something but she must have got confused because, before I had a chance to think, she'd kissed me on the lips. Behind us, her bus pulled up. Liz asked if I was coming her way and would I care to hop on.

After what had happened last time, I'd meant to just say yes, but instead I listened to myself explaining that it wasn't really the right direction and how it would probably add another twenty or twenty-five minutes to my journey time. I'd be far better off waiting for the number 5 as it stops just at the top of my road, although there's a temporary bus stop in place, which means the walk is a couple of minutes longer than usual at the moment, and, sure, it's an inconvenience but the roadworks should only be in place for another two weeks, and it's nothing that cannot be coped with, given a little forethought and planning . . .

I'd missed Liz climbing noisily onto the bus as I was saying this, but, as it pulled away, I noticed her on the top deck, staring grimly out into the distance.

I stood there for several minutes, striking my head repeatedly against the bus timetable, before gathering up my stupidity in search of my own stop and the last bus home.

Saturday June 9th

The Nine O'Clock Water Shed

The NINE O'CLOCK WATER SHED
is the ULTIMATE solution for your ablutions!
Now YOU can ENJOY your showers
alongside NEW, FAST, AUTOMATIC daffodils
and OTHER flowers.
Why not SPONGE YOURSELF DOWN
while TRIMMING your PRIVET?
CEDAR-CLAD* to enable FULL NUDITY,
its DENSE ACOUSTIC QUILT allows
MAXIMUM SWEARING
and SCENES some neighbours
may find OFFENSIVE.
STURDY and RAUNCHY, this is a shed
with 18+ PERMISSIONS:
a shed in which to SHED
your INHIBITIONS.

*Also available in Pine, Beech and Quarter-Past Six.

Studio erectus! It took a team of four experienced shed-builders a whole day to assemble it. They didn't finish it until nine o'clock this evening. I'm not surprised; it's not so much a writing shed as *un palais jardinière des lettres*.

The crew turned up just as Sophie was arriving with Dylan. She had questions.

'What's going on?'

'They've come to assemble a shed. Well, I say, shed. It's more of a studio. Or *un palais jardinière d*—'

'Is that what you've squandered your redundancy money on?' she interrupted. I was sensing a little hostility in her tone.

'I've not been squandering. If anything, I've been unsquandering. This is an investment.'

She snorted. It was not an attractive noise.

'Did you not consider that it might be more prudent to save that money until you have some regular and reliable income?'

Sophie has considered herself an expert on personal finance ever since she once happened to catch an episode of *Money Box* on Radio 4.

'Well, if I get hard up, perhaps Stuart can jump out of a plane for me. Preferably without a parachute.'

That went down as well as somebody jumping out of a plane without a parachute. Sophie made another unattractive snort and flounced off.

By the way, I should say that I am sitting in my shed as I write these words. I may be sitting on the floor but it still counts: I am actually writing in my writing shed! It is magnificent! A Wi-Fi-free oasis for literary endeavour. A cedar-clad creative hub! It is situated right at the bottom of the garden and the cat is yet to discover it. I wish I could say the same about Dave; he has already asked whether it's available to hire for garden parties.

Sunday June 10th

Dave, Martin and Marvin helped me move my furniture into the shed along with the few other bits and pieces I'd assembled. Three hours later, I placed the final volume of Gibbon on the bookshelf and the job was done.

To celebrate, I broke open a new packet of custard creams and put the antique globe mini-bar to use for the first time. Glasses were raised to my future literary success, which promises to shine as brightly as the disco ball Dave had tried to hang from the ceiling until I told him to get down from my writing desk.

It was when they'd left that I made my second resolution of the year: by the time I finish this diary, I will have created something of note in that shed, a work of importance that will silence my critics (Toby Salt) and my doubters (Sophie, myself, etc.).

For once in my life, I need to focus. But I know my own foibles and frailties only too well. The world – with all of its temptations and distractions – must be blocked out for a while. And out of all those temptations and distractions, Liz is the most tempting and distracting of all.

I reached for my phone to tell her I'd be incommunicado for a few weeks; I was sure she'd understand. There was already a message waiting for me from her:

I've changed my mind again.
My new favourite Smiths song is 'How Soon is Now?'.

Again, I couldn't fault her choice. It was six minutes and forty-four seconds of undisputed magnificence (or three minutes and forty-one seconds if you were listening to the somewhat inferior seven-inch single). But I knew there was more to Liz's selection than that. For once, I needed to rise to the challenge:

> I'm sorry. I always go about things the wrong way.
> I promise you I can be better.
> There's just something I need to do first
> and I won't be around for a couple of weeks.
> Perhaps when I'm back we could catch a bus together.
> Brian x

I pressed send and turned off my phone. Draining my glass of wine, I reached for another custard cream.

Eat, drink, and be merry – for tomorrow I write!

Monday June 11th

Not quite the first day I'd hoped for, if I'm honest.

Tuesday June 12th

Still settling into my new environs.

Wednesday June 13th

I think my chair was too low. I've adjusted it now.

Thursday June 14th

I don't think it was the chair.

Friday June 15th

Saturday June 16th

Dylan came over. I am finding it very hard to write with all these interruptions.

Sunday June 17th

I've started to read Gibbon's *Decline and Fall of the Roman Empire*. It has 1.5 million words.

Monday June 18th

Still reading Gibbon. It's taking longer than I thought.

Tuesday June 19th

I have discovered that the Roman Constitution in the Age of the Antonines is not nearly as interesting as it sounds.

Wednesday June 20th

I threw Gibbon Volume III at the window today and now there is broken glass all over the floor of my writing shed.

Thursday June 21st

I need to find something to write about. Anything.

Friday June 22nd

....

~~Broken Glass~~

~~This glass, which~~
~~is broken~~

....

Saturday June 23rd

~~A Glass, Broken~~

~~Every day is a shard of glass~~

Sunday June 24th

~~The Glass That Shatters~~

~~The glass that shatters~~
~~Like glass~~

Monday June 25th

Spent the morning in A&E, having a piece of glass removed from my left foot.

Tuesday June 26th

I am surrounded by £10,000 worth of stupid shed.

Wednesday June 27th

4'35"

'How's the writing going?' asked Darren, as we sat waiting for the performance to begin.

'Very well, thanks,' I lied. 'Still very much at the ideas stage but that's actually where a lot of the work gets done.'

'So what is it you're writing exactly?'

'Well, it's . . . look, there he is!'

My merciful, ministering angel had just appeared on stage.

Daniel Blink: erstwhile student of Philip Glass, and one of the world's leading exponents of minimalism. We stood up to applaud him and then settled ourselves in for the performance.

It was while he was playing a cover version of John Cage's composition 4'33" that I felt my literary constipation unblocking itself. I had the sudden inspiration to translate that piece into poetic form. I'd written a similar piece a while back but had never been entirely happy with it.

I shifted in my seat as 27th Club's lyrical laxative kicked in. Darren had to persuade me from leaving early so eager was I to get back home. After Blink had taken his bows, Darren confessed that he felt rather circumspect about minimalism.

'It left me wanting a little more,' he said. I agreed with him, more or less.

I hurried home to write my poem, keeping well away from the shed. It ended up being slightly longer than Cage's piece as I didn't want to stop when in full flow. I may revisit it and edit it down one day. I wrote it on the sofa, beneath a cat, wallowing in front of *Wallander* and the sound of two weeks of ignored messages and notifications pinging into my phone.

Thursday June 28th

....

This is the Title of this Poem

and this its first line
and while this poem is perhaps
not one of my best,
it still has its moments,
such as the surprise appearance in line six

of a capybara, snuffling in long grass,

and a beautiful descrption
of the dance of light upon sun-dappled Umbrian stone
in line eight.
It also contains, in this very sentence,
the striking incongruity of Charlemagne,
kneeling solemnly at the altar

in Saint Peter's Basilica, juxtaposed
with a muddy puddle, in which lies
one of Jeremy Clarkson's driving gloves.
In spite of all this delicate brushwork,
this poem has generally been poorly received,
described by the *Sunday Times*

as 'irritatingly self-referential'
and the *Guardian* as 'promising much
but delivering little'.
Considerable *schadenfreude*
has been experienced on Twitter
concerning the typo in line seven.

Yet this poem harbours
no delusions of anthologized grandeur,
waits not for recital,
cares not to be remembered
for more than thirty seconds
after being read.

This poem is just happy to be here,
to have filled these pages
which were all so much nothing before.

....

It feels good to be writing again. I've been careful to do this with the curtains drawn so I can't see my shed and my shed can't see me. The cat seems pleased by my return to the house and I'm finding Mrs McNulty's daytime sawing nostalgically soothing.

Less comforting were the messages on my phone that had accumulated during my confinement. There was a series of five messages from Liz, each successive one showing a steady increase on the Umbrage scale. The tone of the final message, though, had moved from annoyance to resignation:

I guess that's it then.

At first I couldn't understand why she was so upset but then, in my outbox, I noticed my message to her from 10th June. It was marked as undelivered; I must have turned my phone off too soon.

I looked again at the words I'd written as they teetered in my outbox, suspended in a permanent state of nearliness, like a metaphor for something that never quite happened.

Friday June 29th

....

Newcastle Brown Ale

This is how I remember it. He appeared
on my fifth week here, asking for food.
He'd washed up on the beach to the south of me;
I'd seen his footprints in the sand,
several days before. I'd been troubled by these,

like an astronaut who discovers giant steps
upon a not-so-lonely moon.

He strung up his hammock next to mine
and slept fitfully.
Later, he told me his name was Gordon –

although he should like to be called Sting –
and I noticed his thighs, welted
and swollen from the tentacled attentions
of jellyfish. One night, he told me of his dreams
of blue turtles

but by then I had tired of him:
the constant wrapping and unwrapping
of the tide-carried twine around his finger,
his insistence, as we swung gently in our beds,
that we put on the red light

as a beacon to passing boats,
that habit he had of standing so close to me.
On his last night, I watched him
as he slipped the note inside the bottle,
and launched it over the surf,

and, when its brown glass disappeared
underneath the waves,
I smashed the oar down upon him
until he'd no more breath to take.
Six weeks on, when the helicopter came,

there was nothing of him,
picked dry as he was, bones shining
beneath an invisible sun.
Every year, I raise a bottle to my lips
and set him free. This is how I remember it.

One might have imagined that, having had all this free time on my hands, the task of finishing *Robinson Crusoe* in time for the monthly book group meeting would have become somewhat easier. It's a reasonable assumption but one that doesn't take into consideration the fact that Mr Bloomer was only able to deliver my edition of *Robinson Crusoe* this morning, on account of it being 'extremely rare' and 'difficult to source'. It was also 'extremely expensive' and that was 'difficult to stomach'. I didn't dare take it along with me to the meeting this evening for fear of it being doused in best bitter and essence of wasabi.

The rest of the group seem increasingly irritated with me at my failure to read the monthly book. On the pretence of not being able to squeeze anyone else around the main table, they made me sit by myself at a smaller table, shipwrecked on the rocks of guilt, marooned on my own personal island of shame. I'm surprised they didn't call the police.

Saturday June 30th

In a Parallel Universe[*]

there is
parallel parking
for all of the cars

and
gymnasts drink
in parallel bars.

[*]this poem was sent by parallelogram

Dylan and I watched a film this afternoon called *Donnie Darko*, in which a 'tangent universe' erupts out of our own universe. It was all rather complicated but thankfully, Dylan explained to me various theories concerning alternative fictional universes. I nodded my head vigorously along to his words as if I understood him.

It made me think that in one of the alternative universes out there, there is an alternative world in which an alternative Brian Bilston is, at this very moment, enjoying an episode of unalloyed passion on an alternative sofa (one without the custard-cream crumbs) with the Liz from this world (although one who has been modified to return his text messages).

The Brian Bilston who lives in this world, and who is currently sitting on an unalternative sofa with an unalternative cat on his lap, writing in this, his miserable unalternative diary, utterly resents that alternative Brian Bilston, and hopes he puts his back out.

July

Sunday July 1st

Audley End

Yes, I remember Audley End –
The name intrigued me, I don't know why,
As the train pulled up beside it.
It was the first day of July.

The doors beeped. An announcement
Was made. I stepped down from the train,
Unwittingly. The sign I saw
Said *Audley End* – only its name

Was then followed by other words,
Ones to strike a note of caution.
Five words to fill a heart with dread:
Alight here for Saffron Walden.

And, for that minute, a church bell tolled,
Close by, and round it, clangier,
Louder and louder, all the bells
Of Essex and East Anglia.

It being one of those uncommonly pleasant and sunny English days, I decided to take myself off upon a train journey. The destination was irrelevant; what counted was the time to sit and reflect, to watch the countryside rattle by from the window of my three-quarters-empty train.

Two and a half unwonten hours later, I got off in search of air. The station was called 'Audley End' and seemed as good a place of disembarkation as any other. It was only having strolled to the end of the platform and read the poster pinned to the white lattice fence that I recalled the station was but a short stroll to Saffron Walden where, it appeared, a Poetry Festival was about to begin. What a stroke of luck! I'd forgotten all about this event, but there were some excellent poets on the bill (as well as some awful, pretentious ones).

I checked into the hotel on the high street and unpacked the clean shirt and cardigan that I'd carefully folded and placed in my suitcase last night, hanging them in the wardrobe to prevent further crumpling.

Monday July 2nd

Saffron Hall was busier than I'd imagined. Some ticketing issue with one of the more interesting, popular poets, I supposed, had meant that festival visitors had been given some free tickets to Toby Salt's talk instead. I squeezed in at the back of the auditorium, hidden beneath my balaclava.

A rather weaselly man with a goatee beard and nasal condition introduced Toby Salt. This was Django, editor and owner of Shooting from the Hip. He described Toby Salt as 'one of this country's finest poets'. I was thankful that my balaclava muffled my laughter.

Toby Salt began, as he invariably does, with a Petrarchan sonnet. It concerned itself with human fragility and the restorative power of Lake Como. I concerned myself with the crossword which I had brought with me to fill just such moments of tedium. I fished out my dictionary to check my answer to 17 down:

NUDNIK (noun): a tiring, dull or boring person.

As I was pencilling it in, I noticed that the rest of the audience, rather than staring embarrassedly at their shoes or gazing blankly into the mid-distance, appeared to be actually enjoying this stuff. A lengthy exploration in free verse on the nature of hermeneutics was greeted with a ripple of warm applause. There were gasps and strangled cries at his graphic retelling of the story of the Rape of the Sabine Women. Selected readings from his advance proof copy of *This Bridge No Hands Shall Cleave*, which he shook in the air like a TV evangelist, provoked tears, laughter, melancholic reflection and a thunderous response from the audience.

And it was then, amidst the sighs and swoons, the squeals and the whoops, that I saw Liz. She was gazing up at him, with an expression paused somewhere between unexpected admiration and unbounded wonder. I scrambled blindly to my feet, and out of the auditorium, my mind reeling with its imprint of her beautiful, treacherous face.

Tuesday July 3rd

Somehow, I took the first train of the day out of Audley End. To distract me from myself, I attempted to write a poem about the view from my carriage window:

> A pylon looms up suddenly like a sini-
> Two birds puncture the early morning blue as th-
> Cows stare into the distance and wonde-
> Fields sleep drowsily, waiting for-
> Buddleia bubbles up along the tr-
> A woman waves at her youn-
> Some buildings.
> Graffitti.
> King's Cross Railway Station.

It was no use. The world was passing me by too fast and everything was hopeless.

Wednesday July 4th

I had a dream that I'd murdered Toby Salt.

Liz was running a workshop on how to lay out a newspaper. We were looking at text alignment and I was experiencing some difficulties with a ragged right side. Toby Salt began to mock me.

I'd always been a marginal figure, he said. I should climb back into the gutter where I belonged.

Liz laughed at his awful puns. I flushed angrily, then proceeded to bludgeon him with the keyboard from an old nineteenth-century Linotype machine.

I ran out into the street in panic and bumped straight into a newspaper seller, who was brandishing the evening edition. I stared at the headline: 'POET FOUND MURDERED!'. The front page had been printed in red ink. I inspected it more closely. It wasn't red ink, it was blood. It looked like poet's blood.

I woke up with a shudder and consulted my *Dream Dictionary*. But there was nothing in it about Linotype machines and so I am none the wiser as to what it all might mean.

Thursday July 5th

My phone buzzed. There was a message from Liz:

Are you around for a drink tonight?

We need to talk.
I need to know where we stand.

I felt like responding that I knew exactly where *she* had been standing, i.e. next to Toby Salt at an inexplicably oversubscribed poetry reading in Saffron Walden. But I restrained myself; I am not one to bear grudges. My reply was measured and courteous:

Can't make tonight.
There is an old episode of *A Touch of Frost* on ITV4
that I'm planning to watch.

There were no further messages from Liz so I can only assume that has drawn a line under the matter.

Friday July 6th

I nearly forgot about bin day! The distant rumble of the lorry woke me up and I jumped out of bed in horror. I got my bags out just as the bin men were pulling up in front of Mrs McNulty's house. The Man at Number 29 had his bags neatly stacked outside and awaiting collection.

I went back inside and attempted to write a poem; an exercise in futility, as it turned out, as I was interrupted constantly. Every five minutes or so, I would be forced to check my phone only to discover that – yet again – there was no message from Liz. She kept up this stream of non-communications through the day. It was very infuriating. After many hours of this, I looked down to see the unripened fruits of my labours: a sequence of discarded first lines and no more.

I put them in a drawer where I keep all the abandoned first lines of poems I shall never write. Perhaps one day I shall make a book out of them.

Index of First Lines

Also, I am bleeding profusely so please stay for a while 8

Carter called again today, enquiring of his ladder 22

For that was the winter we listened to Enya 31

her eyes were a question mark, her mouth a semi-colon 36

I am a bowl, chipped at the rim 43

I remembered Newport Pagnell and wept 5

I see you forgot the fabric softener again 25

In the vacuum between when and how, I squat 3

Me and you in matching tank tops 39

Oi Oi! 78

Our love is a broken oatcake 61

Please don't do that, it's disgusting 27

She loved his unfinished similes like 52

That, my dear, is a diphthong 73

The sky is darkening and yet the dove 11

Today, we shall make strudel 4

Whither the hair tongs? I have seen them not 19

Saturday July 7th

I opened the door to Dylan. Standing next to him was a man clad in Lycra. He looked to be in his late thirties. His jawline was chiselled and his cheekbones delicately planed. He was as healthy as an Alp and wore the look of somebody who knew his way around a velodrome.

'Brian!' he exclaimed. 'Stuart! Stuart Mould!' He pointed to himself then reached forward and shook my hand before I had the chance to withdraw it. I could sense him taking in my shabby tartan dressing gown and Mr Men mule slippers.

'Sophie sends her apols but she's got a few things on – haven't we all! – and said you wouldn't mind if I brought Dylan over for once! Sometimes you just gotta be pragmatic! That which works, works!'

He looked at me expectantly for a response. I silently willed him to go away.

'Err . . . anyway, Bri, I've got an eighty-mile bike ride ahead of me! Fundraiser for Syrian orphans! You know how it is! So great to meet you at last! Absolutely *love* those slippers!'

He bounced off down the path. I went back inside to Dylan.

'How do you put up with it?' I asked.

'I don't know,' he replied glumly. I realised that it had been several weeks since I'd heard Dylan mutter a single inspirational quote. There was hope for him yet.

Sunday July 8th

This month's book is *The End of the Affair* by Graham Greene.

I have decided not to return to Bloomer's, having taken something of a dislike to the shop after receiving a rather brusque letter concerning my overdue payment for *Robinson Crusoe*.

It felt good to be back in the bookshop on the high street although, as is customary, I came away with rather more than I'd intended: Carson McCullers' *The Heart is a Lonely Hunter*; Elizabeth Smart's *By Grand Central Station I Sat Down and Wept*; Harold

Pinter's *Betrayal*; Joseph Conrad's *Heart of Darkness*; and John Gray's *Men Are From Mars, Women Are From Venus*.

I also bought a book entitled *Deaths of the Poets*. This was a rather morbid exploration of the stories behind the demise of famous poets: Dylan Thomas and his eighteen straight whiskies, Sylvia Plath and her Primrose Hill gas oven, John Berryman and his leap into the frozen Mississippi, and so on. It is grisly but fascinating! Who'd have thought there could be so many ways for a poet to snuff it?

Monday July 9th

Revolution, Inc.

This social movement protest is brought to you
in association with Pepsi –
putting the pop into popular demonstrations
for generations.

If all that shouting is making you hungry,
try the all-new McDonald's GuevaraBurger®,
available now at all major marches.
Just look out for the Golden Arches.

We are also delighted to inform you
of our 3 for the price of 2 offer
available on placards at the moment –
choose from a wide range of slogans,

including 'APPLE EACH DAY KEEPS THE FASCISTS AWAY',
'STARBUCK THE SYSTEM NOW'

and 'POWER TO THE PEOPLE, POWERED BY GOOGLE'.
Stay fresh and youthful

even when the police are being brutal
with the soothing balms
of Clinique's 'Revolutionary You' skincare range,
cleansing tyranny since the Ancien Régime.

We hope you enjoyed this protest brought to you
in association with Pepsi,
but before you go, why not enter this survey
for a chance to win a better world.

....

The arrival of *Well Versed – The Quarterly Magazine for the Discerning Poet* becomes more foreboding every quarter and today's issue was no exception. My poem was unplaced, as per usual. And there, of course, was the competition winner, Toby Salt, with the latest impenetrable example of his inexorably rising star.

1905

Порви все портреты, rage, my comrades / place the
telephone back upon its cradle / I spent these years waiting
for you / like the crocodile who basks / inside the handbag
/ fashioned from its own hide! / The walls are crumbling
now / Even Mme. Vissilovich knows that / She with her
head full of wool / and her hands that are never still /
Hush! царские солдаты идут / It is safe here / inside the
past / where the future cannot find fault / Safe behind this
barricade / of paper/ Watch how it burns! / This paper /
These walls that crumble / The future that turns in / upon
itself / And the bear who weeps / his tears of iron.

What on earth does all this mean? Even the boffins at Bletchley

Park would be baffled. Toby Salt's prize is a hamper from Fortnum and Mason. I hope he chokes on his salted caramel Florentines. He will be even more insufferable than usual at Poetry Club tomorrow. Beautiful, funny, perfidious Liz will be there, too. I don't think I'll go.

Tuesday July 10th

I went. I was persuaded by a news item this morning which suggests that people who read and listen to poetry are likely to live longer than those who don't. Poetry reduces stress levels, researchers claimed; its rhythms and cadences alleviate high blood pressure. My own experience seemed to contradict this but I may be the exception that proves the rule. In the absence of any other discernible lifestyle choices regarding healthy living, I decided to brave it.

Fortunately, Toby Salt wasn't there. He was being interviewed on the radio. I hope the listeners were warned that exposure to his poetry may result in dizziness, diarrhoea and vomiting. In his absence, he'd given Mary some invitations to hand out for the launch of his *This Bridge No Hands Shall Cleave* next month. I crumpled mine up in my cardigan pocket.

Liz and I didn't exchange a single word all evening. I thought her poems lacked their usual fizz and heady allure. I tossed off a light-hearted piece about the pain of betrayal and rejection, but my heart wasn't really in it either.

After we'd all had our turn, we sat down to discuss arrangements for the Poets on the Western Front trip, which is now only three months away. Mary took the chair.

'First up, finances,' she said. 'Brian, how much have we raised?'

I consulted my notebook. 'We now have £9,855.27 in the bank.'

Kaylee whistled. 'That's ten grand, to all intensive purposes,' she said, impressed.

'Yes, but don't forget that nearly half of that is ring-fenced for Dr Miller and his expenses,' I said.

'And have you been in touch with him to finalise the itinerary?' Mary asked.

'Not yet, I'm afraid,' I said. 'I've been very busy recently. But I'll get that done by next month's meeting – things are easing up.' I glanced at Liz. 'Some of my previous commitments have reneged on me.' I was struck by a pistachio shell.

Mary quickly moved the agenda on.

'Chandrima and Kaylee,' she said, 'you had something to share with us all.'

'We've put together a suggested reading list for the trip,' explained Chandrima, pulling some sheets of paper out from her bag. 'Kaylee has organised the books and poems by theme.'

I glanced at the headings: Imperialism and Jingoism. The Exploitation of the Working Classes. Women to the Rescue! Death and Futility.

'That should be very helpful. Thanks very much to both of you,' said Mary. 'Anything else from anyone?'

Douglas put his hand up.

'I was wondering,' he said, a little bashfully, 'whether it might be a good idea for us to dress up as infantrymen while we're over there – in order to experience at first-hand what life would have been like for the poets in the trenches.'

After some discussion the idea was vetoed, although Douglas was granted the concession of being allowed to wear a Brodie helmet for the duration of the tour.

Wednesday July 11th

I have now had time to reflect upon developments over the last few weeks – or 'Saffrongate' (as I inwardly refer to it). I must admit to being surprised – and, frankly, a little disappointed – to see Liz there, hanging on Toby Salt's every word. Things between us had been going along so promisingly up until 'Shedgate' (as I inwardly refer to it) but I wonder now, in hindsight, whether the breakneck pace of our affair had frightened her.

We are all free to make our own choices, however – no matter how stupid and ghastly they may be (and it is hard to think of a choice that is stupider or ghastlier). Regardless, I'm not the kind of person to harbour ill-feelings even if it does seem as if I've been led up the garden path (and all the way to 'Gardengate', as I inwardly refer to it).

But if there's one thing I refuse to do, it's to dwell on such matters. Yes, sure, Liz and I had some good times but that's all in the past now. I need to look forward, not back. It's time to move on.

Thursday July 12th

I was spending the morning busily moving on when I came across a playlist that I'd compiled for Liz. It had taken me days to put together. I'd planned to send it to her weeks ago but had never quite got around to finishing it.

I consider myself something of an expert in such matters, regarding the playlist as one of the most powerful weapons in my armoury of love. Years ago, it was a series of perfectly constructed compilation cassettes that were able to break down Sophie's defences. It's not simply a case of bunging one song down after another and hoping for the best. Each track needs to be carefully deliberated over and assessed, appraised for content, fit and flow. Every song choice represents a tiny glass fragment of your inner self; put them all together and the playlist becomes a window into one's soul.

◀ **You've Got Me Dangling On A String**
Chairman of the Board • A Little More Time

♪ **I Just Don't Understand**
Spoon • They Want My Soul

♪ **(You Make Me Feel Like) A Natural Woman**
Carole King • Tapestry

♪ **Even Though**
Norah Jones • The Fall

♪ **I'm A Man**
Bo Diddley • Bo Diddley

♪ **I Can't Stand Up For Falling Down**
Elvis Costello & The Attractions • Get Happy

♪ **I Don't Know What to Do**
Pete Yorn, Scarlett Johansson • Break Up

♪ **You Ask Me**
B.B. King • Ladies and Gentlemen

♪ **Stupid Questions**
New Model Army • Thunder and Consolations

♪ **I Haven't Got a Clue**
Ann Rabson • Saxophone Blues

♪ **Who Let The Dogs Out?**
Baha Men • Who Let The Dogs Out?

♪ **Where Have All The Flowers Gone?**
Marlene Dietrich • The Essential Marlene Dietrich

♪ **Do You Really Want To Hurt Me?**
Culture Club • Kissing To Be Clever

♪ **How Long Has This Been Going On?**
Audrey Hepburn • Funny Face

♪ **Is She Really Going Out with Him?**
Joe Jackson • Look Sharp!

♪ **Please Please Please**
James Brown • Get On Up

♪ **Say It Ain't So**
Weezer • Weezer

♪ **What Becomes Of The Brokenhearted?**
Jimmy Ruffin • Jimmy Ruffin

♪ **Should I Stay or Should I Go?**
The Clash • Combat Rock

I could have spent the whole day listening to it while staring dejectedly out of the window. But, having moved on from Liz and the whole Saffrongate thing, I didn't do that at all.

Friday July 13th

I was staring dejectedly out the window, listening to a playlist, when the doorbell rang. It was Mrs McNulty in a state of some excitement. She'd come over to inform me that my cat has been possessed.

'Possessed?'

'Yes. By an evil spirit. Or maybe just by another cat.'

'What makes you say that?'

'I saw her today in the garden and she's not herself. Just look at her!'

I looked at the cat. She looked very much like my cat, asleep.

'I think you're barking up the wrong tree.'

'My point exactly. That's what she was doing.'

'I thought you said she was possessed by an evil spirit or another cat?'

'Well, the evil spirit might belong to a dog. Or a cat with a sense of mischief.'

I remembered it was Friday the 13th. Mrs McNulty gets even crazier on such days. I ushered her out of the house with a hasty promise that I'd look into the matter in hand before she called the RSPCA or a priest.

Saturday July 14th

Dylan and I heard the VW Beetle sound its customary parp as it rounded the corner and Dave, Martin and Marvin were gone, leaving behind a trail of beer cans, cymbals and surgical gloves in their wake.

We went back inside and I saw Dylan surveying the mess in

the sitting room: the carpet was covered with records, most of which had been left out of their sleeves and were covered in cat hair; on the sofa lay plates of half-eaten food and empty tubs of houmous; piles of books towered precariously on the floor and it was clear from even the briefest of glances that a number of titles on the bookshelves themselves had fallen out of ISBN order; custard-cream crumbs were everywhere, having settled on the room like a layer of biscuity dandruff.

Dylan sat me down and gave me a talking to. He's worried about me, he says. Even Mum is worried about me, he says. I have *lots* to be positive about, he says. I need to think about all the *good* things around me, he says, and talks about my poems and the cat and how much he enjoys our Saturdays together. Most importantly, he says, I mustn't stop hoping.

He has written me a poem. It's called 'Hope on a Rope'. He asked if he could include it in my diary. I watched him quietly as he wrote it down:

If you don't

want to lose hope,

tie it to a rope and pull

yourself to safety. Because

hope has the power to lift

you up – whether your

problems are

light or

w

e

i

g

h

t

y

Sunday July 15th

I got my house in order. For once, I did not fight the chores but embraced them with renewed vigour: laundry, ironing, vacuuming and cleaning. It was late afternoon by the time I'd finished. I sat down and picked up *The End of the Affair*.

And I read it. Not quite all of it but, by the time I turned out the light, I was within whistling distance of the final page.

Monday July 16th

The cat has gone missing. I was reflecting on all the progress I'd made yesterday when I realised that it was achieved with – or perhaps, because of – the absence of cat. I rattled her food bowl at regular intervals throughout the day but with no success. I have checked all her usual sleeping places. I must confess that I am worried; this is not like her at all.

In brighter news, I have finished reading *The End of the Affair*. This month, I will actually be going to book group having read the book!

Tuesday July 17th

It's my birthday on Friday. Most years I do what I can to avoid it, shunning all human contact three days before and after its occurrence. But this year, in an attempt to re-establish my life on a more positive footing, I've decided to grasp it by the celebratory nettle and host a small party.

I have sent invitations out to Mary, Chandrima, Kaylee, Douglas, Darren, Tomas, Mrs McNulty, Dylan and the Man at Number 29. I also wrote an invitation out to Liz but then thought better of it, scrunched it up and threw it in the bin: there is only so much that my new growth mindset can withstand. I would have invited Toby Salt but the party invitations came in a pack of ten and I'd run out by the time I got to him.

There's still no sign of the cat. I do hope she returns in time for the party. She would feel sad to have missed out on the opportunity of all those fresh laps.

Wednesday July 18th

I went to ask Mrs McNulty whether she'd seen my cat. She was in the middle of vehement denial of any involvement in its disappearance, when I noticed a piece of paper pinned to a door off her hallway. On it was written "EXORCISE ROOM" in shaky felt-tip pen.

'I didn't know you had a gym, Mrs McNulty,' I said, striding past her and following the steps down into her cellar.

And there was my cat, surrounded by candles on top of a wooden crucifix-shaped table. She was fast asleep and smelt of sage. Beside her was a book entitled *Spiritual Warfare: A User's Manual*, with the pages open at some kind of prayer or incantation.

I picked up the cat, went back up the stairs and confronted Mrs McNulty.

'What have you been doing to her?'

Mrs McNulty fiddled distractedly with the umbrella stand in her hallway.

'MRS McNULTY!?'

'Let's just say she'll be having no more problems with evil spirits,' she declared, winking and tapping her nose, before proclaiming triumphantly: 'There'll be no more barking from her!'

I held onto the cat tightly and hurried out the door. If anyone was barking, it was Mrs McNulty.

Thursday July 19th

I have received six items of post today, all of them bills. Among them was a reminder from Bloomer's about my outstanding payment for *Robinson Crusoe* and an invoice from the hotel in Saffron Walden for undeclared mini-bar items from my final evening there. I fail to understand how the invoice can be so big when the fridge had seemed so small.

I put the invoices under my bed in a box with all the other ones and got on instead with my party preparations.

Friday July 20th

Birthday Party, Alone

Wearing my most daring tank top,
I arrived downstairs fashionably late,
at a quarter to eight;

the invitations that I forgot to send out
some days before
clearly stated it was to begin at 7:34.

I put on 'Russians' by Sting.
It wasn't long before the party
was in full swing.

Hanging out in the kitchen
with the Cheese Singles
I met the Pringles,

whom I thought delightful,
far better company than the rather nonchalant
wild mushroom vol-au-vents.

Six skittish tins of Fosters enticed me
to play a game of Hold the Parcel
(forty-two minutes – a new record),

Musical Statues (until I got cramp
attempting to out-statue a Victorian floor lamp),
and finally, Sardine,

in which I hid in the airing cupboard
for three days, on an inexpertly folded sheet
until I found myself.

....

Nobody came, of course. The list of excuses seemed entirely valid: Mary had her grandchildren visiting; Kaylee was at a talk on domestic abuse; Chandrima had judo; Darren, salsa; Tomas was giving a lecture on Wittgenstein's *Philosophical Investigations*; Mrs McNulty was off to the bingo; the man at Number 29 dropped a note through my letter box to tell me he was going to be away on a course on effective planning and could I put his recycling out. Dylan rang to wish me a happy birthday, at least, but then apologised for not being able to make it. It is also Stuart's birthday today, apparently, and Sophie had got them all tickets to a new West End musical.

It was only Douglas that I felt disappointed with. He didn't even bother to tell me that he couldn't make it.

As I sat beneath the disco ball in my shed, my growth mindset felt itself under severe pressure once more. But, thanks to a combination of vol-au-vents, cheap lager and *The End of the Affair* (which I have begun to re-read) I powered through. On reflection, this constitutes one of my more successful birthdays of recent years.

Saturday July 21st

Even my Saturday newspaper contains added Salt. He gazes smugly out at me from the *Literature & Culture* section, as he shares with the world what he'll be reading on his holiday this summer. What a pretentious selection of books! They should put signs up on whatever Mediterranean beach he'll be lying on:

'READ AT YOUR OWN RISK'

'SLIPPERY METAPHORS'

'BEWARE: SUBMERGED MEANING'

They're not for the likes of me. I'll follow my usual practice of leaving my reading to the lottery of a holiday cottage bookshelf: all those potboilers, page-turners and bodice-rippers, with their pages crimpled from sun-cream and god knows what other kinds of liquids.

Dylan is off to Marbella for two weeks with Sophie and Stuart over the summer. I'd originally had hopes of something grand for the pair of us, too, but with another three bills arriving just this morning, I've had to downsize my dreams to a week in a cottage just outside Scarborough. Dylan took the news pretty well, all things considered.

Sunday July 22nd

Having now read *The End of the Affair* three times, I thought I'd attempt to get back on civil terms with the book group by sharing with them a deep analysis of its major themes, talking points, and literary strengths and weaknesses. I began work on the PowerPoint slides today. I think I shall print out packs for Thursday rather than bring along my own projector screen: how sad would that be!

Taking inspiration from Kaylee's First World War reading list, I've organised the slides into the following sections:

1. Betrayal
2. Guilt and shame
3. The corrupting power of human love
4. Suffering
5. Death
6. Irony

All in all, we should be set for a fun evening.

Monday July 23rd

WE DEEPLY REGRET TO INFORM YOU

TELEGRAMS IN THEIR THOUSANDS
THE HEARTS OF LOVED ONES SINK
ALL THAT WASTED PAPER
ALL THAT WASTED INK

A hashtag is trending in my heart and it goes by the name of #DouglasRIP.

Chandrima called to tell me the news. He had met up with some fellow re-enactors last Thursday morning, she said, as part of a documentary commemorating the Battle of the Somme. Douglas was one of the first of the 'Tommies' out of the trenches but fell within seconds, amidst the smoke and pyrotechnics the production team had conjured up that morning. He lay there for four hours, face down in no-man's-land, before one of his fellow re-enactors realised there was something wrong. It was thought he'd had a heart attack, perhaps triggered by the shock of a flare whistling overhead.

It is so very sad but this is how he would have liked to have gone, said Chandrima, seeking to console. I know exactly what she means: Douglas in uniform, on the battlefield, fighting for Queen, Country and Television Production Company.

Tuesday July 24th

It was in a state of Douglaslessness that I loaded up the dishwasher and scoured the work surfaces. And, as I did so, I found myself meditating deeply on the meaning of existence and the nature of death. What if I was suddenly struck down as I re-ordered this cutlery basket, for instance; what might others say of me? I imagined my gravestone:

BRIAN BILSTON
He never quite managed
to seize the day.

> But he sure stacked a dishwasher
> in an orderly way.

I found myself asking questions that went straight to the very heart of things. Sensing that this might be prime poetry-writing territory, I wrote them down:

a) what purpose serves a life?
b) what constitutes a life well-lived?
c) is happiness a social construct?
d) is there any rinse-aid left?
e) where do we go to when we die?

I thought long and hard. This was difficult stuff and the search for answers exhausting. After a few hours my brain could take no more; I looked down at what I'd written in response.

a) don't know
b) not sure
c) probably
d) no idea
e) maybe check the cupboard under the stairs

I may have got some of the answers muddled up but it was a start, I suppose.

Wednesday July 25th

Ink Nothing of It

In that cheap rented room, he lay for weeks
upon the threadbare carpet, half-hid,
underneath virgin printer paper sheets
and some empty inkjet cartridges.

The finer things in life I always did lack
because of the cyan, magenta, yellow and black.

'I knew him when he was up at Cambridge,'
said one at the funeral, 'Not a loner,
then, by any means. Popular, quite rich.
And, back in those days, quite free of toner.'

Pity me, the penniless, penurious fellow,
because of the black, magenta, cyan and yellow.

In his twenties he would do what he liked,
never stopped to think before he would print.
In full colour, too, not just black and white.
The money bled away faster than ink.

I am off-colour, off-line, off-print, off-centre
because of the yellow, cyan, black and magenta.

Along with the body they found a note,
taped to the printer and stained with blood:
'I have run out of ink, money and hope,
and now I am running out for good.'

There's nothing left at all of who I am
because of the yellow, magenta, black and cyan.

My finances are fading faster than the pages that emerge from my inkjet printer. I began to print out *The End of the Affair* packs only to find my fine-tuned analysis streaked with nothingness. The subsection on The Roman Catholic Novel in the Twentieth Century was particularly affected and my Suggestions for Further Reading barely legible. I cycled into town, blanching as I handed over the money for new toner cartridges.

Thursday July 26th

Love Letters Carved in Rock

For you, no ordinary stick of rock,
not some standard candied stock
from a faded seaside town,
no kiss-me-quick before I drown.

Instead, this home made confection,
its letters engrained to perfection.
Five years I spent to create this art!
Your name runs through its heart,

as it runs through mine. Red strips
of sugar, glucose, water mixed
into molten calligraphic stasis,
white rock pouring in the spaces

to shape the letters of your name.
For you're as sweet as candy cane
and my love is – what do you mean
that's not how you spell Siobhan?

Anyone can make a mistake. That's what I kept telling myself, anyway, as I sat quietly at the end of the table, listening to them all discuss *Brighton Rock*. That business with Liz at the beginning of the month had knocked me about a little – and I must have muddled it up in my head. Sure, that work on the Roman Catholic Novel in the Twentieth Century hadn't been wasted, and a cynical worldview seemed to permeate through both books, but I didn't have much to give beyond that. I could have counted all the characters I knew from *Brighton Rock* on my little pinkie.

It wasn't until I was halfway home that I took the handouts out of my bag. I stuffed them in a bin.

Friday July 27th

It was all Darren's fault. We should take 27th Club on tour, he said, and make a proper weekend of it. It had sounded so liberating a few months ago, as we anticipated our very own epiphanic Woodstock, in which we not only discovered a new soundtrack to our lives, but somehow better understood who we *truly* were, while sitting in a field somewhere deep in the haze of a golden English summer.

We hadn't envisaged that the weather might be like this – lashing rain and blackened skies – nor that we would spend six hours queueing on the M62 for the turn-off to Hull. For much of the day, all we'd seen was Cars, Traffic and The Jam.

And we certainly hadn't foreseen that confusion over the ticket-ordering which meant that we weren't off to Tribeca, hipster festival of experimental music, after all, but Tribfest, advertised as the UK's 'second' largest annual gathering of tribute acts.

By the time Darren had managed to pitch his tent in the driving rain and I'd settled into my yurt, the first day was nearly over, and we only just managed to catch the end of Phoney M murdering 'Rasputin'.

Saturday July 28th

....

Pyramid Stage

I

think

he was

twenty-one

years of age /

when he went through

his pyramid stage. He did

not know what triggered that /

strange urge to be a ziggurat. He

reached his apex then had a seizure. /

I think about him to this day. Amazing Giza.

....

I feel like I've landed in one of those parallel worlds that Dylan sometimes talks about. Everything in it is the same as this world, only a little bit more rubbish. It rains here, only heavier. There is mud here, but it is gloopier. Instead of the Pyramid Stage, we have the Triangle Stage. And then, of course, there are the bands: Proxy Music, Fleetwood Mock, Mad Donna, The Velvet Underpants, Sample Minds, Punk Floyd, New Hors d'oeuvres, The Heebie Beegees.

The only noticeable improvement in this new world is that I live in a yurt. I found myself spending an increasing amount of time in it as the day wore on. Darren tells me that it's not in the spirit of things, and I'm missing out on the authentic festival experience. Still, I couldn't help but notice his look of envy when he visited my spacious accommodation – with its underfloor heating, Wi-Fi and shower-room – in the middle of the night, to tell me about the leak in his tent. Water had been pouring in for several hours, he said, and, judging by the state of him, it appeared it had.

But friendship knows no boundaries and so I sent him away with an old T-shirt of mine, having discovered it at the bottom of my suitcase, which was lying unpacked on the Egyptian cotton sheets of my spare bed.

Sunday July 29th

Everybody Yurts

When the day's been long and the night,
The night chills you to the bone.
When you're sure you've had enough
Of mudslides, well hang on.
Let your tent pegs go, let me please advise
That everybody yurts sometimes.

Sometimes standard camping's wrong.
It's only suited to the strong.
When the ground is hard as stone,
And it feels like ten below.
If you think you've had too much of this life, well hang on.

'Cos everybody yurts. Take comfort in king-size beds.
Everybody yurts.

No frozen hands. Oh no. No more frozen hands.
From sheep's wool, it's wove.
Oh, oh, oh, wood-burning stove.

If you think you may not survive, and your tent is not that
strong,
When you think you've had too much of this life to hang on.
Well, when your body hurts most times,
As you try to rise . . .

Everybody yurts sometimes.
And everybody yurts sometimes.
The cold's gone, cold's gone.

Darren was strangely irritable today and barely had a civil word
to say to me. I suspect this may be due to the heavy cold he seems
to be coming down with. But we hung in there as best we could,
sticking around for the headline act, an R.E.M. tribute band
called Are.We.Them?

They were clearly not. Sophie and I had seen the genuine article all those years ago. Only a few hazy images of their
performance have stayed with me: Peter Buck with an electric
mandolin; Michael Stipe bizarrely wearing a football shirt; a
cover played in tribute to Kurt Cobain. But I remember everything
else about that night: Sophie in her denim jacket and DMs; the
way she jumped up and down in excitement as they walked on
stage; the look of wonder on her face as she watched the day's sun
sink slowly behind the stadium; the journey back, with Sophie's
head in my lap as she slept; and the reflection in the bus window
of me, smiling back at myself, a shiny, happy person.

Monday July 30th

Breaking News

The news seems broken now,
nearly every day.
I shall gather up its pieces
and throw it all away.

Breaking news: I am broke.

My front door was almost wedged shut by the stack of mail that greeted me on my return. Amongst the reminders of unpaid bills for books, hotel bills, shed furnishings and luxury yurt accommodation was a bank statement coloured in red.

My redundancy money has gone and my overdraft limit is exhausted. There remains £10,000 in the account for the 'Poets on the Western Front' trip but that, of course, is untouchable. I need money – and quickly – before the mortgage payments and utility bills drag me further under.

Incredibly, the sun has emerged from all this rain; it shines down and gently mocks me.

Tuesday July 31st

The Met Office is forecasting a heatwave. I am in search of a brainwave. I have been attempting to identify possible solutions which might alleviate my financial difficulties. I didn't get very far. I looked at the list I'd written:

1. Sell all my books.
2. Hire out my stupid, useless writer's shed for garden parties.
3. Get a proper job again.
4. Earn money from writing.

Option 1 is possible but ill-advisable given the structural support provided to the house. Option 2 is also possible but income may be sporadic. Option 3 is possible but would squat on my life and crush my soul. Option 4 has proved to be impossible, and so I have decided to pursue that further.

August

Wednesday August 1st

Chandrima has suggested that all members of Poetry Club should read a poem at Douglas's funeral tomorrow.

I sat on the garden bench with a dozen anthologies spread out in front of me, slowly reddening under the mid-day sun. It took me ages to find anything appropriate; most of the popular funeral poems seem overly morbid, maudlin or mawkish, and I'm not altogether sure that's what he would have wanted.

I tried Kipling but couldn't find anything quite right. In the end, I settled on Noel Coward's 'Mad Dogs and Englishmen'. He would have enjoyed its comedy and redolence of colonialism.

Thursday August 2nd

....

Funeral Shoes (Stop all the Crocs)

Stop all the Crocs, cut out these foam clogs,
Don't let your footwear go to the dogs,
Silence the pavements from the Crocs' fearsome slap,
Bring out the dustbin, put your Crocs into that.

Let the easyJets gather and circle in glee
To write on the sky the words CROC: R.I.P.
Organise parties and grand cavalcades,
Host dinners, bake cakes, throw victory parades.

He was her North, her South, her West and East,
Her Mini-Milk, her Fab, her Chocolate Feast.

But such thoughts were all packed away in a box,
From the moment she saw him wearing Crocs.

Crocs are passé now: discard all your pairs;
Lob them onto the waves, recite a prayer.
Watch them drift out to where sea and sky meet,
And beg for forgiveness from your poor feet.

Douglas's funeral was not well-attended. Poetry Club represented about half of those gathered together to say their farewells. But amongst the others assembled, much consideration had gone into providing him with the kind of send-off he would have wanted: there was a guard of honour; his coffin was draped in the Union Jack; the 'Last Post' was bugled. And then it was the turn of Poetry Club with our selections: Rossetti, Dickinson, Barrett Browning, Tennyson, Wordsworth. Toby Salt read an extract from Sun Tzu's *The Art of War*, in its original Chinese.

We walked across the road together to the pub. As Toby Salt's footsteps clacked behind me, my loathing of him reached new levels. I was munching on a cheese sandwich and wondering what kind of monster wears crocs to a funeral when Liz came over.

'Funerals aren't much fun, are they?' she said.

'Not much,' I said. 'About as much fun as weddings, I suppose.'

She looked at me for a moment.

'What is it that you're afraid of, Brian?' she asked.

I wasn't quite sure what she was getting at so I started to murmur things at the carpet.

'Death. Life. Spiders. Toby Salt's poetry. These cheese sandwi—'

'Happiness?'

I looked up sharply. I knew the answer to that.

'Happiness is a social construct. Probably.'

Liz sighed. From the corner of the pub, I could hear Toby Salt's voice droning on about his new book. Any moment now, he'd start bellowing out a poem.

'Is it?' she said. 'Is it really? And what about me? Am I a social construct, too?'

'No, of course not! You're—'

I tried to think of the right word. *Real? Palpable? Beautiful? Treacherous?*

'You're—'

Tangible? Corporeal? Sexy? Amphibious?

'You're—'

Amphibious? I was just thinking random adjectives now. For once, I had Toby Salt to thank as I heard him launch lustily into a Petrarchan sonnet and, mercifully, I was snapped out of my reverie.

'Sorry, Liz. But I've got to go. It's been really good talking to you again.'

I fled the pub, cursing myself and my stupid brain. Words, why do you always fail me when I need you most?

Friday August 3rd

Dylan is in Marbella from tomorrow with Sophie and Stuart. He has sent me a link to where they're staying. It's a villa with two heated pools, three bathrooms, a Jacuzzi, an on-call maid and dinner service. There is ready access to a local golf course.

I thought again about the prospect of our week together in sodden North Yorkshire. He'll find it such a let-down, which I suppose is how he must find me.

If only there was some way I could make a success of my writing. I looked out at my shed's accusatory silhouette. It occurred to me that I'd been going about it all wrong: it's not about *where* I write but *what* I write. I've just not stumbled on the right topic or format yet. I closed my eyes and focused for three solid minutes but could make no further progress.

Saturday August 4th

I think I have it!

I'd been moping around, worrying about my money problems, and thinking about Douglas's funeral and our poetry readings, when the answer suddenly came to me . . . DEATH!

It had been a real struggle to find a good poem for the service. The selections were fine as far as they went but they all seemed a little too familiar, impersonal and rather dated. There is, it would seem, a real dearth of decent modern poems about death.

This was the gap in the market I'd been hoping for! Could I write something that might corner the funeral market in the way that, say, 'Happy Birthday' had the whole birthday thing sewn up? Or Slade's 'Merry Xmas, Everybody' dominated the festive season? If I could, I'd be quids in.

The more I thought about it, the more advantages I could see. I wrote out a mini-business plan, including a section on market potential:

> 1. *Everyone dies at some stage in their life, typically at the end of it. That's a large market segment to go at, particularly if this segment could be targeted pre-death.*

2. *Everyone experiences grief and bereavement. This represents a fantastic opportunity for a poem written with tact and sensitivity.*

3. *Competition is weak and divided. Existing death poems have typically been written out of personal experience rather than a cool assessment of market requirements and an in-depth understanding of the voice of the customer.*

I sat back in front of an old episode of *Rebus*, smiling to myself. I just had to write the thing now.

Sunday August 5th

First up with any new project: a visit to the bookshop. I bought a new anthology of poems on death and bereavement as well as a few other titles: *Grieving for Dummies*; Elisabeth Kübler-Ross's *On Death and Dying*; *Death: A Graveside Companion*; *Coping with Loss*; *A Guide to London Cemeteries*; and James Joyce's *The Dead and Other Stories*.

Arriving home, I realised I'd forgotten this month's book group selection: *Fight Club* by Chuck Palahniuk. I went back to the bookshop to pick one up and, while I was at it, Allan Ginsberg's *Howl and Other Poems* and three walking maps of the North Yorkshire coast. It had been an expensive day but I managed to find the money from somewhere.

Monday August 6th

It is proving much harder than I thought to write a really good funeral poem. It's very easy to move from the universal to the personal and – as a result – potentially limit a poem's audience. To circumvent this problem, I am considering a multiple-choice format:

Farewell, my dear departed *father* / *mother* /
sister / *brother* / *granddad* / *granny* / *lover* /
auntie / *uncle* / *cousin* / *friend* / *associate*·
(· please delete as appropriate).

I will miss your *generosity of spirit* /
good sense of humour / *patience beyond limit* /
growth mindset / *assorted flaws and imperfections* /
joie de vivre / *Fleetwood Mac record collection*

not to mention those *beautiful blue eyes* / *green eyes* /
brown eyes / *grey eyes* / *powerful, muscular thighs* /
bow ties / *wimples* / *dimples* / *broad hips* / *soft lips*.
You were unique. A one-off. You will be much missed.

But Death, alas, snatched you from us *far too soon* /
after a good innings / *last Tuesday afternoon*.
And we gather here in this *church* / *crematorium* /
cathedral / *cemetery* / *multi-faith emporium* /

synagogue / *prayer room* / *forest clearing at midnight*
to wish you well as you go *into Allah's light* /
on an exciting new journey / *with God's good grace* /
screaming into the void / *to a better place*.

I've given it a provisional title of 'Farewell to [Insert Loved One's Name Here]'.

I considered its merits: it keeps its options open; it's multi-faith; it could be extended to include other scenarios without too much difficulty; it's designed to reach the broadest audience possible. But I couldn't help thinking that once the multiple-choice answers have been decided, there's not a whole lot here. Also, is it *too* impersonal? Might it be perceived as opportunistic?

No, I wasn't happy with it, I decided. I'd just have to have another go at it tomorrow.

Tuesday August 7th

....

Beat Poets

Some say it's for their own good
but I don't think you should.

....

Some say I threw the first punch. Some say I threw the only punch. Some say it was all academic anyway as poets aren't very good at punching and that's why I missed and grazed my hand on the bench behind him.

It was Toby Salt's comments about Douglas that did it. But I was already in an agitated state of mind; I'd spent the whole day wrestling with death but the words still weren't falling as I'd hoped. By the time I turned up at Poetry Club, I was in a foul mood.

Toby Salt had already told us that this was probably going to be his last Poetry Club.

'I've moved on, you see,' he said. 'Important things are happening and I'm not sure I can commit any more to this.' He gestured disparagingly at the shabby back room.

Chandrima looked crestfallen. Mary irritated. Kaylee sullen. Liz cross. I felt my mood lifting.

'It has a certain charm, of course,' he went on, 'but it's all rather small-town stuff whereas I now operate on, shall we say, a different plane.'

'A different plane,' repeated Chandrima dejectedly.

'Well, yes. You know, with the radio and TV, the broadsheets, the festivals and competitions. And my poems operate at something of a loftier altitude to the ones here. You must realise that.'

'A loftier attitude,' said Kaylee, sulkily.

'Take Brian with his funny little poems about goodness knows what! They're hardly going to win any prizes, are they?!'

'Prizes,' repeated Liz, disdainfully.

My irritation had begun to return.

'The scansion! Those rhymes! He'd struggle getting those printed on greeting cards!'

'Greeting cards,' repeated me, properly riled now.

'It's not just Brian. I mean, take Douglas. How he wasted not just my time – but yours – with his ridiculous hoplophiliac ramblings on military conflicts through history. There was a man without a single poetic bone in his body, one far more interested in fighting and viol—'

And that's when I punched him. Or tried to. But I slipped on the collection of pistachio shells underneath my chair as I lunged forward and my fist went whistling past his ear. The others restrained me from inflicting further damage upon myself while

Toby Salt looked at me with amused contempt, shook his head, then walked out of Poetry Club for ever.

Wednesday August 8th

I looked again at the words I'd fought with yesterday. I'd been attempting to create a more contemporary feel to the whole dying thing:

You are gone from the world. I feel so alone.
My head is a rock. My heart is a stone.
Then I think of that summer, our apartment in Rome.
With me, in your thrall, and you, on your phone.

The motif of the mobile phone would make it play more strongly with Generation X and Millennial audiences, I hoped.

The memories come as if to atone:
A daytrip to see the Millennium Dome,
Long walks on the beach, our feet in the foam.
With love in my heart, and you, on your phone.

But was that wise? If I was honest with myself, the market share of those segments, in death terms, was not nearly as significant as that all-important ageing baby boomer market.

But then came that day, the last you'd have known.
You in the street and a car coming home.
I think you may well have been on your phone.
With me, at the wheel, and the smash of your bones.

The whole business of the poem's narrator running over their lover was also troubling me. It did not strike me as the stuff of elegies.

Now, on your coffin, we have thrown our last stones.
Sleep soundly, my love, with the worms in the loam.
I pray where you've gone is a free Wi-Fi zone.
With you, in the ground, lying next to your phone.

I looked at my own phone from the relative safety of the sofa. There was a message from Liz:

Are you OK?
What a pompous idiot Toby [Salt] is!

Well, you weren't thinking that in Saffron Walden, when you hung on his every word, I considered retorting, but I am not by nature a mean-spirited or vindictive person. I replied with the rather more conciliatory:

All fine here!
Good riddance to him.

And I was fine, not least because the last laugh was on him. I'd looked up the word he'd used yesterday:

HOPLOPHILIAC (noun): a person who harbours an unnatural love of guns and other firearms

And it just happened to be the solution to 15 across of the crossword.

Thursday August 9th

I checked in to Twitter for the first time in several centuries. In my absence, my following has blossomed. There are now forty-three people hanging on my every tweet. Toby Salt has nearly five thousand followers. His page is a relentless mudflow of self-promotion: his latest competition success; upcoming book signings for *This Bridge No Hand Shall Cleave*; another piece in the *Guardian*.

I returned to my funeral poem but progress continued to be slow. At some stage I must have drifted off to sleep on the sofa because I fell into a dream. I was a police inspector called in to investigate the death of a poet, who'd been found in suspicious circumstances. He was lying on the floor in the hallway of his apartment, with the pages from his latest book stuffed into his mouth. At the post-mortem, his body was found to contain traces of many harmful toxins, a lethal cocktail of dactyls and spondees and several lines of iambic pentameter.

I think all these deliberations on death are beginning to have a deleterious effect on me.

Friday August 10th

I read 'Now I Am Dead' again:

> Now I am dead,
> please do not weep for me.
> Your tears won't bring me back,
> now I am dead.
>
> Now I am dead,
> you can clear out all my shoes.

I'll not need them where I am going,
now I am dead.

Now I am dead,
don't forget to do the bins on Friday
(this week is general landfill),
now I am dead.

Now I am dead,
you can crack on with that loft extension
I'd never much cared for,
now I am dead.

I seem to have fallen into the trap again of making it too personal, although there may be themes within it that resonate universally (death, the bins, etc.). At least, there's a decent balance of poignancy (*'your tears won't bring me back'*) and practicality (*'you can clear out all my shoes'* etc).

All the same, I don't feel very confident that I've cracked it. Regardless, I've sent all three poems off to a few local funeral parlours to see if they might be interested in including them in any information packs they may hand out to grieving customers.

Saturday August 11th

....

Catastrophe

don't know
what drives me crazier,
your amnesia
or pyromania

even now
I still think about
the time you forgot
to put the cat out

Dylan told me that Stuart hired a Maserati in Marbella so they might better experience the 'majesty of the Sierra Blanca foothills'. He said this somewhat pointedly, as we boarded our third train of the day. In total, it took four trains, two buses and one three-mile walk to make it to our North Yorkshire idyll, a mere fourteen hours after setting off.

It was pitch black when we arrived and it took us another forty minutes and one irritable late-night phone call to the owner, Mr Briggs, to locate the front door key, which we found under a brick in the disused barn next door. The cottage is beautiful, though – and will be even more so once we locate the Wi-Fi password.

Tomas is house-sitting for me and will look after the cat. In turn, the cat will be Tomas-sitting. Last year, I asked Mrs McNulty to help and the cat has yet to forgive me. It was also the first time that the RSPCA were alerted to my Twitter presence.

Sunday August 12th

Our holiday hasn't had the most auspicious of beginnings: a day spent in vain pursuit of the Wi-Fi password. Mr Briggs was hopeless. He was pretty sure it had an 'a' and an 'l' in it, and quite possibly a 'p' or should that be a 't'? I grilled him about the names of his first pet, his mother's maiden name and the name of his primary school, but we are no nearer to the truth.

Dylan got fed up with waiting me for me to crack the code and headed out for the afternoon, having borrowed one of my walking guides. I would have joined him but holidays aren't all about doing what you want.

Monday August 13th

....

Gérard Depardieu is in Pieces!

Gérard Depardieu is in pieces!
He is dreaming of the Remora 2000 again,
steering it solemnly past the gobies,
while sharing silent jokes
with the clown tangs.

Gérard Depardieu's head is all jumbled!
He is no longer sure
of the Remora 2000's thruster capabilities
and at what kind of depths
it can safely operate.

Mais regardez! Voilà une tête flottante!
Tell the catfish he is coming!
He is slowly assembling!
Tell them Gérard Depardieu
is getting himself together at last!

....

The incessant rain has forced us to avail ourselves of the cottage's entertainment facilities (excluding the Wi-Fi, that is, as we are yet to crack the password), the full list of which is as follows:

1) Three VHS video cassettes: *Babe: Pig in the City*, *Pokemon: The Movie 2000*, and volume 2 of a box set of *The Thornbirds*.

2) One slightly soiled paperback copy of *A Surgeon in her Stocking* by Tina Solomon, a Christmas tale from Mills and Boon's *Medical Romance* series.

3) Board games: Monopoly (without the board), Scrabble (without the tiles) and Noel's House Party, still wrapped in its original cellophane.

4) A 500-piece Photo Jigsaw Puzzle of Gérard Depardieu in a Submersible. At this stage, it's unclear to us whether this is complete or not, although we have yet to locate Gérard Depardieu's left ear.

This must seem a far cry from Marbella for Dylan but he's putting a brave face on it all and doing his best to keep my spirits up.

Tuesday August 14th

On Reading a Mills and Boon

His fingers ran down its spine tentatively,
a surprising sensitivity contained
within those powerful, muscular digits.
'Read me,' it gasped.

Preliminary material was dispensed with.
Plunging in, his hands reached firmly
beneath the covers, spreading its pages wide,
as he sought out its hot inky centre,

and buried himself deep within it.
It was all over before you could say
'our love became a burning mist'.
They lay in silence, limp and ashamed.

....

We found Gérard Depardieu's left ear after all, alongside the
racing car and the boot in the Scrabble box. But we were unable
to find a section of the submersible's on-board computer, which
as the jigsaw box informed us, can automatically maintain a fixed
depth as far down as 610 metres for up to ten hours. We also have
a piece left over: it is blue with three nobbly bits.

By the evening, the rain had abated but not soon enough to
prevent me from making inroads on *A Surgeon in her Stocking*. It
was the last thing that beautiful but feisty midwife Ellie Forbes
wanted, but when brooding Italian surgeon Alessandro Montieri
walked into the obstetrics ward that December and back into her
life, she couldn't help but think that all her Christmases had
come at once.

I read sections of it out loud to Dylan; we haven't laughed so
much in ages.

Wednesday August 15th

....

O do not ask if I am beach body ready

O do not ask
if I am beach body ready.

Observe how the folds
of my stomach ripple
like the wind-pulled waves.

Rub your hands
over these pale buttocks,
sand-smoothed by time.

Note my milk-white limbs
like washed-up whalebones,
stranded and useless.

Consider these tufts of hair
on my back and shoulders
which sprout like sea-grass.

And listen to the lapping
of my socks
at the shores of my sandals.

And still you ask me
if I am beach body ready?

....

We made it to the beach and laid out our towels in the drizzle. We
bit into our hard-boiled eggs and gazed out at the grey sea.

'Why did you and Mum split up?' asked Dylan, still staring off
into the distance.

I paused while I considered this.

'I think she thought me to be something of a disappointment.'

'A disappointment? In what way?'

'Not in any specific way. Just generally. A general disappointment. Like a film you've looked forward to watching for ages, and
then you see it, and you realise it wasn't worth the wait. The plot
makes no sense, the dialogue is stilted, the casting's all wrong. A
bit like *Babe: Pig in the City*.'

He smiled. This time, it was his turn to pause and reflect.

'Did you used to write her poems?'

'Your mother was the reason I *started* writing poems. I'd write her one every day.'

'Then what happened?'

'She stopped reading them. Or I stopped writing them . . . I forget which.'

'Why?'

'You see, poetry . . . it doesn't really solve anything. It shines its light on things but it doesn't give answers. It was never going to keep us together.'

'I'm glad you're a poet.'

'I'm not a poet. I'm just somebody who write poems.'

'Same difference,' said Dylan, and we packed up and headed back to finish reading *A Surgeon in her Stocking*.

Thursday August 16th

....

The Incidence of Oxymorons

Alone together at last,
I told her how I thought that –
in my unbiased opinion –
the incidence of oxymorons
in the English language
had been growing smaller.

That's old news, she said,
claiming it had been the case
for almost exactly ten years.
Strongly held convictions
were thrown across the room.
Things got pretty ugly.

But this felt strangely normal;
ours was a bittersweet relationship,
a tragi-comic civil war
of violent agreements
and deafening silences,
going nowhere.

....

For the first time in years, I dreamt about Sophie. We were argu-
ing. I'd spent the day writing poems for her to find when she
came back from work, scattering them around the house like
confetti. She wondered why the fridge was empty when I'd promised I'd go shopping and why the house was in such a state when
I'd promised to tidy up.

She said it would be good if 'just for once' I could drop the
'obsession with poetry and join the rest of us in the real world.'
Later, I found a Post-it note she'd left on the kitchen table. It said:
'Brian, I give up. Can't live with you anymore. I am off to Mum's'.

It was the saddest haiku I had ever read.

Dylan woke me up.

'I've got my results!' he shouted. 'Seven A*s and two As!'

I hugged him and held him close. Later, we headed out to pick
up the trail through the woods until we reached the foss, the
sudden thunder of its fall drowning out the last vestiges of my
troubled sleep.

Friday August 17th

We followed a different route today, tracing the slow curves of the
river until it broadened like a fan as we neared the coast. We
searched the bank for stones, flat and oval, the size of our palms,

and launched them down the river, with varying degrees of success. Legs bent, I watched the stone as it sliced shallow scoops out of the water – one, two – and Dylan started talking – three, four – about how they were moving to America – five, six – the stone barely touching the surface – seven, eight – travelling further and further – nine, ten – disappearing from sight.

Saturday August 18th

We handed the keys back to Mr Briggs, who laughingly told us he'd remembered the Wi-Fi password after all! It was BRENDA678. Brenda being the name of his favourite Large White Yorkshire pig and 678 being the number of pounds that she weighed.

Travelling back, Dylan and I avoided all reference to yesterday's conversation, but it hung uncomfortably over us all day, like a bag strap dangling from the overhead storage compartments of a succession of trains (three). Sophie made no mention of it either when I dropped Dylan back. I got home and closed the door, surrounded by a heap of unpaid invoices, junk mail and funeral-parlour rejection letters.

Sunday August 19th

I took a closer look at the funeral-parlour replies. They all started with the phrase *'It is with much regret'*. The one exception came from Jenkins & Pain (strapline: *It's a Grave Business*).

I read the brochure that they'd enclosed:

Here at Jenkins and Pain,
we know what it's like to lose a loved one,
so why not leave us to take the strain,
while you get on with your mourning.

We handle all aspects of corpse logistics –
from the mortuary table to the grave –
at prices you won't want to pass on.
You'll be dead made up

at our discounts on restorative cosmetics.
Or why not take advantage
of our Bury One, Get One Free offer?
Don't look a gift hearse in the mouth!

But whatever it is you're looking for –
interment or entombment,
aquamation or incineration –
Jenkins and Pain are at your disposal.

But the accompanying letter snuffed out any faint heartbeat of
encouragement; for the 'small fee' of £300, they will carry copies
of my poems in their reception area. I put it in the bin with the
others. It is clear that my funeral-poem idea – or Project Death as
I had inwardly come to think of it – is not going to be the instant
money-spinner that I'd supposed.

With a heavy heart, I began to update my CV. It is time to
re-join the great majority.

Monday August 20th

It has been nearly fifteen years since I've had cause to update my
CV. What's troubling is the paucity of changes I've had to make to

it: the substitution of the words 'solutions' for products; a more contemporary font. If curriculum vitae means 'the course of life', then the course mine has followed appears to have been a dull and meandering one.

CURRICULUM VITAE REVISITED

Personal Statement Haiku

Underachiever
seeks work to fend off bailiffs
and boredom of life.

Experience

Current Position   Sitting on a sofa
is where you'll find me at,
while writing this CV
trapped beneath a cat.

Previous Positions

Recent times: Supine. Horizontal. Prone.
Lying prostrate on my own.
Sprawled. Reclined. At my ease.
Angled (one eighty degrees),

Before that: Slouched. Slumped. Bent-backed. Stooped.
Hunched. Humped. Bowed and Drooped.

Even earlier: Walking. Crawling. Catatonic.
Sitting. Lying. Embryonic.

Education   I hold a lower-second class
combined honours degree
in Theoretical Woodwork
and Sociocultural Apology.

Hobbies & Interests   Music. Reading. Crosswords. Memes.
Football. Murder. Custard Creams.

I suppressed nearly all the references to poetry. Most employers won't even look at anyone with such a background; there is a strong correlation with untrustworthiness and unreliability.

Tuesday August 21st

'Do poets use LinkedIn?' was a question I'd often pondered in quieter moments, along with:

'Do Poets drive?' (conclusion: not if they can help it)

'*Should* poets drive?' (conclusion: probably not)

and 'Who would win in a fight between Auden and Eliot?' (conclusion: unsure – although it would probably end not with a bang but a whimper).

But as I looked today at my LinkedIn account for the first time in five years, the answer seems unequivocally yes, if Toby Salt is anything to go by. He has 500+ connections, including radio and television producers, newspaper and poetry magazine editors, arts correspondents, publishers. I have three connections: Tomas, Timothy Pain from Jenkins & Pain Funeral Directors and Cora Nesmith from the Mongolian Yurt Company.

Wednesday August 22nd

I was idly perusing the job pages today, minding my own business, when I was disturbed by an unwelcome intruder in my kitchen.

Radio 4 had been on all morning and I'd already absorbed programmes on the Dewey Decimal classification system and a debate concerning the ethics of driverless cars. But the schedule appeared to have moved on, and a vaguely familiar voice emerged over the airwaves, amidst background sounds of stamping, hammering and whirring. I heard the words 'This Bridge No Hands Shall Cleave' and I realised I was listening to the nasal tones of Django from Shooting from the Hip. It was a programme on the history of letterpress printing and Django was talking from a print shop in Swansea, where Shooting from the Hip produced their artisanal, hand-crafted special editions.

'Letterpress printing is one of the great lost arts,' he was saying. 'In construction, it is as beautiful as a Toby Salt poem. First, one must—'

I switched it off in irritation and took a look at my phone. A notification on LinkedIn! I'd barely finished 'optimising' my LinkedIn page – or making it fractionally less pessimised: had I worked some magic already?

I took a closer look and sighed deeply: the message was headed *Stuart Mould has invited you to join his professional network.*

Please send help! I am being assailed in my own home.

Thursday August 23rd

I'd been stuck in the house for four days and I needed to get out. I called Tomas to see if he wanted to meet up. He was busy, unfortunately, but asked whether I'd be interested in coming along to a lecture he was giving this afternoon on Wittgenstein's *Tractatus Logico-Philosophicus*, in between cleaning shifts. I sat at the back, near the exit, struggling to understand a single word he was saying. I looked at the rest of the audience. A lot of nodding was going on. I was trying to stop nodding off.

'But, of course, we place our own interpretation on the world around us,' Tomas was saying. 'Wittgenstein knew this. "The world of the happy," he wrote, "is quite different from the world of the unhappy".'

That was something I could understand.

I thought about the world of Toby Salt with his new book and his prizes and his media appearances.

I thought about the world of Stuart Mould with his positivity and his relentless acts of charity and his unflagging confidence that things will get better.

I thought about my own world. How I'd messed things up with Sophie. How I'd messed things up with Liz. How I'd squandered all my money. What my world might be like without Dylan in it.

And I thought about how the world of the unhappy is quite different from the world of the happy.

My phone pinged. Another LinkedIn message from Stuart. He's has been endorsing my skills. It's all a sham, of course; if he was being truthful, he'd have endorsed me for Blundering, Bungling, Fluffing and Muffing.

Friday August 24th

I have now applied for fifteen jobs in total. These include roles as various as quantity surveyor, solutions engineer, accounts assistant, project manager, haberdasher, window dresser, trainee hair stylist, Oxford Professor of Poetry and several customer-facing roles in the fast-food industry.

In other news: I have had another LinkedIn recommendation from Stuart Mould and I seem to have put out my bags for recycling on the day for general landfill.

Saturday August 25th

....

Stuart Mould has invited you to join his professional network

I.   *Stuart Mould has invited you to join his professional network*

He is wearing a tuxedo and the smirk
of a man unfamiliar with the concept of rejection.
Stuart Mould has four thousand and fifty-eight connections.
Small wonder given he holds the keys
that unlock the door to inner peace.
It's all there in his results-driven profile.
It appears Stuart Mould will go the extra mile
as your Life Coach and Dream Architect.
I don't know why but I click accept.

II.   *Stuart Mould has endorsed you for the following skills*

Marketing ✓ Leading Teams ✓ Targeting ✓ Weaving Dreams ✓
Scuba diving ✓ Semaphore ✓ Lego building ✓ Harp (Grade Four) ✓
Chess playing ✓ Home baking ✓ Soothsaying ✓ Lovemaking ✓
Balefulness ✓ Masturbation ✓ Aimlessness ✓ Procrastination ✓

III.   *Stuart Mould has written you a recommendation that you can*
include on your profile page

'Bold strides this colossus in the workplace
with footsteps firm and full of flawless grace,
noble of purpose and so fair of face,
greeting PowerPoint with such fond embrace.
O Mighty Strategist! Leader Complete!
The Pivot-fabled Slayer of Spreadsheets!
Analytical Artist! Office Athlete!
Leviathan of the Corporate Elite!'

....

As if it were not enough for him to haunt me in the corporate networking world, he now has to do it in real life, too.

'Hi, Brian!' said Stuart loudly, when he dropped Dylan off this morning. 'How's all that job-hunting going?!'

'I'm not looking for a job.'

'Of course not! You've not been updating your LinkedIn page at all!' he chuckled.

I went to close the door. He put his foot in it.

'Look, Brian. Honestly, any help you need to get yourself on your feet again,' he grinned at my slippers as he said this, 'then just say the word! I know things have been hard for you.'

He gave me a sympathetic look then put his hand on my shoulder.

I shrank back and he appraised me once more.

'Don't feel too bad about failure, Brian. It's just a petrol stop on the road to success! Anyway, I need to go! Charity free-running event! Young carers and vulnerable children!'

He parkoured off and I retreated back inside to Dylan.

We proceeded carefully. All mention of What Dylan Told Me When We Were Skimming Stones was avoided. If no one talks about it, it can't happen. Everyone knows that.

Sunday August 26th

....

Six Haiku Book Reviews

I
Did not finish it.
Got the pip. Shame. I had such
Great Expectations.

IV
Woolly yarn about
the history of tank tops.
A Farewell to Arms.

II

Dystopian tale.
Neon leg warmers and Wham!
Nineteen Eighty-Four.

III

A group of lions
struggle to find acceptance.
Pride and Prejudice.

V

.well aged hasn't it
:*Button Benjamin of Case*
Curious Re-read

VI

Pop group clones itself.
It all ends in tragedy.
The Thirty-Nine Steps.

....

It is now Toby Salt's turn to invade my personal space again. His ferrety eyes stared out at me from the pages of the Sunday review section. I proceeded to draw on him: horn-rimmed glasses and a large phallus emanating from the top of his head. Next to his photo is a five-star review (presumably out of a hundred) by the paper's poetry editor, Sefton Warbrick, who writes:

> *This Bridge No Hands Shall Cleave* is a remarkable *tour de force* by one of this country's finest emergent poets. Let's be clear, this is not a volume for everyone; the uninitiated won't be getting their hands dirtier by attempting to fathom its inner cadences, the beauty of its lyrical lilt, its ghostly echoes of Eliot and intimations of Ovid. Let's leave them to the twelve-bar blues of their democratic doggerel, playground poesy, and sing-song simplicia. If poetry is the new rock 'n' roll, then God help us all. What Salt gives us is opera.

I wondered whether Liz has ever caressed Toby Salt's magic flute. After a few minutes, I looked down at the paper and noticed

how my ballpoint had punctured the page and ripped Toby Salt's
stupid papery face to shreds.

Monday August 27th

Bloodshed

They found him, several days on,
head stoved in by his Remington,
sitting as if slumbered at his desk,
were it not for that ungodly mess
which had seeped into his sonnet.
And there, cut out and pasted on it,
at the centre of this macabre scene,
was Matthew Chapter 5, Verse 13,
the initials BB scribed underneath.
The Bible Butcher, thought the police.

We were waiting for Meet Me at the Gallows, a Goth band from
Cheadle. Darren had turned up wearing a high-viz urban gilet
and carrying a large fluorescent sign on a pole which said STOP:
CHILDREN CROSSING.

'Sorry. New job starts next week. Had to come straight from
the training course,' he explained. 'Didn't have time to go back
and change.'

I nodded my head as imperceptibly as I could in the hope that
no one would notice that we knew each other.

'By the way,' Darren went on, 'Stuart tells me you're looking for
a job at the moment.'

I shrugged indiscernibly.

'Only the instructor today mentioned they had a couple of vacancies, if you're interested. Pay's not great but the hours are short.'

I looked off into the mid-distance.

'Anyway, what I'm saying is that I could put in a good word for you on the whole lollipop front.' He winked and then tapped a finger on the side of his nose.

I was about to raise my left eyebrow silently in response when he thrust his giant lollipop at me and shouted, 'Go on! Give it a go! Try this one for size!'

Only the sudden arrival on stage of Meet Me at the Gallows saved me. I used the distraction of their presence to edge steadily away from Darren and establish a human shield of goths around myself. I could see him glowing in the distance as the band launched into their crowd-pleasers: 'The Bloodied Veil', 'The Rose that Blackens on the Branch', 'Suicide in Crouch End', 'I Can See Blood Upon Your Hands', 'The Bible Butcher', 'Crumbling Bones'.

All in all, a really fun evening for all the family. Four stars. Would recommend!

Tuesday August 28th

I lay on the sofa and waited for the job offers to roll in. Somehow, in the middle of all this excitement I must have dropped off to sleep because the next thing I knew, I found myself in an airport, waving goodbye to Dylan.

Everyone was smiling sympathetically at me. The airline staff allowed me go right up the door of the Airbus A320 but a sudden shove from behind and I suddenly found myself on the plane and Dylan, Sophie and Stuart were waving *me* goodbye. I staggered to my seat and watched the flight attendant perform her flight-safety demonstration although the plane was somehow already up in the air but then I looked more closely and saw that the flight attendant was actually Liz and she was grinning at me, and the plane began to nosedive and my seatbelt was missing and I reached underneath for my life vest but it wasn't there, and then the door of the cockpit flew open and there was the pilot and it was Toby Salt, and he and Liz both started to laugh hysterically beneath their oxygen masks, and then I woke up.

I looked it up in my *Dream Dictionary* but as it's an old edition it only references the Airbus A319 and so I was none the wiser. What on earth can it all mean?

Wednesday August 29th

....

Aura Boringalis

an admission:
my aura is beset
with grey emissions
I have such drab
and dreary
energy fields,
my inner dullness
is revealed.
i fear my chakras
have congealed.

....

Mrs McNulty's sawing has reached new levels. Whereas once it was restricted to the daytime (as laid down in the Daylight Sawing Time Act (DST) that we'd agreed three years ago), forming a not unpleasing accompaniment to my household chores, she is now to be heard woodworking away into the small hours of the morning. I've long given up asking her what exactly it is that she's making as she just cackles in response to any enquiry.

I went around to complain. As she opened her door to me, she recoiled backwards unsteadily.

'Your aura!' she hissed. 'It's black!'

I wasn't altogether certain of what an aura was but I had a sudden flashback to old Ready Brek television commercials. I looked at my sleeves, my jeans, my shoes.

'Mrs McNulty, I'm dressed all in black. Are you sure you're not confusing my aura with my clothes?'

'Don't you see? This means it will happen soon!'

'What will?' I wondered whether she was referring to the annual street party, flyers for which had been posted diurnally through my letter box, and which I'd been doing my best to ignore.

'You have so much negative energy.'

I found it hard to disagree. The street party was nothing but a nuisance.

'Your energy fields have turned black! That can only mean one thing: death is coming!'

I realised she'd moved on from talking about the street party. I attempted to bring up the subject of her sawing but she slammed the door in my face before I could continue. I went back in, thinking dark thoughts, and waited for news of a job.

Thursday August 30th

Three rejection letters arrived today. I headed off to book group in pugilistic mood.

Frustratingly, they broke the first rule almost straight away and began to talk about *Fight Club*. They then proceeded to break the second. I yelled STOP! and went limp but they carried on regardless. If I'd known they were going to talk about it, I'd have taken the time to read it.

I sat there sullenly with my dry roasted peanuts for the rest of the evening, unresisting to their jabs concerning my lack of commitment, slowly getting punch drunk.

Friday August 31st

It is Friday night. I am sat at the kitchen table, with four more rejection letters spread out around me, and with a cat on my lap and a glass of wine in my hand. In order to get everything into perspective, I have made a list of all the good and bad things to do with my current situation:

Bad Things

1. I am broke. I have squandered my redundancy money on a writing shed I do not use. This is all thanks to Toby Salt's advice in a poetry magazine.
2. My attempts to become a writer have been a total failure. Unlike Toby Salt's, whose rise to fame is as dramatic as it is inexplicable.

3. I now have to find myself a proper job again (see 1 and 2, including Toby Salt-related sub-points).
   I appear to be unsuited to every vacancy.
4. I have messed things up with Liz. Although this is mainly Toby Salt's fault.
5. Dylan is leaving. This is because of 'Stuart' although there must be some kind of Toby Salt connection in there somewhere. Perhaps they are brothers.
6. I have forty-three followers on Twitter. Toby Salt has 7,872.
7. I am on the verge of being kicked out of book group on account of not reading the books, due to all the distraction with this Toby Salt business.
8. I did that thing I shouldn't have done.

Good Things

1. Poetry Club is now mercifully free of Toby Salt.
2. The cat still loves me.
3. I have this bottle of wine.

Dylan once told me to concentrate on the positives so I shall try to do just that. I will pour myself another glass of wine and write a poem to cheer myself up.

The pleasure of a glass of wine
to toast the passing of the week;
the merlot serves to wash away
its sour and sweat-soaked reek.

Sitting back I let it soften
the dog-toothed edges of my mind,

thwarted frown, unfurrowed brow,
I pour another glass of wine.

I try not to think of TobyS alt
&my disused writing shed,
replenisch my glass a fewmore times
untilthe bottles onlydregs

two emptied botttles infront of me
so rubbage around   in the cubpoard
find 2stellas and some whiskers
drinkem down! like a drinky think
sing bomenhian raspberry
yes! I loveyou cat!

mommajustkilllledaman
gin
theres some
SCARABOUCHE!
gin
nothing
   nothing really
matches

    any way the windows

September

Saturday September 1st

A bell was clanging in my head. I attempted to open my eyes. The operation met with limited success.

I tried again. The clanging continued. It was coming from downstairs, I realised.

I crawled downstairs and opened the door. Dylan was there. With Sophie.

'Brian, we've been waiting outside for ages,' she said.

'I . . .' My voice trailed off because I couldn't think of any more words.

'Can I come in for a few minutes? We need to talk.'

I made a vague invitational gesture and they came inside. I noticed them both appraising the empty bottles and cans strewn across the kitchen floor. Dylan went into the sitting room to stroke the cat while I stayed with Sophie in the kitchen and watched as she made tea.

She started talking about their plans. My mind wandered back and forth as she spoke but I heard the key words: America – January – Stuart. They were followed by vague reassurances about the future: Cheap flights – Holidays – Skype. But I'd almost stopped listening by that stage.

I hadn't spoken a single word throughout. Sophie thought it best perhaps if Dylan didn't stay with me today. She understood that this would be a shock for me. It was a lot to absorb in one go. She wondered whether it might be helpful for me to talk to somebody about my problems. A professional. She knew that I didn't really like talking about things but, who knows, it might be of some use.

I continued to sit in silence, heard them leave.

Sunday September 2nd

This month's book may have been *The Picture of Dorian Gray* by Oscar Wilde but it was *The Pictures of Toby Salt* that were foremost on display as I made my way around the bookshop. There were posters everywhere, advertising the launch of *This Bridge No Hands Shall Cleave* on Thursday.

I did my best to lock up the picture of his stupid face in the attic of my mind and focus on the rest of my shopping: *Chatterton* by Peter Ackroyd; *Kidnapped* by Robert Louis Stevenson; *A Time to Kill* by John Grisham; *In Cold Blood* by Truman Capote; *Murder Most Vile: 18 Shocking True Crime Murder Cases*; and, because it was on special offer at the till, *The Little Book of Hugs*.

Monday September 3rd

My unsuitability for employment knows no bounds; I am a jack of no trades and a master of none. The rejection letters keep flooding in. Four more today, including this one from the University of Oxford:

Re: Your Application for the Position of Oxford Professor of Poetry

> Dear Brian,
> Thank you for applying / I hope you don't find this too
> distressful / but your application was unsuccessful / Your verse
> is unsatisfactory to the nth degree / a cross between a dog's
> dinner and a catastrophe / It's the kind of drivelling doggerel
> / more suited to a sheet of bog roll / Your villanelles are vile /
> your haikus quite hopeless / your sonnets have as much class
> as soap-on-a-rope. Yes / and I'm afraid your ballads are
> bollocks / We wish you suffered from more writer's blocks.

You write about buses and bin bags and crocs / you think
you're profound but you're actually pro-lost. / And as for your
poems on Clarkson, they're close to litigious. / On the plus
side, your spelling's quite good / and your output's prodigious.
Yours sincerely,
Professor A. P. Brearley

In other news, Toby Salt has tweeted that he has been
appointed Poet-in-Residence for the BBC.

Tuesday September 4th

....

Thief

You caught me stealing a glance at you.
Ordered me to empty out my pockets.
I shook my booty onto the table:

a swiped charge card,
a nose I'd pinched,
one poached egg,
a ruler (half-inched),
a gaze I'd shifted,
some spirits lifted,
and selected other stolen moments.

You told me to stop thieving
and start behaving.

Fat chance.
I've even nicked myself
shaving.

....

Oh, what have I done? What on earth possessed me to do it? All is lost, irretrievably! I am cast out! I am forsaken!

I had meant to pay it back. It was only a temporary measure until I was back on my feet. There were yurts and holidays and all those books to pay for, and as soon as I'd landed a job or earned some money from my funeral poems, I was going to put that £10,000 back. With interest, probably. Everyone would have been happy. I didn't think this would happen. Not this.

I thought the response to my poems had been more muted than usual. I sat back down to silence. Mary was the first to break it:

'Where's the money gone, Brian?' she hissed. All eyes were on me.

'I don't – I don't know what you mean?' I stammered.

'Yes, you do. *Our* money. Our *battlefields* money. I checked the account and it's all gone.'

'Oh, *that* money!' I replied, thinking how I might calm the situation down. 'Dr Miller needed it. To sort out all the payments and everything.'

'I've spoken to Dr Miller already,' she said, stonily. I stared down at my pistachios, knowing the game was up. 'He's been trying to get in touch with you since April. He's not received a penny from you.'

I glanced up. Mary was furious. Liz had turned away in disgust. Kaylee looked as if she was going to thump me. Disappointment dripped from Chandrima's eyes.

I tried to explain but Chandrima interrupted me before I'd even got as far as the yurt.

'I think it is best if you leave, Brian.'

'And don't reel your ugly head in here again,' said Kaylee, 'except to give us our money back, you stupid, pathetic, self-centred mother—'

I was out the door before she'd finished so I had no idea how her sentence ended.

My sentence was just beginning.

Wednesday September 5th

not a poem

this is not a poem
only a combination of words
broken up in such a way to make

you think it is

spacing is important
as is the series of

line breaks
that I have skilfully
manoeuvred on the page (note, too, the absence of
upper-case characters

see how
they make it seem
deeper somehow)

it is still not a poem, though
enough of this now

What the hell *is* poetry anyhow? The tearing open of a heart? The
baring of a soul? The sharing of a universe? Or is it all mere pos-
ture and pantomime?

Ask someone who cares.

I have far more important things to think about.

I am thinking about how I have been cast out.

I am thinking about how all I hold dear is slipping away
from me.

I am thinking about everything that has led me to this point.

And I am thinking about Toby Salt.

And I am thinking about when to do it and where to do it.

And I am thinking about how it might be done.

Monday September 17th

Nothing to See Here

I was carefully coating my life
with a thick layer of creosote,
when – suddenly – out of the blue,
nothing much happened of note.

Life somehow got back to normal,
its rhythms flat and mundane,
but one evening – to my surprise –
nothing much happened again.

Now they come with endless abandon –
I'm spinning around like a top –
all these incessant non-happenings.
Oh, how I wish they would stop.

Nothing much to report today. Just like yesterday and all the days before.

I absolutely did not go out to the shed again.

Tuesday September 18th

An awful night's sleep. Another ghastly dream to destroy the night and haunt the day to come. I have been dragging the ghost of it around with me all day. Not as far as the shed, of course. No, not that far because I obviously didn't go back in there today.

Wednesday September 19th

Take this Hand in Yours

Take this hand
in yours,

bury it
beneath the trees,

and I will get
the rest of him

out of the
deep freeze.

Midnight. I was in a forest, digging. Digging further and further down into the blackness. The thing I'd carried with me from the shed was lying next to the hole. It had been wrapped in an old, moth-eaten blanket. Digging. I had to keep digging. The grave needed to be deep. Deep beyond discovery. And, as I drove the spade into the soil once more, I sensed the thing beneath the blanket begin to twitch and come to life . . .

I woke up with a gasp. All further sleep was futile. I picked up *The Picture of Dorian Gray* to take my mind off things. It made me think of all the secrets we carry around with us and how many of them ever see the light of day.

Other people, that is. Not me. I have no secrets. I'm an open book.

I wear my heart on my sleeve.

Thursday September 20th

....

The Man with the Enya Tattoo

Precious, secret watermark
above my left elbow.
Your ink flows like a river,
as multi-channelled as your vocals.   *Fade away, fade away, fade away . . .*

My dark-haired Donegal beauty,
you've been mine since nineteen eighty-nine,
the year the world held its breath
at your mystical feet.   *Please fade away, fade away, fade away . . .*

No, of course you do not embarrass me!
I cover you up only to avoid
a chill in my upper arm.
Do not cry now. Your ink will run.   *Fade away, fade away, fade away . . .*

Hey, Eithne Pádraigín Ní Bhraonáin!
Guess what, my pretty Celtic pixie?
The scientists have named a new species
of fish after you! In the Orinoco River!   *Please fade away, fade away,
fade away . . .*

....

The rejection letters are still rumbling in; to think of all that hard
labour wasted in the pursuit of gainful employment. And people
wonder why I rarely roll my sleeves up!

   After I didn't go out to the shed, I checked in to Twitter for the
first time in ages. My Twitter following seems to have stabilised at
forty-three. I may have reached my social media pinnacle but
Toby Salt hasn't. His numbers continue to rise; he now has more

than ten thousand followers, despite not having tweeted for nearly two weeks.

Perhaps, at long last, he has run out of things to say.

Friday September 21st

In Vimto Veritas

I am sorry
but I have no real ale
or genuwine left.

I would offer you
some proper tea
but all proper tea is theft.

Dave, Martin and Marvin are back. They popped round to ask whether I could lend them a teabag. We shared a pot of tea and they talked about their studies. It's their final year, and they're planning to really get down to things this time: no more heavy drinking, no more parties, just good old-fashioned studying. By the time they'd left and their guests had begun to arrive next door, they'd somehow managed to deprive me of the three-quarters-full bottle of red wine that was out on the kitchen table, as well as an unopened bottle of white and six beers that were in the fridge.

Saturday September 22nd

Another disturbed night filled with disquieting dreams. Even Dylan has noticed how tired I look. I was expecting another team talk from him but it seems he's through with the whole motivational-speech business. Stuart's unflagging positivity has really begun to irritate him, he told me. I sympathised. That kind of relentless cheeriness can wear anyone down.

We began to plan our remaining Saturdays together, while we still have them. We decided that we'd go to the zoo next week. We used to go there a lot, before the break-up with Sophie and before his childlike wonder metamorphosed into something more adolescent and moody.

Today, though, we dripped around indoors. I asked him whether there was any homework I could help him with but he said he'd rather watch a film.

We settled down to watch *Invasion of the Body Snatchers*. I put my arm around him. We had nothing to hold on to – except each other.

Sunday September 23rd

The deadline for this quarter's *Well Versed* competition is tomorrow. The chosen topic is 'guilt'. I sat for a few hours mulling this over before deciding to give it a miss this time around.

Monday September 24th

Où est Toby Salt? Il a disparu! Pooof!

He didn't even make it to his own book launch, by all accounts. The assembled rabble in the bookshop that evening waited two hours for him but he never showed up. They all shuffled off home, dejectedly clutching their unsigned copies of *This Bridge No Hands Shall Cleave*.

I discovered this upon opening the door this afternoon to a magnificent beard, beneath which was a man. The beard was vibrant, well tended, possibly perfumed: everything, in fact, that mine hadn't been. Its owner introduced himself as DI Lansbury and then nodded at his assistant behind him, a younger, fresh-cheeked figure, who he announced as Detective Sergeant Tuck.

They were making some general enquiries of anyone who happened to have seen Toby Salt in the last month or so. His disappearance had been causing some concern although they assured me there was no reason to view it as suspicious.

I told them I hadn't seen him since early August, the last time he'd visited Poetry Club. Sergeant Tuck scribbled this down in his notepad.

'And you're sure you've not seen him since?' asked DI Lansbury, his beard moving effortlessly in rhythm with his jaw.

'Absolutely,' I replied, smiling and unblinking.

'And can I just ask what you were doing on the evening of Thursday 6th September?'

I thought for a moment.

'Let's see. I think I'd have just had a quiet night in. Yes, that's right. I remember now. I was watching *Murder, She Wrote*. It was the one in which she investigates the murder of a popular neighbourhood greengrocer, who was found choked to death on his own kumquats. Do you know you share your surname with Angela Lans—'

'Yes, of course I know that,' he snapped, with some irritation, as if this coincidence may have been mentioned to him before. 'A night in? I don't suppose you have any witnesses for that, do you?'

'Um, no, I don't. Apart from the cat.' I laughed loudly. He didn't join in.

'That's fine. Not to worry, sir. As I say, we're just making routine enquiries. It's not as if we've found a mutilated corpse, is it!' he joked, staring intently at me.

I smiled uneasily. 'Quite,' I said.

'Now Sergeant Tuck just has a few brief questions to ask you for our records.'

I helped him fill in the form, experiencing that uncomfortable feeling of exposure I somehow always get when my particulars are taken down.

Tuesday September 25th

....

Custard Creams: A Love Sonnet

How do I scoff thee? Let me count the ways.
I dunk thee in my morning cup of tea,
thy vanilla centre dost gladden me
and gives me strength to face the darkest days.
My hunger for thee contains no bandwidth,
we meet at breakfast and elevenses,
at three o'clock and half-past-sevenses,

divine delectable biscuit sandwich.
Thou dost pick me up whene'er I stumble.
Thou dost make me feel I'm not a misfit.
Thou art always there. Thou dost never grumble.
To be with thee, my whole life I'd risk it,
For my love for you shall never crumble,
My beloved creamy custard biscuit.

....

There are times when there is simply no substitute for a custard cream. These times are typically from 7am to 10pm, at the following intervals: 00, 15, 30, 45. There is something about their vanilla-custard filling and the baroque carving of the outer sandwich layers which lends itself to the practice of contemplation and study. And never had I felt more in need of them than today.

They couldn't seriously believe that I had something to do with Toby Salt's disappearance, could they? But there was something in DI Lansbury's manner which suggested they did. Regardless, the main thing was to play it cool. No one was pointing their finger – not even a Rich Tea finger – at me yet.

I went out into the garden to check up on things in the shed.

Wednesday September 26th

....

The Picture in the Attic

I kept it in the attic –
under lock and key –
a youthful, fresh-faced picture

of who I used to be.

And this face you see before you,
I dragged around my life –
growing wrinkled, gnarled and ravaged –
for its vicissitudes were rife.

But meanwhile, in the attic,
that pure and hopeful face,
immune to life's misfortunes,
bore not one single trace.

For years I hid it from her,
but in shame I did confess.
She listened to my story
then said, 'That's because it's a photograph, you idiot.'

....

I hadn't finished the book, of course, but I went anyway. I'd
hoped to try and ingratiate my way back into the group through
the use of some of Wildean witticisms:

'To fail to read one book may be regarded as a misfortune; to
fail to read *every* book looks like illiteracy.'

'I never travel without my diary. One should always have
something sensational to read on the bus.'

'I can resist anything except pistachios.'

But they fell on resolutely deaf ears. The group turned to me
after they'd finished their discussion. I was to be given one last
chance: read next month's book and make a proper contribution
– or I was out.

The book: *No Bridge These Hands Shall Cleave* by Toby Salt.

I stared morosely at the pub's wallpaper. It was dreadful. One
of us will have to go.

Thursday September 27th

'I hear they're all heading off, then?' said Darren. We were pre-gig and for once he was not holding a big luminescent sign.

'Yes.' I gave him a look that suggested I didn't want to talk about it.

'America,' he said, with an involuntary whistle to emphasise the enormity of the word.

I intensified my look.

'Long way, that,' he continued. 'Very long way.'

'Have you seen this guy before?' I asked him, in an attempt to change the conversation. We were waiting for Little Floyd Wetherspoon to come on stage. He was a blues singer who was reinterpreting the genre for the modern age.

'Still, at least it's east coast. Three thousand two hundred and sixty-five miles to Boston, it is, or thereabouts. From Heathrow, that is.' 'I've heard Wetherspoon's not his real name. He adopted it in an unsuccessful attempt to secure a nationwide deal with the popular pub chain of the same name.'

'The flight time isn't so bad,' he mused. 'Seven hours. But don't forget you need to factor in all that hanging around at the airport, both sides. And then there's the cost!' He whistled again.

'I don't know for sure about the "Little Floyd" bit. But that sounds made up, too.'

'Must be hard for you. An ocean between you and your son. A whole ocean.'

I was considering accidentally spilling my pint on him when there was some activity on stage and a man of remarkably average height and stature launched into 'Can't Get My Wi-Fi Working'.

The other rumour I had heard about Little Floyd Wetherspoon was that he'd sold his soul to the devil in return for the gift of the blues. I thought about the shed and whether I had left the door firmly locked and bolted behind me.

Friday September 28th

....

hipster cop

hipster cop
with his hipster well-cropped mutton chops
has a favourite case, for sure,
you won't know it
it's too obscure

hipster cop
with his hipster thrift-shop beach flipflops
rehabilitates hardened villains
he makes them listen
to early dylan

hipster cop
buys hipster chips from hip hop chip shops
gangland bosses he just don't dig
he prefers their petty crimes
before they got big

....

After another troubled night, I opened the door again to DI Lansbury and Sergeant Tuck. They seemed preoccupied with the antics of Mrs McNulty, who was leaning out of her bedroom window, shouting, 'It was him! It was him! He's the one you want!'

I ushered the police officers inside quickly and mumbled an apology.

'That's just Mrs McNulty from next door!' I told them, chuckling and shaking my head. 'She's such a character! Utterly bonkers, of course, but we all love her around here, the lovely crazy woman!'

I noticed DI Lansbury glance at Sergeant Tuck, who proceeded to write something in his notebook. He then asked:

'Do you know anyone who might have wished to harm Mr Salt, sir?'

I pretended to think carefully before replying.

'No, I don't. Although I could think of plenty of people who might have wanted to harm his poetry!'

Neither man laughed at my joke. I could see DI Lansbury's magnificent beard noticeably bristling.

'How about yourself, sir? We've had it on good authority that you and Mr Salt had a small altercation the last time you met.'

Damn them in Poetry Club.

'Well, I wouldn't quite call it that. Just a mild disagreement about the nature of poetry. That kind of thing happens all the time amongst poets. We're a passionate lot!'

He looked back at me, considering this statement.

'So it would appear, sir. If anything does occur to you, then please don't hesitate in giving us a call, will you? We're beginning to think that Mr Salt's absence may have been of a rather more permanent nature that we had originally thought.'

They left. Next door, Mrs McNulty was busy unfurling a bedsheet from her bedroom window, on which she'd written 'HELP! I AM LIVING NEXT DOOR TO A MURDERER' in red marker pen.

Saturday September 29th

Arklife

Competence was my reference as the scriptural voyager
on what is known as – Arklife!
And the monkey coop can be avoided if you take a route
straight through what is known as – Arklife!
Shem's got puma poop, he gets intimidated by the dirty chickens
They love a bit of it – Arklife!
What's that buzzard starting?
You should cut down on your squawklife, mate. Get some exercise.

All the creatures, so many creatures
They all go two by two,
two by two through their Arklife.
Know what I mean.

I get up when I want except on Wednesdays
when I get rudely awakened by the bison – Arklife!
I put on my apron, inspect myself for fleas,
and I think about lemurs and cows – Arklife!
I feed birds, fish, insects. I also feed the mammals, too,
it gives me a sense of enormous well-being – Arklife!
And then I'm happy for the rest of the day,
safe in the knowledge that I've remembered
to feed the unicorns at the end of it.

All the creatures, so many creatures
They all go two by two,
two by two through their Arklife.
Know what I mean.

It's got nothing to do with your horse dung durch technik, you know.
And it's not about you goldfish, who go round and round and round.

Our day at the zoo passed in a blur. We lingered with the lions, hung out with the Humboldt penguins, loitered splendidly with the slender lorises, lounged languidly with the langurs, moseyed with Geoffrey's marmosets (Geoffrey didn't seem to mind) and tarried with the tamarins.

We had hoped to see the silverback gorilla but he stayed in his enclosure all day, watching re-runs of *Taggart* on his television. I shook my head. Imagine a majestic creature wasting its life in such a way!

On the bus back, I asked Dylan about how he was feeling about America.

'I don't want to go,' he said, turning his head to look out the window.

'But won't it be exciting? You've always wanted to go there.'

'Only to visit, not to live. All my friends are here. I won't know anyone.' He pressed his head against the glass.

'Oh, you'll soon make friends,' I said. 'Lots of them. Never forget the hold an English accent has over an American.'

'But they won't be the same as my friends here. Everything will be different.' He paused to reflect a moment. 'They don't even put an "s" on the end of "maths".'

'Well, that's because they need it to put on the end of "sports".'

Dylan smiled briefly.

'Ah, yes. Of course. But you know what I mean.'

'I do. Believe me, I do. I know it can be hard to make friends. Change is difficult. But it'll be an adventure, too. Sometimes shaking things up is good. You don't want to spend your life being dictated to by the waste-collection schedule. Or when your next book group meeting is. Don't measure out your life in coffee spoons!'

'Or in Wetherspoons.'

'That's true enough. I guess what I'm saying is . . . just don't end up being a nobody like me, that's all. You're young and clever, funny and kind. Do something with your life. Be a somebody!'

'That sounds like the kind of thing Stuart would say. Anyway, you are a somebody,' he protested. 'You're my dad! And besides, I'd much rather end up like you than Stuart.'

'I should think so, too,' I said, managing to restrain myself from high-fiving all the other passengers. 'I like to think that if I've taught you anything at all, it's to maintain a healthy suspicion of anyone who wilfully chooses to play *The Best of Huey Lewis and the News* in public.'

Dylan smiled again and we settled back into thoughtful silence while the seats around us slowly emptied and we waited for our stop to come.

Sunday September 30th

....

Last Night, Sleepwalking . . .

I broke my arm
when I fell off a fence.
Got taken off
in a somnambulance.

....

Dave brought me back inside at 4am. He was smoking in his garden when he heard a noise from over the fence. He peered over and saw me in my dressing gown. I was talking to someone inside my writing shed, as I rattled the door and angrily fumbled with my keys. He told me all this after he'd guided me back to my kitchen and made me a cup of tea.

Stress and anxiety can contribute to sleepwalking, according to Dave, and he advised me to take it easy. He says Mrs McNulty thinks it has more to do with the presence of a full moon but we agreed that seems unlikely.

October

Monday October 1st

Versions, He Wrote

I

The record was lodged
deep down his throat:
REM's first album.
Murmur, she wrote.

II

Hairy hobbit foot,
severed. No note.
Who was behind this?
Mordor, she wrote.

III

Stuffed in his mouth,
an inspirational quote:
'Happiness in execution'.
Goethe, she wrote.

I locked up the shed and came back into the house.

I lay on the sofa. The cat lay on me. A youthful Angela Lansbury appeared on the screen. I looked at the television guide: it was an old version of *The Picture of Dorian Gray*. She was in the role of Sybil Vane. I started watching the film but must have drifted off. She was on stage, singing old music-hall numbers –

'My Old Dutch', 'When Father Papered the Parlour', 'A Little Bit of Cucumber'.

The audience swayed along in time, loving it. All of a sudden, the music stopped and the lights went down. Ghostly chimes began to ring out. The band struck up again but this time their accompaniment was more sinister and brooding. Sybil Vane turned and fixed her eyes on me, and began to sing:

Take a little walk to the edge of town

Go across the tracks

Where the viaduct looms

Like a bird of doom

As it shifts and cracks

I recognised it. It was by Nick Cave and the Bad Seeds. The song continued. When she reached the words:

But hidden in his coat

Is a red right hand

the stage lighting turned red, thunder rumbled, and a bell tolled loudly. She lifted up her own right hand and pointed at me. It was then that I noticed the rest of the audience; their music-hall high spirits had long since disappeared, usurped by fear and anger. They turned their eyes upon me. Terrified, I shifted back in my seat as they closed in upon me . . .

My shout woke me up. The cat slept on as I groped for a custard cream.

I didn't bother looking this one up in my *Dream Dictionary*.

Tuesday October 2nd

They'll be hard at it right now. Mary will be revealing the secrets of one of her six husbands. Kaylee will be kicking the ass of injustice. Chandrima will be lighting up the moon. And Liz will be making the world go weak at the knees.

I'd toyed briefly with the idea of showing my face but quickly reconsidered as I remembered the look on Kaylee's.

I thought about them all gathered together and redoubled my efforts.

Wednesday October 3rd

DI Lansbury and Sergeant Tuck were back again. Mrs McNulty can't have seen them approaching this time as I could hear her sawing busily next door. DI Lansbury's beard sparkled with freshly shampooed lustre.

'Sorry to disturb you once more, sir,' he said, 'but we were wondering if you'd given any more thought as to whether you knew of anyone who might harbour ill-feelings towards Mr Salt.'

'Oh, still missing, is he?' I said casually. 'No, I really can't think of anyone. Hard to imagine him being given a second thought, to be honest. He was a bit of a nonentity.'

'You've not noticed anyone exhibit strange or erratic behaviour around him. Say, at one of those poetry festivals he'd go to.' He paused then shot me a quick look. 'In Saffron Walden, for instance.'

Our eyes locked briefly before I shifted my gaze quickly away. How on earth did he know about that? I fumbled for a reply but his attention had been grabbed by my diary, which lay open at my desk. He leant towards it and read aloud a line from it:

'*"I wondered whether Liz has ever caressed Toby Salt's magic flute."*'

He flicked through more of its pages and then scrutinised its Hello Kitty cover.

'Is this *your* diary, sir?' he asked with faux innocence.

'Well, it's more, er, kind of, yes, it is.'

'Very useful things, diaries! They help to tell us what happened when – if they're written truthfully, of course. And they can be very revealing of the inner mind.'

'Quite.'

'Any chance we could have a look at it back at the station? See if there's anything in it that can help us track down Mr Salt? Or at the very least it may help us understand what goes on in the creative mind, so we can put ourselves in the poetic shoes of Mr Salt, as it were?'

'Well, no, actu—'

'Wonderful! Thank you very much. Tell you what, you've only got a few pages left in it so why not keep it for a few more days and we'll pop by and collect it next week? In the meantime, Sergeant Tuck can see about picking you up a new notebook. We wouldn't want your writing to suffer while we take this one into custody!' he said, amused at his own joke.

After they left, I sat back down, closed my eyes, and silently cursed the day – 1st January – I'd started to write this stupid thing.

Thursday October 4th

Last year I spent National Poetry Day wrestling with a pivot table. This year, I am waiting for the dishwasher to be fixed. This is the humdrum, unglamorous side of poetry that is often hidden from ordinary members of the public. Many people have the notion that writing poetry is all about striding across meadows, notebook in hand, or quietly observing the world from coffee-shop windows. It is indeed mainly these things but with unfathomable pivot tables and blocked dishwasher pumps thrown in.

The repair man didn't turn up until 4pm. All that waiting around in the house for his arrival meant that I couldn't pay a visit to the shed today. But after yesterday, that was something of a relief.

I note that Toby Salt had been due to give a talk about the nature of poetry today at the Royal Festival Hall in front of four hundred people. Only he won't be doing that now on account of him being dead.

Probably.

Friday October 5th

....

crimeweave

upon retiring
from the mafia,
Don Corleone
wove aquatic mammals
out of raffia

i learnt this news
when he made me an otter
i couldn't refuse

....

I was shuffling around in my dressing gown when there was a knock on the window. It was the Man at Number 29. He gestured towards the top of the street with his thumb. There was the bin lorry and I'd forgotten to put my bags out. Five frantic minutes later, I collapsed back inside following a successful carpet-slippered pursuit of the lorry. How the mighty have fallen!

After that, I couldn't settle to much. In the end, I accepted my fate and curled up on the sofa with the cat, watching films all day – *Godfather I and II*, *The Wicker Man* and *Ring of Bright Water* – drifting in and out of sleep and yet more unsettling dreams.

Saturday October 6th

Quite why Dylan wanted to visit Buckingham Palace, I don't know. Maybe he wanted to say goodbye to his English 'heritage' before he left it all behind. Or perhaps it was more personal than that; a subconscious impulse triggered by buried memories of childhood bedtime stories. He used to love it when I'd read A. A. Milne's *The Christopher Robin Versebook* to him; his favourite poem was 'They're Changing Guard at Buckingham Palace' and we'd often talked of going there although we never quite managed it. Until now that is.

The palace was being renovated; there was scaffolding everywhere and many of the staterooms were closed for refurbishment. The extravagance and opulence that remained only served to make the whole place shabbier somehow and it seemed like an apt metaphor for the state of the nation. By the end of the visit, following my running commentary on our surroundings, I felt Dylan had made real progress in viewing what he'd seen through more cynical and jaded eyes.

On the bus back, we took it in turns to give A. A. Milne's poem an update:

They're renovating Buckingham Palace –
Christopher Robin went down with Alice.
Past understaffed wards and cash-strapped schools,
'The Sèvres Porcelain sounds really cool,'
wrote Dylan.

They're renovating Buckingham Palace –
Christopher Robin went down with Alice.
The queues were as long as those for food banks,
'There's Vermeers, Van Dycks and even Rembrandts,'
wrote Brian.

They're renovating Buckingham Palace –
Christopher Robin went down with Alice.
Outside, the homeless were all moved along.
'The Grand Staircase, I've heard, is cast from bronze,'
wrote Dylan.

They're renovating Buckingham Palace –
Christopher Robin went down with Alice.
'You know so much 'bout the palace and grounds.'
'Got a book from the library before it closed down,'
wrote Brian.

Getting home, I considered whether I should renovate my
diary, too; give the entries a fresh layer of plaster, slap some paint
over them. But unless I ripped the whole thing up and started
again, I knew DI Lansbury would see through the cack-handed
restoration to the grime underneath.

Sunday October 7th

....

On Locating the Poetry Section in a Bookshop

Poetry? Let's see . . . yes, fourth floor.
No, I'm afraid there's not a lift.
We used to keep them all down here
but they're ever so hard to shift.

All those gloomy meditations
on the meaning of life and death!
Putting customers off, they were.
Now it's all celebrity chef

and lifestyle books – *they're* selling like
warm focaccia. But, as I say,
fourth floor – sandwiched between Transport
and Religion – out of harm's way.

....

I'd rather have bought a book on erectile dysfunction. But the job is done and now I have it (*This Bridge No Hands Shall Cleave*, that is, not erectile dysfunction).

It took me a while to find the poetry section, which had been relocated since I was last in the bookshop and now resided in the quietest corner of the uppermost floor. There was a stack of signed copies of *This Bridge No Hands Shall Cleave* on the table, left over from the aborted book launch. I slipped one discreetly into the middle of the pile of books I was carrying, which included Dante's *Inferno*, G. K. Chesterton's *The Innocence of Father Brown*, Ian McEwan's *Atonement* and a couple of self-help guides on how to beat insomnia.

At the counter, I made it very clear to the bookseller that

Toby Salt's book wasn't for me but an uncle who I didn't like very much.

Monday October 8th

....

How to get Pikachu onto a Bus

Above all, be gentle.
Explain why the journey is necessary
in calm and reassuring tones.
Remember, Pokémon are not natural bus travellers
preferring instead to hide
in the overhead luggage compartments
of high-speed trains.

A double-decker is best.
Boarding a minibus or local 'hopper'
may result in feelings of claustrophobia
and cause Pikachu to evolve prematurely into Raichu,
particularly should a passenger
be carrying a thunder stone.

Remember to ensure
you have the correct travel documentation
as anime restrictions may be in place
upon designated routes.

If all else fails,
lay a trail of apples to the door
and then quickly bundle him in,
being mindful at all times
of the risk
of electrical discharge.

....

DI Lansbury's beard appears to change with the seasons. Today I detected autumnal reds, yellows and oranges within it, hitherto unnoticed. I wondered whether it might sprout snowdrops in January.

He was here again with Sergeant Tuck to pick up my diary.

'Don't worry, sir, we'll have it back to you in a few days once we've given it a good read through. Sergeant Tuck has got you this to keep you going in the interim.'

Sergeant Tuck had wrapped it up as if he were giving me a birthday present. The new notebook had a cover which featured some kind of creature from Japanese anime; yellow with red cheeks, black-tipped long ears and a lightning-shaped tail.

'Sorry about that, sir,' said an apologetic Sergeant Tuck. 'They were all out of "Hello Kitty" ones and that was the nearest I could find.'

DI Lansbury picked up my old diary from the desk to put in his briefcase but not before he'd noticed the folder that was underneath it. It was a manila folder, plain and unremarkable, except for a label in the top right-hand corner upon which was written the words 'Project Death'.

He stared at it for about ten seconds.

'Ah, would you mind if we also borro—'

'Go right ahead. Just take it,' I snapped. 'Take it all.'

Tuesday October 9th

The thought of DI Lansbury and Sergeant Tuck making free and easy with my diary feels like a violation of my private space. The forensic nature of their scrutiny unsettles me, the embarrassment of a life examined and found wanting.

Wednesday October 10th

How to Read a Poem

Always have a drink in your hand,
preferably a large one
(the drink, not the hand).

Before commencement of reading,
delicately frisk the poem.
It may contain an incendiary device.

Begin at a word of your choosing.
proceeding methodically through the others,
or haphazardly, according to taste.

Wring the meaning from it,
being careful not to cut yourself on a metaphor.
Rinse and repeat several times.

Dispose of it safely on completion
in your nearest radioactive waste depository,
or on a local bookshelf.

I made a start on *This Bridge No Hands Shall Cleave*.

It is only sixty pages long and contains sixteen poems. I had
expectations of finishing it by lunchtime but, by the time I put it
down this evening, I'd only managed to make it through the first
two poems. I have re-read each of these approximately thirty
times in an attempt to understand them. This is proving to be a
futile exercise. They have now become just a series of uncon-
nected words floating around the page. Two hours alone were
spent on:

your bright kimono face and lacquer box remonstrations
in courtly Zenobian tones of sepia. The door closes.
Use me not as your plinth.

I'm finding it harder work than *The Guardian Bumper Christmas Cryptic Crossword*. I hope there will be a prize for finishing it.

Thursday October 11th

....

Baby on Board

This badge proud-pinned to my lapel
may proclaim 'Baby on Board' but it fails to dispel
the mistrust that sits around me. Suspicion crams
itself into the carriage. They'd rather see me hang.

Me! With my aching back and Monday morning sickness,
these need-to-go-to-bed eyes, and a belly that thickens
beneath my shirt like the skin on a rice pudding,
and causes my trousers to involuntarily unbutton.

Me! A clearly pregnant man in his forties, unshaven
with three days' stubble who is experiencing unruly cravings
for pistachio ice cream and shredded wheat.
But no, not a single 'please, DO have this seat'.

I suppose that's what happens in these post-truth days;
No one believes anything another says.
Inside, I feel something stirring.
I clutch at straps for the remaining journey.

....

I was standing on a tube train, six months pregnant. No one offered up their seat to me in spite of the badge pinned to my lapel clearly stating my condition. My fellow passengers shifted uneasily in their seats, staring at their feet, not wanting to catch my eye. I glanced down again at my badge. It now read 'Murderer on Board'.

I studied my fellow commuters more closely. I realised I knew them all; Dave, Martin and Marvin, Mrs McNulty, Tomas, Darren, Dylan, Sophie and Stuart, everyone from Poetry Club and book group, DI Lansbury and Sergeant Tuck. And there in the corner of the carriage, sat next to the only available seat, was Toby Salt. He was caked in blood, head dangling at an impossible angle, while he read the latest issue of *Well Slaughtered: The Quarterly Magazine for the Discomfiting Murder Victim*. He looked up, smiled strangely at me and gently patted the seat next to me. The train roared into a tunnel, and as a sudden blackness engulfed the carriage, I woke up with a shudder.

I consulted my *Dream Dictionary*. The dream's significance seems clear: don't take a job which involves a lengthy commute.

Friday October 12th

The phone rang. It was DI Lansbury.

'Sorry to bother you, sir, but we've been reading your diary and we just wanted to ask you a few quick questions.'

Deep breath. Here goes, I thought.

'Sure. Fire away.'

'We were struck by the absence of limericks. Is there any reason for this?'

'Um, not really. They're just not my thing, I suppose.'

'He said, *"They're just not my thing, I suppose"*,' repeated the inspector. I could hear Sergeant Tuck scribbling in the background.

'Next. Did you know that the second line of your haiku for Scorpio on 31st January actually has eight syllables?'

'No. No, I didn't.'

'Sergeant Tuck spotted that. He suggests you may simply want to change that line to "experience angers you".'

'Does he? Right.'

'Another thing, the poem "Bloodshed" on August 27th. Do you realise that the initials of the poem's murderer, "BB", as well as standing for "Bible Butcher", might equally be seen as an abbreviation of your own name?'

'That's a coincidence.'

'He claims it's "a coincidence". I heard more scribbling. 'And a very extraordinary one at that! Finally, is it true that you have a tattoo of Enya on your arm?'

'What on earth has that got to do with your investigation?'

'Nothing at all, really. We were just curious. But I think we now have our answer! Anyhow, we will be back in touch once we've done some deeper intertextual analysis. Goodbye!'

He hung up. I tried to put the conversation out of my mind but it was too ridiculous. All these questions about my diary. It's as if it's become a set text for an English 'A' level paper.

Questions for Further Study

1. Consider the poem *The Day My Dog Spontaneously Combusted*.

What does the dog's tragic death tell you about
the author's attitude towards animal welfare?

2. Discuss how Bilston plays with form and structure in a number of his poems.

   Present your answer in the shape of a pipe.

3. How believable is the character of Mrs McNulty?

   Use crystals to divine your answer,
   but please remember to show your workings.

4. *'I think that I shall never meet / A poem lovely as a tweet'*

   Discuss Bilston's attitude towards social media.
   Answer in no more than 280 characters.

Saturday October 13th

Stuart was back. He arrived with Dylan and then mooned around on my doorstep, grinning broadly. It was World Smile Day today, he told me. But, then again, why shouldn't it be every day?

'Not only does smiling spread happiness,' he went on, 'it's physically good for you! It boosts your immune system by decreasing cortisol in your body!'

By this time, I was in full grimace mode. He looked at me, then slapped me on the shoulder and carried on regardless.

'Cheer up, Brian! Did you know that it takes seventeen muscles to smile but forty-three to frown?'

I began to do some calculations in my head to work out how many it would take to hit him but before I'd finished, he took his leave.

'Can't chat all day, I'm afraid! Things to do! Bungee jump! Abandoned poodles!'

Back inside, I saw Dylan eyeing up my Smiths records. I took *Hatful of Hollow* out of its sleeve and placed it on the turntable.

Sunday October 14th

Tomas called me up and we went for a walk. I told him of Toby Salt's disappearance and the police's unhealthy interest in me; how I felt as if they were trying to trap me; how I was worried I might find no way out.

Tomas cogitated for a while.

'You know,' he said eventually, 'Wittgenstein once declared that "a man will be imprisoned in a room with a door that's unlocked and opens inwards; as long as it does not occur to him to pull rather than push." '

'What are you suggesting?' I asked. 'Are you saying that I should investigate what's happened to Toby Salt?'

He shrugged. 'It's up to you. But if you were able to find out what had happened to him, then maybe you will have opened the door.'

'Tell me, Tomas, do you have a Wittgenstein quote for every occasion?'

He shrugged once more. 'When we can't think for ourselves, we can always quote.'

'Wittgenstein again?'

He nodded.

Monday October 15th

I watched an episode of *Sherlock* to get myself into an investigative mood.

I thought about Sherlock's famous precept: when you have eliminated the impossible, whatever remains, however improbable, must be the truth. After that, I started working my way through all the impossible – and mildly thrilling – reasons for Toby Salt to have disappeared: abduction by aliens; time-transported to a Stalinist labour camp; mauled by dinosaurs; carried off by stoats; turned into an actual pillar of salt by a modern-day witch or wizard; and before I knew it, it was time for bed.

Tuesday October 16th

DI Lansbury was on the telephone again.

'Good afternoon. You do realise that "yurt" is a noun not a verb, don't you, sir?'

'Yes, of course. Why on earth are you asking me that?'

'*Everybody Yurts*. 29th July. Sergeant Tuck pointed it out. Doesn't really make sense, does it? People don't yurt. They stay *in* yurts.'

I sighed. 'Is this why you're calling me?'

'Ah, no, not really. That was just something that's been on my mind, that's all. I was calling because I was wondering whether Sergeant Tuck and myself might pop round again. We have a few more questions to ask you in connection with the investigation.'

'What kind of questions?'

'Oh, nothing to worry about, I'm sure. Just a few gaps and

other things in your diary that we're a little confused about. I'm sure it can all be easily explained.'

'I see.'

'How about tomorrow morning? About eleven?'

'Yes, OK.' He hung up. I took a deep breath then gathered up my cleaning equipment and headed out for the shed.

Wednesday October 17th

DI Lansbury pointed at my diary. 'And how do you explain these missing eleven days?'

I gave him the line I'd rehearsed on the cat the day before.

'I ran out of things to say. Writing in a diary every day takes its toll. Especially with all the poems.'

He raised an eyebrow. His right one. Sergeant Tuck was writing away.

'Not that many poems. You'd intended to write one every day.'

I sighed. 'It was harder than I thought it would be. Things kept getting in the way.'

He looked disappointed in me.

'But why then rip the pages out in September? You didn't do that earlier in the year when you'd had that spot of bother with your new shed and you couldn't write.'

'I didn't like the idea of all that white space in my diary.'

DI Lansbury's beard looked sceptical.

'You do know that this is exactly around the time that Toby Salt disappeared, don't you?'

I didn't say anything.

'Anyone who might have seen you coming and going during

this week? Someone who could confirm you were just going about your normal business.'

I thought about Mrs McNulty. She must surely have seen me going back and forth from my shed.

'No. There's no one I can think of.'

DI Lansbury looked over at me. 'Anyway, what's that you're writing?'

'Today's poem.' They both came over and pondered it. It read:

<blockquote>
my calendar is a colander
the numbers collect
in the bowl
while

time

      itself
drains

  through the

holes
</blockquote>

'It's like your poem "Leak-end" on 13th May,' said Sergeant Tuck, 'but not nearly as successful. That original poem, although perhaps a little crass in its construction and naive in its world-view, at least had a semblance of novelty in its mimicry of the slow drip-drip of time. This one here is covering exactly the same ground but in a far less interesting way.'

'It's not finished yet,' I replied testily, 'Anyway, like I said, it's not very easy to write a poem every day.'

I saw them out the door and then ripped up my poem. Perhaps if the police spent more time catching criminals and less time analysing poetry, the world would be a safer place.

Thursday October 18th

First, I checked Toby Salt's Twitter feed. There wasn't much to get excited about. Promotional tweets mainly, plugging his new book and various festival appearances. A new poem published in *Poetry Today*. A link to a piece in *Speculum* concerning the role of political metaphor in contemporary Iranian poetry. Pseudo-intellectual banter with other priests of high culture, deploring the democratisation of the art form. Retweets of praise from Django at Shooting from the Hip. And then, from 5th September, silence.

Next, I called Liz. I had slim hopes that she'd reply. But to my surprise she did:

'You've got a nerve. Have you got our money yet?'

'I'm working on it,' I told her. 'Look, I'm sorry. I messed up.'

'Not for the first time.'

I let that pass. I asked if she had any thoughts on what happened to Toby Salt.

'No idea. I haven't really spoken to him since that evening he was so obnoxious and you tried to punch him but fell over.'

'Do you think he's dead?'

'Maybe. He's not the kind to hide his light under a bushel for long.'

'Do you think I killed him?'

'You?' She laughed. 'No, I don't! Remember, I've seen you in action, Brian.'

I let that pass, too, but I sensed a thawing.

Friday October 19th

....

My Life: A Footnote

        *

        †

        *

        †

        ‡

....

The autumn issue of *Well Versed: The Quarterly Magazine for the Discriminating Poet* flopped apologetically through the letter box. As I turned to the competition pages, it was a relief not to have to endure the usual metamorphosis of blind hope falling away into eye-opening despair. I was delighted to see that, for once, Toby Salt had not won. Nor had he even been listed among the shortlisted. He had so dominated those *Well Versed* pages that it seemed at last as if there had been some rebalancing in the poetic cosmos.

I flicked through the rest of the magazine. There was an article on Toby Salt's disappearance on pages 2 and 3. Pages 6 and 7 were given over to a review of *This Bridge No Hands Shall Cleave*. It got five stars. On pages 13–15 was a transcript of a lecture given

---

 *   Even in the pages
 †   of my own biography,
 *   my life would be nothing
 †   but a footnote
 ‡   at the end of chapter 3.

by Toby Salt earlier in the year entitled 'Beauty and Didacticism in 1950s Hungarian Poetry' and on page 24 there was a feature on his new role as Poet-in-Residence for the BBC. This article, in turn, referenced page 31, where a new Toby Salt poem was displayed, commemorating his appointment.

It didn't seem fair somehow. Not when I would have given my right arm – and that's my poetry arm – for a mere mention in a footnote.

Saturday October 20th

....

Poem for World Sloth Day

He's snoring as he dangles
from his special branch
by his toes, hanging loose:
he's tree-hugging and nap-taking,
a long-limbed recluse.

....

It is World Sloth Day, according to Twitter. Dylan and I celebrated the occasion by watching nature documentaries whilst working on our sloth mindset. Not once did he pester me to go out for a walk or to help with his revision. It would seem that my son is finally doing some growing up.

And so we sprawled on the sofa all afternoon, dunking custard creams into mugs of hot tea, as scenes unfolded involving very different kinds of life on Earth: an iguana pursued across rocks by sinister racer snakes; an Emperor penguin, protecting his egg through the long, bitter winter; and a sloth itself, clinging to his branch as if his very life depended on it.

Sunday October 21st

Poem for World Sleuth Day

Exploring all the angles,
he's from Special Branch
and his tie's hanging loose:
he keeps slogging, it's back-breaking,
this long skim for clues.

It is World Sleuth Day, according to me.

For the modern detective, sleuthing is no longer about dusting for dabs, finding toothpicks in hedges and acting on hunches. That's old-school. Nowadays, it's surfing the net for potential clues while trying not to get too distracted by adverts on how to remove stubborn stains from your shed floor.

Toby Salt's disappearance is getting to be big news: there are features in all the major newspapers. It is widely conjectured that Toby Salt has snuffed it, most likely in suspicious circumstances. Fuelling this view was DI Lansbury:

'There is one particular line of questioning we are pursuing vigorously,' he was quoted as saying. 'A certain gentleman is helping us with our enquiries.'

And a certain diary is helping them, too, no doubt.

Annoyingly, most of the articles go on to mention how well *This Bridge No Hands Shall Cleave* is selling. This strikes me as ghoulish, the way people are rubbernecking at his words like that, while his head lies smashed on the steering wheel at the crash scene that is his poetry collection.

I mean that metaphorically, of course.

Monday October 22nd

Conspiracy Theories

But let us consider this poem more closely.
Given the steadiness of the author's hand,
it seems clear that it cannot have been written
from the location of the grassy knoll,

as often supposed, but more likely
from the vantage point of an upstairs window,
perhaps even multiple windows. The theory
that there may have been several authors

involved in its composition should not be ruled out
at this stage. For more on the poem's capacity
to summon evil spirits when recited backwards,
please refer to my YouTube documentary.

Some have questioned whether this is a poem at all
and argue the existence of another poem – a *better* poem –
that didn't make it onto the page we see before us.
It is hard to refute these claims.

DI Lansbury and Sergeant Tuck arrived unannounced this time and asked if they could take a look in my writing shed. They believe it may be 'pertinent to the enquiry'.

'Well, I'm afraid you can't,' I told them. 'A writer's shed is his castle. You'll need a warrant.'

DI Lansbury sighed. His beard rippled gently like a field of wheat in a late summer's breeze.

'OK, then, sir. If you're going to be like that, we'll get one.'

'How's the case going, by the way?'

'Very well, thank you,' he replied tetchily. 'We have a couple of theories that we're in the process of validating.'

'Such as?'

'One is that Mr Salt has been murdered in a *crime passionnel*. A sudden fit of rage from a rival, jealous of his literary acclaim.'

'Oh, right,' I said, with as much indifference as I could muster. 'Although it seems unlikely that anyone could get themselves worked up over Toby Salt. What's your other theory?'

'It's Sergeant Tuck's, actually.'

Sergeant Tuck stepped forward. 'Have you ever read *Fight Club*, sir?'

I sighed. 'No. You know very well I haven't.'

'Well, in *Fight Club* there's this character called Tyler Durden. He's brash and popular and the book's narrator finds himself in thrall to him. Anyhow, it turns out that Durden himself isn't real but merely a projection of the narrator's mind! Durden is simply an imaginary construction who incorporates all the qualities that the narrator would like to possess had he himself been blessed with that kind of talent and self-confidence.'

'So your second theory is that Toby Salt doesn't actually exist?'

'. . . Yes.'

'Then why are you looking for him?'

There was a long silence, during which DI Lansbury looked at Sergeant Tuck with mounting irritation.

'We'll be back on Wednesday with the search warrant,' he said.

Tuesday October 23rd

I have now reached page 17 of *This Bridge No Hands Shall Cleave*.

If information scientists were to conduct a study of my reading habits, they would formulate a law which states that:

The strength of enjoyment derived is inversely proportional to the quantity of words on the page.

Page 14 contained no text at all; my joy was unbridled.

But I continue to persevere: my long-term future at book group depends on it. Also, I can't help thinking that somewhere in this book is the key to help me unlock the mystery of Toby Salt's disappearance.

Wednesday October 24th

While they rummaged around in my shed, I continued my online scavenging for clues. I became distracted and was in the middle of creating a poem out of suggested Google searches when they returned.

Sergeant Tuck, in particular, seemed most interested in what I'd written so far:

How can a poet make money?
How far can the human eye see?
How can I fill my dog up?
How soon is now? Search me.

Why does Gatsby stop giving parties?
Why am I always hungry?
Why is the carpet all wet, Todd?
Why do goats faint? Search me.

'These are all Google searches, you say?' he asked.

'Yes, that's right. If you type in the first couple of words, Google offers you a list of previous searches other users have made that begin with those same words. I'm selecting the lines for my poem out of those.'

'That's quite experimental.'

'It's called a "found" poem,' I told him. 'That's when you apply words from a non-poetic context and—'

'Right, that's enough!' shouted DI Lansbury. He looked fed up. His beard was looking slightly bedraggled today. The search of my shed had obviously not gone quite as he'd hoped.

'Well, your shed all seems to be in order, sir.'

Inwardly I breathed a sigh of relief.

'Although there were a couple of things . . .'

Inwardly I unbreathed my sigh of relief.

'It appears you've recently had a window repaired. I notice that the glass does not match the frames of the others. Glass broken in some kind of struggle, perhaps? A violent altercation?'

'Gibbon.'

DI Lansbury laughed contemptuously. 'With all respect, sir, do you really expect me to belie—'

'Edward Gibbon, sir,' interrupted Sergeant Tuck. 'Author of *The History of the Decline and Fall of the Roman Empire*. Mr Bilston threw it at the window on 20th June. It's in his diary. It was Volume III, if I remember correctly.'

'Thank you, Sergeant,' said DI Lansbury, even more peeved. 'Just one more thing. On the subject of books, we found this on your shelves. We thought it a somewhat unusual addition to your garden library.'

From out of his pocket, he produced *A Surgeon in her Stocking* by Tina Solomon.

My stomach lurched.

'An unusual book,' he continued, 'for someone so apparently erudite as yourself, sir.'

'Well, we all need a day off occasionally,' I replied, with a nervous laugh. The inspector eyed me closely.

'Indeed. Or eleven days,' he said, putting the book back in his pocket. 'If you don't mind, I'll take this back to the station with me. I have a feeling this could be important.'

They left. I reached for the custard creams, distractedly.

Thursday October 25th

I was only halfway through *This Bridge No Hands Shall Cleave* but I strode to book group with the unshakeable confidence of a man who knows when a book is unfinishable.

I arrived to find everyone had finished it except me. More than that, they were able to talk about it for three hours. I sat on the fringe of the group, playing with my pistachios, retreating into my shell. Occasional phrases penetrated my outer layer: 'lyrically fecund', 'difficult but enriching', 'timeless and yet *so now*'.

My silence hadn't gone unnoticed and, when the evening had finished, we all knew it was over for me. 'Bye, Brian,' one of them said, 'hope to see you around some time. Oh, you've dropped something.'

I stooped to pick up the postcard that had fallen out of my book, inserted it back between its pages, then walked out of the door and away from book group for the very last time.

Friday October 26th

Pumpkin

he carried a candle for her
and so she would call him
'pumpkin'

that his head was huge,
fleshy and orange
were further contributory
factors

On my way back from getting some new materials for the shed, I stood back to admire the sight next door. Mrs McNulty's front garden explodes with pumpkins at this time of year (not a euphemism). The jagged, jarring noise of her wood-sawing temporarily makes way for the restrained and civilised muffle of her pumpkin-carving. She loves Halloween and makes a big effort with jack o' lanterns, fake cobwebs, skeletons and (what is presumably) fake blood on her driveway.

I always feel a little sorry for her, though. She never gets any trick-or-treaters; parents have long memories and tell their children to give her house a wide berth at Halloween, particularly after what happened to poor Susan Watkins in 2007.

Sangue Sulle Tracce

[translated from the Italian]
Pepe lies dying in the arms of Carlotta by the side of the running track. Enzo's javelin is embedded deep within his chest. Pepe's vaulting pole lies forgotten on the ground. The 3000m steeplechase continues around them.

Also, I am bleeding profusely
so please stay for a while
and hold me, my pretty heptathlete!

Be mindful of the javelin
that protrudes from the very heart of me.
How it pierces me so!

Careful! There is blood on your running vest!
You may find yourself disqualified!
The judges are harsh here.

And now for one final time
I must launch myself into the sky.
Oh, do not cry, my little athlete.

I hear them calling you.
It is time for your shot put.
Leave me now and let me jump.

After I'd taken Dylan back home, I met up with Darren. He'd entered a competition and won VIP tickets for a modern opera, entitled *The Pole Vaulter of Turin*. We watched it from one of the balcony boxes. Our tickets meant we avoided the crowds and the queues and got served first at half-time. Darren pointed to his ticket and said the phrase 'access all arias' ten times in the course of the evening.

Neither of us had a clue what was going on. It was like *This Bridge No Hands Shall Cleave* with added wigs, make-up and mezzo-sopranos. The only scenes I vaguely understood were the death ones, of which there were six, although I had no understanding of who was dying, or for what reason.

Everywhere I go, it seems, death is never far behind. It never used to be like this. Perhaps Mrs McNulty is right after all.

Sunday October 28th

I know I should be doing all I can to establish my innocence with DI Lansbury and Sergeant Tuck but it feels like I've reached a dead end. I left messages with Mary, Chandrima and Kaylee to see if they might have any theories about what may have happened to him but unsurprisingly none of them have called me back.

I reached for the crossword instead. There were still seven clues I had yet to solve. I looked at the most recent words I'd written into the grid from a few weeks ago – APANTHROPY, LOGANAMNOSIS, CLEPSYDRA. I could no longer remember what any of these words meant. I stared at it for ten minutes until the black and white squares began to swirl in front of me like a revolving chessboard and I threw it on the floor in disgust.

Why did I bother with it?

Monday October 29th

Haiku Horrorscopes

Aries
That decision not
to believe in poltergeists
comes back to haunt you.

Taurus
You are invited
to a skeleton party
but meet nobody.

Gemini
Please be aware of
the whereabouts of werewolves.
Treat with wariness.

Cancer
Murderer at large.
Eat your cornflakes with caution.
Cereal Killer.

Leo
Is the world a blur?
Curse the day that you were Bourne?
Possessed by Damons.

Aquarius
Evil ghostwriter
forces you to read his book:
Life of Michael Gove.

Virgo
You let a vampire
into work. Boss furious.
Get it in the neck.

Libra
Your day is awful.
Chased by flesh-eating zombies.
Leave brolly on bus.

Scorpio
Trick or treaters call.
You choose trick. Oh the horror!
It's *Mrs Brown's Boys*.

Sagittarius
Good news! Islanders
want you as their special guest
at wicker craft show.

Capricorn
You're buried alive
with your phone. Get top score on
Candy Crush Saga.

Pisces
Morrissey's ghost calls.
His one concern: some ghouls are
bigger than others.

Mrs McNulty has posted her customary Halloween horoscopes

through the door. She has highlighted Cancer with a green marker pen. It reads:

> At this time, the Moon–Jupiter opposition straddles your natal Ascendant–Descendant and your Vertex lies forebodingly conjunct with Venus. Meanwhile Neptune is conjunct the 9th house cusp and opposing the 3rd house cusp. It may be an idea to start saying your goodbyes to the loved ones around you while you still have the chance.
>
> On a brighter note, Pluto and its associated penumbra is conjunct your antiVertex and you may find yourself being paid an unexpected compliment.

This is the most positive forecast that I've received from Mrs McNulty for some time.

Tuesday October 30th

....

On Tender Hooks

Let me cut to the cheese:
every time you open your mouth,
I'm on tender hooks.

You charge at the English language
like a bowl in a china shop.
Please nip it in the butt.

On the spurt of the moment,
the phrases tumble out.
It's time you gave up the goat.

Curve your enthusiasm.
Don't give them free range.
The chickens will come home to roast.

Now you are in high dungeon.
You think me a damp squid:
on your phrases I shouldn't impose.

But they spread like wildflowers
in a doggy-dog world,
and your spear of influence grows.

....

To my surprise, Kaylee answered my call.

'What you been up to, Bri? You been robbin' the British Legion of their poppy fund?'

I could sense some hostility in her tone.

'You got our money yet?'

'Nearly.'

'Anyway, you got anything important to say or is this just a curtsey call?'

I asked her about Toby Salt and whether she had any ideas what had happened to him.

'Dead as a doorknob, I reckon.'

'Why do you think that?' I asked.

'Far gone conclusion. His book's only just published. People want to talk to him about it. He loves himself too much to stay away from all that voluntarily.'

'What do you think happened to him?'

'Murdered, I s'pose. Half a million people get murdered every year. That's one a minute. I know these things. I wrote a poem about it once.'

I remembered. 'But who could have done such a thing?'

'Dunno. Maybe someone had taken a dislike to him. Jealous, maybe. Couldn't stand the thought of him being so successful. Decided to extract his revenge on him. Can you think of anyone like that, Bri?'

She put the phone down on me and I was left alone with the silence.

It was a mute point.

Wednesday October 31st

I opened the door to a vampire, a werewolf and Donald Trump. Dave, Martin and Marvin shouted 'TRICK OR TREAT!', holding out their sack, but reared back a little when they saw me.

'Cool outfit, Brian,' said Marvin.

I looked down at myself. I was wearing nothing out of the ordinary, although I had slipped a tank top on, as the cold weather had begun to bite.

'Norman Bates!' said Martin. 'Brilliant.'

I was about to correct them but thought better of it.

'Oh, you know. Halloween,' I muttered.

I could hear Mrs McNulty cackling next door. I gave them each a small sandwich bag containing a solitary custard cream and was pleased to see their disappointment as I did so.

November

Thursday November 1st

Next door's Halloween party was still raging on even as the morning sun was bravely daring to peek its head above its rooftop duvet. In honour of All Saints' Day, I tried to have the patience of one but there are only so many times it's possible to hear 'Monster Mash' before murderous thoughts emerge.

I said a prayer in the hope that the saints might intervene:

O holy saints, I thank you.
St Eadfast and St Alwart, for always being there for me.
St Urdy and St Able, for making me stand on my own two feet.
St Agger and St Umble, for helping me to keep going even when
                                                  the journey was hard.
St Ubborn, for teaching me to stick to my principles.
St Alactite, for giving me something to look up to.
St Alagmite, for keeping me grounded.
St Artle for your endless surprises.
St Atistics for showing me that deviation can sometimes be normal.
St Ockholm-Syndrome, for holding me in thrall.
St Raddle, for always letting me see both sides.
St Upendous, for just being terrific.
And St Anza, for introducing me to poetry.

Whether it was my prayer or not, the music died down next door shortly afterwards and the final St Ragglers left. I went out to the shed to continue the unsaintly task I had begun.

Friday November 2nd

The money arrived in my bank account today. There's enough in there to settle my Poets on the Western Front debts although whether I will now be accepted back into Poetry Club, I don't know.

Mr Bloomer and Cora Nesmith from the Mongolian Yurt Company will have to wait for future instalments.

Saturday November 3rd

Villainelle

A hero is fine but boring as hell.
Where is the fun if there isn't a foe?
A good story needs a villain as well.

Heroes win out and they then get the girl.
The end of the tale we already know.
A hero is fine but boring as hell.

Luke without Darth is a difficult sell.
The Lion and the Wardrobe's plot is too slow.
A good story needs a villain as well.

Sherlock's OK but Moriarty's a swell.
A Joker-less Batman, I'd gladly forgo.
A hero is fine but boring as hell.

Every Beowulf needs their Grendel.

Borg sans McEnroe? I'd have to say no.
A good story needs a villain as well.

Harry's less dull under Voldemort's spell
And Jekyll is best when Hyde's in full flow.
A hero is fine but boring as hell.
A good story needs a villain as well.

....

No Dylan today. He was going to see Stuart compete in an iron man triathlon. Ugandan cleft-lip and palate sufferers. I confess to feeling rather let down by this: we have so very few Saturdays left. For him to spend one of them in the company of that serial over-achiever rather than me (a cereal over-eater) is hard to stomach. He had been doing so well, too.

I buried myself in the Saturday newspaper as distraction. I was reading yet another article about *This Bridge No Hands Shall Cleave* and how well it was selling when I was struck by a sudden notion: perhaps, in a similar fashion to how he felt threatened by *my* verse, Toby Salt in turn had his own rival in the poetry world, someone upset by his own rise to prominence.

A faint memory stirred of Sefton Warbrick's recent review. I quickly found the section I wanted:

"And it may be time for Bramwell Price to step down – as gracefully as he can – from the stage. For we have a new *Il Divo* waiting in its wing, and his name is Toby Salt."

Bramwell Price. For many years considered the *enfant terrible* of British poetry. A man famed as much for his violent temper and petty feuding as for his verse. Just the kind of poet to take umbrage at Toby Salt's inexorable rise. I checked online. He was giving a reading next Thursday. There were plenty of tickets still available.

Sunday November 4th

I continued with my research. It seems that there *had* been literary fireworks between Bramwell Price and Toby Salt. Toby Salt had reviewed Price's latest collection *Spunk* in one of the broadsheets and absolutely panned it:

> Price's continued efforts to shock us – while entertaining enough, perhaps, back in the early 90s – now seem nothing more than a puerile cry for attention, a desperate plea of relevance to an audience, who have long since moved on. It seems the *enfant terrible* grew up to be nothing but an *enfant ennui*.

Bramwell Price responded in typical fashion in the following week's letters column:

'Toby Salt is a twat,' he wrote laconically.

I must admit I rather like the sound of this Bramwell Price.

Monday November 5th

....

The Bonfire

As I warmed myself by its fire,
I noticed on that burning pyre
a poem of mine, long since penned,
now in flame from end to end

and next to it, another one,
the words alight and quickly gone,
its rhymes and rhythms up in flame,
just like the letters of my name.

Only then did it dawn on me,
the whole thing was my poetry,
a blazing bonfire of *bon mots*,
all my writing up in smoke.

More and more got thrown upon it:
haiku, villanelles and sonnets.
The people's faces overjoyed
to see my work at last destroyed.

They hoisted up an effigy,
which turned out to be really me,
lighting up the evening sky.
Brian Bilston: what a guy.

Dave, Martin and Marvin invited me to join them at the local bonfire night celebrations but I turned them down, on the pretence I had a poem to write. What I didn't tell them was that I've been terrified of organised firework events ever since I was a child. Even the smell of candyfloss sends me into a flap.

Instead, I settled in to watch *Prime Suspect* but dropped off to sleep on the sofa, beneath the cat. I had a dreadful dream in which all my poems were set on fire and everyone cheered. I looked this up in my *Dream Dictionary* but the book is clearly faulty and I have put it in my bag for Oxfam.

Tuesday November 6th

'Oh, look. The black sheep has returned,' said Mary as I walked in through the door.

I wore a cowed, hangdog expression as I silently returned the money to each of them.

'You're a dark horse,' said Kaylee. 'Where did that come from?'

I kept my mouth shut.

'I thought we'd have to wait donkey's years for it,' said Chandrima.

'Can't have been easy,' said Liz to the rest of the group, 'being ostrichised like that.'

They laughed but stopped when I tried to join in.

I asked whether I might sit and hear a few poems but Mary said that perhaps under the circumstances, it might be better if I left; it should not be forgotten that I was responsible for the cancellation of the club's Poets on the Western Front trip. They would discuss whether any re-enrolment might be possible in my absence. Besides, she said, there was only one free chair and they had a new member joining them later.

I glanced back as I reached the door. Liz was smiling at me. I walked home, with a spring in my step, and unread poems in my duffel-coat pocket. Somewhere, amidst the hurt and anger, I detected the faint traces of forgiveness and the beginning of my rehabilitation.

Wednesday November 7th

I had just settled down to watch *Countdown* when the phone rang. It was DI Lansbury.

'You are the salt of the earth,' he said. 'But if the salt loses its saltiness, how can it be made salty again? It is no longer good for anything, except to be thrown out and trampled underfoot.'

'I beg your pardon?'

'Matthew. Chapter 5, Verse 13,' he said.

'Sorry, I don't quite follow.' The consonants and vowels were being doled out.

He sighed. 'You mention it in your poem "Bloodshed".'

'Do I?' I said, looking at my letters and writing down *'splat'* on my piece of paper.

'You do, indeed.'

One of the contestants had got a seven-letter word, the other a six.

'Any reason for that particular choice of Bible quotation, sir?'

The contestant with six letters said the word *'pistol'*.

'Can't remember.'

'He says he can't remember,' said DI Lansbury. I could hear Sergeant Tuck in the background.

The contestant with seven letters said the word *'spatula'*.

'Anyway, sir, we just wanted to let you know that we've not forgotten about either you or your poems. In fact, you might say that you are our "rhyme" suspect.'

He was still chuckling as he put the phone down.

Susie Dent had got the word *'autopsia'*. I wrote the letters into 18 down of the crossword. 'An alternative word to "autopsy",' she told us, 'a post-mortem examination of a corpse.'

I went back out to the shed to review where things had got to.

Thursday November 8th

My meeting over-ran. By the time I got there, Bramwell Price was climaxing with a piece from his seminal collection, *Emanations*. The room was half-empty and it was clear that this was a poet whose star was on the wane, no matter how forceful and arresting his ejaculations were.

The audience dissipated quickly at the end of his performance and I seized my chance.

'That was quite something,' I said.

'Was it really?' he replied disinterestedly. 'That's a deeply unfashionable view to hold these days, you know.'

'Yes. After what Toby Salt had said about you, my expectations were low. But . . . wow! That was . . . terrific!'

I knew it hadn't come out quite right. His eyes narrowed as he looked at me. '*Who* are you?'

'A new fan?' I tried.

'Well, whoever you are, understand this. Toby Salt is someone of absolute inconsequence to me. And before you ask: no, I *don't* have any idea where he is. He could have disappeared up his own arse for all I care. One more thing, if you don't leave right now, I'll call security.'

I wasn't in the mood to be scuffled so I made myself scarce. But I left the building with the knowledge that Toby Salt's disappearance had left Bramwell Price a very worried man.

Friday November 9th

....

Why I No Longer Write Love Letters

Oh b oody he !
My keyboard has a broken ' '.
It seemed to work OK ast night,
as far as I cou d te .

h n ! The ' ' has g ne as we ;
yet an ther key that's damaged.
Such misbeha i ur's ery weird.
And n w my ' ' has anished.

It isn't easy t write ike this.
My w rds are p aced in fetters.
 k! N w th ' ' has disapp ar d!
That's th last f my   tt rs.

Sergeant Tuck has been to collect the typewriter from my shed; DI Lansbury was attending a murder-scene health and safety course in Loughborough, he told me.

Forensics want to take a look at it, apparently, to see how the typography might compare with various correspondence found in Toby Salt's house. I told Sergeant Tuck that he was welcome to it; the keys always got stuck and I'd never quite worked out how to change the ribbon.

Before he left, Sergeant Tuck asked rather awkwardly if he might borrow a few copies of *Well Versed* magazine for 'background reading' so he could try and understand a little more the 'mind of a poet'. I loaded him up with the last three years' worth and was glad to relieve some of the pressure on my bookshelves.

Saturday November 10th

Exclamation Mark

Mark was his name!
He would shout and proclaim!

Every sentence he wrote
would end just the same!

He would assert! He would blurt!
He would ejaculate and spurt!
Each line was a screamer!
A gasper! A slammer! A shrieker!
A literary loudspeaker!!!

It all began to needle and nark!
Why did no one think to question Mark?

....

Stuart was on the doorstep again, exclaiming at me.

'Brian! What a beautiful autumnal day! Such magnificent colours!'

I closed my eyes and willed him to disappear.

'You know, days like this almost make me wish we weren't upping sticks and heading to New England!'

I opened my eyes. It hadn't worked. He was still there.

'Still, what an exciting time for Dylan. He'll love it! Anyway, gotta dash! Sponsored hop! Indonesian lepers!'

Back inside, I asked Dylan about last Saturday but he looked all shifty and tried to change the subject. The poor boy looks increasingly ground down by all of Stuart's high energy and positivity. I played him some Radiohead to help restore his equilibrium and then we settled down on the sofa to watch a Mike Leigh film, our happiness warming us like a blanket.

Sunday November 11th

The Book of My Enemy Has Been Selling Rather Well

The book of my enemy has been selling rather well
And I am distraught.
In huge quantities it has been shifting
Like drugs on a street corner, bought
By customers looking for a quick fix
Of culture. My enemy's much-praised effort is stacked
Twenty copies deep on the front tables,
A sticker which denotes '3 for the Price of 2' is attached –
Among all the cocksure and pre-ordained
Paper skyscrapers from big-budget
Marketing campaigns.

His volume – described as a *'tour de force'* –
By the *Sunday Times* poetry critic –
No longer keeps the company
Of Seamus Heaney and Maya Angelou.
That worldly wise lyrical beauty is two floors up.
No, my enemy's acclaimed collection
Prefers to rub its shoulders with Joe Wicks,
The 'Body Coach', and his 15-minute schemes
To keep you lean and healthy.
The book of my enemy has been selling rather well
And I'm as sick as hell.

I may be free from the shackles of book group and its monthly reading impositions but I am not free of the lure of the bookshop. There was a big pile of *This Bridge No Hands Shall Cleave* on the front table – and one in the window, too. Someone must have made an ordering error. Oh dear!

In a new spirit of economy, I was modest with my purchases: Bramwell Price's *Spunk*, Clive James' *Unreliable Memoirs*, Raymond Chandler's *The Long Goodbye*, Joe Wicks' *Lean in 15*, Tolkien's *The Lord of the Rings* and *Travelling to the US on a Shoestring*.

Monday November 12th

I was reading some Tolkien when my phone sounded. I picked it up after just the one ring. It was DI Lansbury.

'Acrostics,' he said.

'What about them?'

'Write them much, do you, sir?'

'From time to time. Why?'

'We've had another look at your diary. And Sergeant Tuck here noticed your entry for 5th September is an acrostic. I must admit that I didn't know what an acrostic was but Sergeant Tuck informs me that it's a type of poem in which the first letters of every line spell out a word or phrase.'

'Sergeant Tuck is correct,' I sighed. 'What does it say?'

'Well, that's the interesting bit, sir. It reads T-O-B-Y S-A-L-T M-U-S-T D-I-E.'

'Does it? I had no idea. What a coincidence!'

'Extraordinary, isn't it? I mean, the odds of the letters forming unintentionally in that way must be, what, a hundred million to one?'

'Yes, quite large, anyway.'

'Do you enjoy word games, Mr Bilston?'

'I suppose so, yes.'

'Well, here's one for *you* to crack today. Rearrange the following words to make a sentence: Watching. We. Closely. You. Are.'

'Mmm . . . you closely are watching we?'

He hung up.

Tuesday November 13th

It is practically mid-November and there are Christmas songs on the radio. Even the cat was disturbed enough to make one of her rare excursions into the garden.

I stayed in the warm and delved further into the murky past of Bramwell Price. The man's got previous: a brawl with an audience member at a literary festival; a charge for assault on a waiter at a central London restaurant; and, most alarming of all, a restraining order placed on him concerning his first wife after he was found to be posting deposits 'of a sexual nature' through her letter box, following their estrangement. Not the kind of poet content to settle a score merely by writing some mildly scabrous remarks and cryptically hiding them within an acrostic.

Wednesday November 14th

....

To the Forty-Three

Oh, my poor and helpless herd,
waiting on my every word,
through all these pointless weeks

without the comfort of my tweets.

Use this time to make a plan.
Get some sleep in while you can.
Read a book. Or climb a tree.
Don't put your life on hold for me.

Easier said than done, I know.
It's always hard to just let go.
But I'll be back before too long.
Despair not. Chin up. Please be *strong*.

....

I'd not looked at my own Twitter account for several weeks. My follower count still numbers forty-three. I wondered whether they'd missed me – or been worried by my absence – but there were no notifications to help me corroborate this. Toby Salt's account was still frozen in time, like a bedroom kept as a shrine to the child who never came home. Bizarrely, his followers were still increasing rapidly. Bramwell Price, it appeared, did not 'do' Twitter. I looked at some photos of cats set against a cosmic background. I watched a video of baby pandas.

It is all pure avoidance, of course.

I know I need to get back to it.

It's just that I'm not sure I can bear to go back in there again.

Thursday November 15th

I lit the wood-burner but the shed is still freezing. You could catch your death in here.

Friday November 16th

....

Alibi

I didn't write this.
Must have been someone who looks like me.
I keep my nose clean, see.
I'm not the type to get mixed up in poetry.
Don't pin this poem on me.

Besides, I was out drowning kittens
when this poem got wrote –
I'd've had my hands round one's throat
around about that time.
So don't say this poem is mine.

....

Sergeant Tuck has visited again. He called to ask whether they might hold on to my typewriter for a little longer as it was proving very useful. I gave him my assent and he seemed unduly pleased.

He was about to leave when he noticed my copy of Bramwell Price's book on the table and asked me if I was a fan.

'Not really my kind of thing,' I said. 'I just like to keep up with what's happening in the poetry world, that's all.'

'I know what you mean, sir,' said Sergeant Tuck. 'I just wondered because DI Lansbury and I met him a few weeks ago. Peculiar chap. He's got a lot of "issues". We thought he might have something to do with Mr Salt's disappearance.'

'Oh, really?' I said, attempting to keep my tone as neutral as possible.

'Yes, that's right. Until we found out he was at an arts festival in Rio at the time. There were photos of him there the whole week. Watertight alibi. Shame, because he was just the kind of person we were hoping might be the murderer,' he said.

He walked off up the garden path.

Saturday November 17th

Dylan tells me that Stuart takes part in an average of four charitable events a week. This year to date, he's raised over £120,000 for over eighty different charities. Perhaps one day there will be a Stuart Mould Fundraiser for Beleaguered Poets.

Sunday November 18th

....

The Postcard

Weather is disappointing as is the food. But Brenda
and I trying to put our best face on things! Been to all
the local attractions, inc. the castle. The hair museum
was a highlight. Brenda had one of her tummies on Tues
which meant I had to dispose of Cyril on my own. The
look on his face when I hit him with that spade! Found
a nice spot to bury him. Will tell you more when we're
back. Beach tomorrow if weather holds then home! Xx

....

If I am being honest with myself, my ISBN classification system has not been a success. It is simply proving far too difficult to find anything. I have decided to adopt a new organising principle – that of page extent. It was as I was in the act of re-sorting my bookshelves – moving all the slimmest volumes to the top shelves in the hope that this would remove Bramwell Price's *Spunk* from my eyeline – when I noticed something sticking out of my copy of *This Bridge No Hands Shall Cleave*. It was the postcard that had fallen out of it at last month's book group.

The postcard was to promote his book. The front was a reproduction of the book cover. I flipped it over, expecting the back to be blank. Instead, I found a handwritten poem on it. I recognised it: it was Toby Salt's winning poem about the wind from January's *Well Versed* magazine.

I stared at it thoughtfully for a few minutes before returning to the problem of my piles.

Monday November 19th

Sophie called me. She thinks something is up with Dylan.

'He spends all his time in his bedroom,' she said. 'He's not been doing his homework. He answers me back. He avoids Stuart whenever he can.'

This was all wonderful news.

'That sounds like completely normal behaviour for a sixteen-year-old boy to me.'

'I knew you'd say that.'

'Well, it is. I was just the same at his age.'

'I can well believe it. I think this is all your doing,' she said accusingly.

'I don't know what you mean,' I replied, mildly bridling.

'You're a bad influence on him. Whenever I ask him what he's been up to at your house, he always says "nothing much". From what I can tell, the two of you seem to spend the whole day on the sofa.'

'Perhaps he's suffering from galeanthropy?' I suggested.

'What?' I could sense Sophie's levels of irritation rising.

'It's 21 across in *The Guardian Bumper Christmas Cryptic Crossword*. It's the belief that you've become a cat. It's from the ancient Greek – galéē, which means—'

'Oh, shut up, Brian. It's not about cats. It's *you*. He's even started listening to The Smiths.'

This was also wonderful news.

'Ah, yes, that may be my influence. Better them than Huey Lewis and the News, though.'

'It's all a big joke to you, isn't it? But this is our *son* we're talking about, with his whole life ahead of him. He could do anything, that boy. He could really make something of himself. And I'm worried that he won't. He'll mess it all up. He'll go wrong. He'll end up like you.'

There. Sophie had said it and now it couldn't be unsaid. There was a brief silence between us before I answered.

'Has it ever occurred to you that he might be acting like this because he doesn't want to go to America?'

She put the phone down on me.

Tuesday November 20th

I took another look at the postcard. It must have been handwritten by Toby Salt as a promotional giveaway at his book launch. There would have been similar postcards inserted in other copies, too. All the same, there was something about it that struck me as significant. I re-read the poem:

A rock for a jail
and nothing but the wind for company.
O Aeolian confidante! Dry my salty locks
and whisper the world into my ear.
The latest stockmarket news.
A child strangled. The shaming of a politician.
The pounding of the letterpress.
The jangle of my jailor's keys as they bounce upon his hip.
But no. These chains. This rock.
What do you bring exactly? Only betrayal.
The dread beat of accipitrine wings,
the shooting pains,
and my ripped-out liver
shining at my feet,
surrounded by rock pools, ruby-red.

A queasy feeling of déjà vu washed over me as I remembered the hours I'd spent trying to understand it earlier in the year. But I'd got nowhere with it then and I got nowhere with it now.

Wednesday November 21st

DI Lansbury had returned and his beard was in an interrogative mood. It was Sergeant Tuck's day off.

'These eleven days that are missing from your diary. Can you tell me again what you were up to?'

'I can't really remember. Just this and that, I suppose.'

'*This and that*? Can't you be more specific?'

'Not really,' I said. 'My mind's a blank. Like my diary was. That's why I ripped the pages out. I wasn't in the mood for poetry.'

'It must have been a difficult period for you. No job. No money. Alienated from all those around you. And there was Toby Salt, a man riding wave after wave of success. You must have resented that?'

'What exactly are you insinuating?'

'Nothing at all, Mr Bilston. Perhaps, though, if you were to be a little more forthcoming, it might help us in knowing where best to focus our efforts in this investigation.'

He left. I stroked the cat thoughtfully and wondered whether I should tell him.

Thursday November 22nd

I continued to wrestle with the postcard and at last it seems that I have made some progress. My *Dictionary of Classical Mythology* tells me that the figure in his poem is most likely Prometheus, chained to a rock by a wrathful Zeus for stealing fire from Mount Olympus and giving it to mankind.

But what was the significance of that? Did it mean that Toby Salt himself was being held captive? Was he Prometheus? If so, where was his rock? And who was his jailor? And why on earth wasn't 'accipitrine' an answer in my crossword?

I opened another packet of custard creams in search of further inspiration.

Friday November 23rd

....

Poem Sequence in E Flat Major

One
word
followed another,
each line augmented,
dressed up, embellished and tormented,
like some poor Chopin polonaise performed by Liberace.
It was only then that I realised my poem had got all Fibonacci.

....

Twitter tells me it is Fibonacci Day, celebrating that remarkable sequence of numbers that governs the population of bees and the shape of snail shells. I set about Toby Salt's poem once more in the hope that I might find some inner pattern or sequence to unlock its mystery – if it *was* a mystery that is, rather than just a sequence of dull, only loosely connected words.

I found myself going around in spirals for the rest of the day.

Saturday November 24th

Stuart had to dash. He was skydiving for Romanian orphans.

'That'll be another one ticked off my bucket list!' he said before proceeding to tell me about a succession of fulfilled dreams, including a journey on the Orient Express, a swim with dolphins and – with more detail than was strictly necessary for a Saturday morning – how he became a member of the Mile High Club.

'But enough about me! What's on your bucket list, Brian?!' he asked.

'At this moment, kicking it, most probably.'

He paused for a moment to reflect on this and then burst out laughing.

'Oh, Brian! Don't ever lose your wicked sense of humour!' he said with a broad grin. 'Anyway, gotta run – or should I say *jump*!'

Mercifully, he bounded off, and Dylan and I sought refuge inside, where we made a pact that should one of us notice any Stuart-like behaviour in the other, we should tell them immediately.

Sunday November 25th

....

Three Thought Experiments

1. If a poem is printed in a book
   but few people buy that book
   and those that do, fail to understand the poem,
   does it really exist?
2. Imagine a cat lying upon your lap.
   It has been lying there for five hours.
   During this time, it has not stirred once.
   Its breathing is imperceptible.
   Is the cat alive or dead?
3. Consider a group of people, each with a box.
   They are told it contains a 'custard cream'.

Each person can only look in their own box.
Might it be possible that each person
has something entirely different in their box?
A 'digestive' or 'malted milk', for example?
What then do we mean by the term 'custard cream'?

I told Tomas about the poem. He was familiar with the story of Prometheus but even he was unable to decipher the poem further or determine whether it might provide some insight into the whereabouts or fate of Toby Salt. But he had a suggestion.

'What Wittgenstein would do, in such circumstances, is conduct a thought experiment,' he said. 'He would concoct an imaginary situation and use that scenario as the basis for thinking through the consequences of a particular hypothesis.'

I gave it a whirl when I got home. I conjured up a scenario in which Toby Salt had been enclosed in a steel chamber, along with a phial of hydrocyanic acid and a radioactive substance. I'd intended to think through the consequences of what might then have transpired, but so pleasing was the scenario to me, I lingered on it for the rest of the day and found myself no further forward.

Monday November 26th

DI Lansbury again.

'We've had a sighting of you, Mr Bilston – on 7th September, the night of Mr Salt's book launch.'

'Oh yes?'

'Yes – from a neighbour of yours, as it happens.'

I sighed.

'She claims she saw you out in the garden. She'd seen you emerging from your shed. Late it was. About 2 a.m., she reckons. And then you decided to have a bonfire.'

'Oh, really.'

'Funny time to have a bonfire, sir, if you don't mind me saying.'

'Yes.'

'I'd like to take another look at your shed. Shall I get a new warran—'

'Yes, why don't you,' I snapped and slammed the phone down.

Tuesday November 27th

All That Jazz

Here's the scene:
we're booted, real hep,
feeling the step,
laying it loose,
Big Leon's noodling in the corner.
Man, that cat! On tubs is Jack,
giving it some
and then some again,
Pretty Boy Lester's gone,
sharp, feeling the heat,
digging deep,
totally wigged,
Leon's sucking his popsicle stick
all slick licks,
until Den, in search of kicks,

suggests we all go out

and find a jazz band to listen to.

....

I have always nursed a deep suspicion of jazz. I think this may be due to the concept of improvisation; the prospect of having to think on your feet without every move carefully researched and rehearsed disturbs me at a profound level. Or maybe it's just the haircuts.

Regardless, Darren and I had to confront it. It had been billed as an evening of free jazz but, annoyingly, we still had to pay at the door. The main draw was a nine-piece ensemble aptly named Vertigo (ft. Dizzy Malone) as they led to complications in my inner ear. The giddiness and nausea felt like an unwelcome reminder of having to read Toby Salt's poetry.

Wednesday November 28th

DI Lansbury and Sergeant Tuck have taken my wood-burner off to forensics 'for further analysis'.

They carried it up the front garden. Mrs McNulty was looking on interestedly out of her window. Dave, Martin and Marvin were at theirs, too, which was unusual as they always seemed to make themselves scarce whenever DI Lansbury and Sergeant Tuck came to visit.

'Let me know if you find a body in there!' I joked.

DI Lansbury and his beard wheeled around simultaneously.

'You find all this amusing, do you, Mr Bilston?' he said.

'No,' I responded sheepishly.

'I'd like to remind you that a man has disappeared – and may very well be dead. Which, as far as I'm aware, is not the usual stuff of comedy.'

'No, it's not,' I said in a small voice.

From the whoop that emitted from behind her net curtain, Mrs McNulty appeared to be most delighted by this whole exchange. There was some support on offer from Dave, who stuck his middle finger up at the policemen's retreating figures as they continued down the path, only to pretend he was scratching his nose when DI Lansbury turned around suddenly and glared at him.

Thursday November 29th

I'd gone back to pondering Toby Salt's poem. I was trying to read between its lines, and wishing it was comprised of only the bits between the lines and none of the actual lines at all, when the doorbell rang and there was Sergeant Tuck. He'd popped round on the off chance I was in so he could return the back issues of *Well Versed* I'd lent him, he said. As he brought them in, I could sense him nervously eyeing up my bookshelves.

'Is there anything else you'd like to borrow while you're here?' I asked, keen to put him out of his misery.

Gratefully, he seized an anthology of twentieth-century poetry, and collections by Emily Dickinson and W. H. Auden.

'I'll get these back to you next week,' he said and skipped off up the path.

I went back inside and took one final look at Toby Salt's post-card poem in search of meaning. It stared back at me in defiance once more. No, that was it. I'd tried. I'd failed.

I ripped it up and threw it in the recycling. The lorry will come for it tomorrow.

Friday November 30th

Bring Your Cat to Work Day

It will look good on your CV, he said.
Pfff. What needs have I but to be fed,
stroked – when I wish it – upon my head,
and a lap that's warm to call a bed.

This is how the photocopier works.
He thinks I'm his goddam office clerk.
I size up the A4 tray as it whirrs.
It's not so comfy. But I've had worse.

Perhaps you could get on with some filing.
I wait until he's walked out the door
and then file myself inside a drawer.
It's peaceful here and I sleep some more.

It's quite cosy here on this keyboard.
There's a spot of sun I stretch towards.
I don't know what he's shouting for.
Hang on a minute . . . is that a mouse?

The deadline was approaching so it was time I got back down to it. Without my wood-burner, I was reduced to working back in the house with all its cat-induced limitations. Did T. S. Eliot have a shed? If not, it's a wonder that he was able to write *anything*.

December

Saturday December 1st

Verb Your Enthusiasm

I remember when it first circumstanced,
this problem that routines with my words:
I was in the kitchen, plating my food,
when my nouns conversioned to verbs.

I friended others with similar troubles;
we workshopped together for days.
Dialoguing in search of solutions,
the long hours flipcharted away.

I now diarise each time they event.
Are they *nerbs* or *vouns*? I'm not sure.
The doctors cannot medication me.
Even to poem provisions no cure.

In a World Cup for languaging weirdly
or a verbing-renowned Olympics,
I'd have podiumed – I'm in no doubt –
if it weren't for those medalling kids.

Dylan was disconcertingly cheerful today. Perhaps, unlike me, he has come to terms with his departure.

He came in brandishing a leaflet. It was for a 'Motivatathon': a rolling twenty-four-hour session of workshops for leading business executives to 'inspirationalise' and 'change-manage' their teams. It is hosted by Stuart Mould, 'Dream Architect', and is all for a good cause. On the leaflet is a list of charities, who will receive 80 per cent of the corporate sign-up fee: Save the Elderly,

Aid for the Vulnerable, Lame UK, the Guatemalan Orphan Trust and so on.

There was a picture of Stuart on it, gazing enigmatically at a lake. I suggested to Dylan that we 'graffitise' his face but he didn't want to join in the fun. He snatched the leaflet up and put it carefully back into his bag.

Sunday December 2nd

For some unfathomable reason, the disappearance of Toby Salt continues to be of interest to the media, as well as the police. You would think they'd have more interesting things on which to report, like the victim of a splashed puddle or a hat being found in a tree.

In today's newspaper was an article about the phenomenon of *This Bridge No Hands Shall Cleave*, which has reprinted six times now since it was published. It's been recommended in all the Books for Christmas pages of the broadsheets and is set to be the best-selling poetry book of the year. It's a relief that Toby Salt is not around to see all this, to be honest; he'd be insufferable.

Monday December 3rd

In an almost-certainly doomed attempt to get ahead of myself, I revisited my list of Christmas card beneficiaries. Each year, it shrinks a little. This year I am down to twelve and that includes all the members of Poetry Club.

I'm not sure whether I can stand any more recipients asking to be removed from my mailing list. Last year, there were three of them, one of whom seriously considered prosecuting me under breach of the 1998 Data Protection Act.

I may need to add DI Lansbury and Sergeant Tuck just to get my numbers back up.

Tuesday December 4th

....

Having Fun with a Clerihew

Archimedes of Syracuse
was keen to tell the town his news.
Naked through the streets he raced,
with clothes displaced.

....

Eureka! I have it! I know where Toby Salt is! At least I think I do.

I'd been flicking through old issues of *Well Versed* in search of some advice on how to write a clerihew when I realised that I knew what was wrong. But I needed Toby Salt's postcard to figure it all out and that had gone into last week's recycling collection.

Only it hadn't, I remembered. On Friday morning, there'd been another knock on the window from the Man at Number 29, who'd pointed out it was a landfill day. I went rummaging in the recycling bag to find the bits and then pieced it all together. It was harder than a 500-piece Photo Jigsaw Puzzle of Gérard Depardieu in a Submersible and far less satisfying. But I finished it.

Whether Toby Salt was still alive was another matter.

One thing was clear: time was of the absolute essence.

I ran myself a bath and consulted tomorrow's train timetable.

Wednesday December 5th

....

Why Poets Don't Drive

Whether motorways, B roads, or backstreets,
there is a road for us all to explore.
Yet each leads – in the end – to the same place.
Yes, Karen, I know we need the A4.

There are some who live life in the fast lane
and some who stick in the middle, unsure.
Others live theirs in a roundabout way.
I know I did, Karen. We'll have to go round it once more.

The road is – in essence – a metaphor.
We journey along it, trusting to luck,
being mindful of others upon it.
Don't be silly, Karen, there isn't a tr—

....

One of the drawbacks of being unable to drive is that it takes me a while to get anywhere. Unlike those heroes you encounter in the movies, I can't just drop everything and hit the open road. Journeys need to be planned – and sometimes delayed – in order to secure a more competitive ticket price, as well as to write a poem and get the laundry up-to-date.

The 4.50 from Paddington arrived in Swansea just before eight o'clock. I checked into a B&B and left a message for DI Lansbury and Sergeant Tuck.

Thursday December 6th

....

Roles

He never got to play
the part of Joseph;
he was one of those kids
that no one noticed.

The type barely seen
and more rarely heard,
no Innkeeper, Herod,
or Second Shepherd.

Not once did he wear
the crown of a king
nor wings of an angel
(although he could sing).

Instead he would be
Brown Cow Number Four,
A Rock or A Bauble,
The Stable Door.

And now – forty years on –
it still made him wince,
for it seemed that his life
hadn't changed that much since.

....

With the exception of once being a rather pivotal turnip in a vegan nativity play at primary school, I don't think I've ever played the role of 'hero' before. But I suppose that's what I must have been to Toby Salt, not that he could quite bring himself to say it – not even after I'd pressed him several times on the matter after he'd been unchained from the letterpress.

The print shop was situated at the rear of a quiet Victorian terraced house in a secluded Mumbles backstreet. There was no sign of DI Lansbury or Sergeant Tuck yet so I thought I'd take a quick look around myself. The house itself was locked but on the left-hand side was an entrance leading into the back yard. This side-door had also been secured but, by climbing up precariously onto the neighbouring fence, I was able to reach over and slide the bolt over to open it.

The outhouse door had been left slightly ajar. There was some-body talking inside. I slipped in quietly. A man stood with his back to me, leisurely loading up various items of crockery onto a tray.

'And how was your breakfast this morning, my bestselling poet?' he said.

Django. I'd recognise his adenoidal tones anywhere. And there, in front of him, sitting on a bench and chained to a nine-teenth-century letterpress, was Toby Salt. The top of his head was bandaged but the rest of him appeared to be disappointingly bruise-free. His head was bowed and he appeared utterly unre-sponsive to all of Django's attempts at conversation.

'I must apologise for the continued absence of Lapsang Sou-chong,' Django went on. 'But I can assure you that I'm on the case. The shopkeeper has high hopes of a delivery this Friday!'

Toby Salt continued to stare at the floor.

'But do not despair,' said Django. 'I bring you better news.' He flourished a newspaper in front of Toby Salt. 'Look,' he said, 'the non-fiction top 10 – you're now at number 4!'

Django, undeterred by the silence which greeted every utterance, pressed on:

'And you are fast closing in on the *Lean and Healthy Cookbook*. Who knows, by Christmas, you could be number o—'

'WHEN ARE YOU GOING TO LET ME GO, YOU MONSTER!?' shouted Toby Salt, livid with rage.

'Now, now, Toby,' replied Django calmly. 'I have told you before that you really should not make such a noise.' He bent down to pick up a cloth from the floor and, as he did so, Toby Salt glanced upwards and our eyes met. I put a finger to my lips in warning.

In my anxiety to hear the conversation, I'd advanced further into the workshop than I had intended; I was now standing only a couple of metres behind Django. But, as he set about re-tying his prisoner's gag, he must have noticed some subtle change in Toby Salt's demeanour that caused him to whirl around suddenly. We found ourselves face to face.

'What!' he snarled nasally. 'Who are you?'

He picked up a printer's block and began to advance on me menacingly.

'Please put that down. It's all over now, Django,' I said, backing away nervously.

'It is for you!' he cried as he raised the printer's block into the air, poised to bring it down on my head. In desperation, I blindly grabbed an object from the table next to me and slammed it into his face. If that didn't unblock his nasal passages, nothing would. Django reeled backwards from the blow, lost his footing and crashed down, cracking his head on the edge of an impressively solid-looking piece of Victorian machinery.

There were shouts behind me as DI Lansbury and Sergeant

Tuck burst into the workshop. They surveyed the scene in front of them. Sergeant Tuck went over to inspect Django's crumpled figure.

'He's out cold but he'll be OK,' he said.

I looked down at my hands to see what I'd struck him with: it was a copy of the commemorative linocut edition of *This Bridge No Hands Shall Cleave*.

'Who would have thought Toby Salt's poetry could be so hard-hitting,' I joked. Disappointingly, nobody laughed. Darren would have enjoyed that line.

'Can somebody PLEASE unchain me from this damn machine?' came a voice from across the workshop.

I went over to Toby Salt.

'Is this what you meant by being at the bleeding interface of literature and technology?' I asked him, in an attempt to cheer him up.

It was at that point DI Lansbury reminded me that kidnapping was a rather serious matter, that Toby Salt would have endured a very traumatic and gruelling experience and that perhaps it would be the best for everyone if I went home and left them to it.

Friday December 7th

I opened the door to the spectacle of DI Lansbury's triumphant beard, and behind him, the doughty Sergeant Tuck, bearing news.

'Django has confessed all,' declared DI Lansbury. 'It was the final act of desperation from a publisher on the verge of bankruptcy.'

'I had no idea,' I said. 'I'd always imagined they were doing well. That's the impression that Toby Salt gave.'

'I've no doubt he did. But all that poetry takes its toll on the finances,' continued DI Lansbury. 'Sales are precarious, margins slender. Then along comes Toby Salt, the best thing to have happened to Shooting from the Hip for years.'

I did my best to keep a straight face.

He went on. 'But there was a cloud on the horizon. Toby Salt's star was rising fast – he was winning awards, writing for newspapers, appearing on the radio and television – and the major publishers had started to circle. Django knew that a small press like Shooting from the Hip wouldn't be able to keep hold of him for long. His only hope was to make as much money as possible out of *This Bridge No Hands Shall Cleave* – and what could be better for sales than a mystery surrounding its author.'

He helped himself to another custard cream before proceeding.

'It worked far better than he could ever have dreamt. After his disappearance, Toby Salt was in the news every day – and as sales of his book increased that became a story in itself. A publishing phenomenon with a self-perpetuating cycle of sales and publicity.'

'But what was he planning to do with Toby Salt when it had all died down?' I asked.

'Who knows! He claims he'd only intended to detain him for a couple of weeks. But then the book orders flooded in, and it all spiralled out of control. I suppose he'd have had to find a way of getting rid of him more permanently.'

I wondered momentarily whether I'd been a little too hasty in uncovering his whereabouts.

'And now?'

'And now, Mr Bilston, we'll leave you alone. Thank you for your assistance and good luck with whatever it is that you do.'

He handed me my old diary back and they took their leave.

Saturday December 8th

....

Christmas without you is

A cracker in need of pulling.
A glass of wine that could do with more mulling.
A stocking that's lacking in presents.
A champagne cocktail without effervescence.
A deep-filled mince pie with no deep-filled mince.
A Father Christmas who doesn't convince.
A Wise Man bereft of myrrh
(substitute gold or frankincense, if you prefyrrh).
A card you've written but forgotten to send.
It's A Wonderful Life without the bit at the end.
An Ernie without an Eric.
Generic
An out-of-tune carol.
A tin of Roses with no Golden Barrel.
A Bowie without a Bing.
A merrily-on-high dong that's lost its ding.
Mistletoe without a kiss.
That's what Christmas without you is.

....

With all the excitement of the last few days, my thoughts had been distracted from Dylan's departure but it all came flooding back as I opened the door to him this morning. My attempts at cheeriness were unconvincing. By contrast, Dylan was in high spirits; I even caught him breaking out into a whistle.

Maybe he's on drugs.

Or maybe he's just looking forward to going away.

I hope he's on drugs.

Sunday December 9th

Mrs McNulty whistled to me from across the fence. Reluctantly, I popped my head over. She handed me a piece of paper containing a series of strange patterns and squiggles.

'Are you feeling OK?' I asked her.

'I've been reading the runes,' she said, 'and it's not good news for you. No, it's not good news at all. They spell. . .' She paused for dramatic effect. '. . . DEATH!'

I sighed. 'Toby Salt has been found now, Mrs McNulty. Alive and well, worst luck. It's no use trying to pin that one on me.'

She looked at me with something approaching sympathy, then shook her head softly.

'Poor boy,' she said. 'My poor boy.'

She reached into her apron and produced a book of Icelandic Christmas songs and fairy tales.

'I was going to give you this for Christmas,' she said. 'But you should have it now. It will help you sleep.'

Monday December 10th

....

Papa Crimblecheeks

A traditional Icelandic lullaby translated from Old Norse

364

Be good, my child, be good,
for Papa Crimblecheeks comes tonight.
Shut tight those snowflake eyes
or he will slit your throat.

The whale pot rocks by the fire
and the wind whistles a tune tonight.
Papa Crimblecheeks is on his way.
Hear the ghosts of children's cries.

Leave a tooth in the baleen bowl.
Keep it by your bed.
Papa Crimblecheeks will walk on by
for he knows you have been good.

Have you seen little Pétur?
He is hanging in the shed.
For he stole Eyhildur's doll
and Papa Crimblecheeks found out.

....

'Sorry to disturb you again, sir.' It was Sergeant Tuck.

I was glad of the interruption. I'd been reading the book Mrs McNulty had given me and I wasn't keen on being alone in the house.

'I've just been wondering how you figured out where Toby Salt was.'

'Oh, that was simple,' I lied and showed him the taped-together postcard.

Sergeant Tuck filled me in on some more of the back story: how Django had forgotten his promise of providing the book-shop with handwritten postcards for the launch of *This Bridge No Hands Shall Cleave*; how he'd returned to the imprisoned Toby Salt and applied some 'pressure' to get him to write them.

I smiled at the thought.

'Presumably, Django was watching him closely,' I mused, 'to be sure that he wasn't able to send a message to the outside world about his incarceration. But then again his writing is so opaque, who can tell what any of it means? I felt, though, that there was something even odder than usual about the poem on my postcard. I'd seen it before in *Well Versed*. But there was something about it that jarred.'

'Which was?'

'For a while I wasn't quite sure. But then, when I chanced upon the original version again, I noticed there were differences between that poem and the one on the postcard. *Gutter press* had been changed to *letterpress*. *Jingle* to *jangle*, like Django. *Thigh* to *Hip*. *Daily agonies* to *shooting pains*. Once I'd spotted the inconsistencies, it didn't take a genius to see where all the clues were pointing.'

'That cryptic crossword you're always doing must have helped.'

'Possibly. But also, a few days before, I'd been listening to some jazz and I'd had a sudden revelation. Improvisation and freedom of expression only works if the musicians have a common base from which to start.'

Sergeant Tuck was impressed, much as I'd hoped he would be because I'd just made that bit up.

'One more thing, sir. Those eleven missing days in your diary: what *were* you up to?'

'Ah. Some things are best kept secret,' I replied enigmatically.

He didn't pursue this further. I saw him eyeing up my anthologies.

'Feel free to borrow anything you'd like,' I said.

As he left, he thanked me profusely, from behind the large pile of poetry books he was carrying and expressed his hope that we might meet again one day soon.

Tuesday December 11th

I have been welcomed back into the soft and crinkly fold of Poetry Club.

Instrumental in my re-bosoming was Poetry Club's latest recruit, Sergeant Tuck – or Henry, as he prefers to be known when he's not on duty. He told them all about how I'd unearthed and untethered Toby Salt. As he narrated my fight sequence with Django, I thought of Douglas and how he'd have embellished the tale with suitable sound effects. I chipped in occasionally with the odd additional detail (again, no one laughed at my 'heavy-hitting' line) but I was content to leave the retelling to the good sergeant.

After the tale had been told, Chandrima hugged me. Kaylee gave me a fist bump. Liz stroked a sleeve of my cardigan, an action that I discovered to be surprisingly erotic.

Mary sat there, seemingly unmoved and impassive, and then cleared her throat.

'When you've all quite finished,' she said, sternly, 'we have a poetry evening to put on. Brian . . .' she paused and I wondered whether she was going to ask me to leave, 'since we've all missed your poems over the last few months, I'd like to suggest that you go first.'

I took some crumpled pieces of paper out of my cardigan pocket and went up to the make-shift stage.

'Here's a poem about the time I kidnapped Mumford from Mumford and Sons,' I mumbled

margin-
alised

I'll
tell you
what
the
thing is

I've spent
too long
on
the
fringes

i'm
on
the
edge,
it's
ever
so

cold,

please

welcome

me

back

367

in my usual, shambling manner, 'planted him in a large pot and decorated him like a Christmas tree . . .'

It was just like old times: Mary treated us to a poem about the time her sixth husband nearly choked to death on a five-pence coin hidden in a Christmas pudding; Chandrima enchanted us with a meditation about the uniqueness of each snowflake; Liz accompanied a poem concerning the pulling of an obstinate Christmas cracker with a series of hand gestures that left me feeling rather hot and bothered for a while; and not even Kaylee's powerful diatribe about an unscrupulous landlord who hires out his barn at an exorbitant price to a young pregnant mother on Christmas Eve was able to dampen the atmosphere.

And then, finally, Sergeant Tuck – Henry, I mean – shared with us something he'd written about the revelation of a corpse hidden beneath melting snow. It had promise but afterwards I gave him a few pointers as to how he might make some improvements to it.

On parting, Mary reminded the group about our Christmas lunch together next week. Chandrima said that she'd try to get in touch with Toby Salt to see if he would like to join us. I hope he does; it would be good to catch up and hear about what he's been up to recently.

Wednesday December 12th

....

On the Shelf

They got straight to the heart of the matter.
'It's no fun here any more,' remarked *Bleak House*, sadly.
'He makes me so angry!' whined *The Grapes of Wrath*.
'I've never felt so alone,' said *One Hundred Years of Solitude*,
for whom reality had long since lost its magic.

'He couldn't even remember my name, *The Idiot*,'
muttered a voice from the Russian literature section.
'That's because he avoids you like *The Plague*,' said another.
'C'est vrai!' came a cry. 'It is like I don't exist!'
Two shelves below, an atlas shrugged.

Meditations of Marcus Aurelius thought for a while.
'But why on earth doesn't he read us?' he pondered.
'Perhaps he doesn't have time because he spends so much of it
in a bookshop,' suggested *Catch-22* ruefully.
'He just needs something to sink his teeth into,' said *Dracula*.

'Let's not give up on him yet.' It was *Brave New World*.
'Who knows what the future may hold?'
After some *Persuasion*, they agreed to give him one last chance.
'Be quiet!' cried *Waiting for Godot* with *Great Expectations*.
'I think that's him coming now!'

....

My next deadline is approaching fast. I gritted my teeth and got down to it as best I could, interrupted only by an exchange of messages with Liz: she's asked me if I'd be interested in joining her book group. After a brief deliberation, I agreed, and then spent the rest of the evening avoiding eye contact with my bookshelves.

Thursday December 13th

A 'memory' flashed up on Facebook today: I'd been tagged in a photograph from an old Christmas office party. There were about twenty of my co-workers on the dancefloor, all linked together to form some kind of human centipede – or 'conga' as I believe it's called. They were all laughing and having fun. You could just about make me out in the background, sat by myself, looking glum. I was attempting to flick pistachio nuts into a jar.

It is funny to think that was only two years ago. It feels so good to have moved on from those days.

Friday December 14th

I've drawn Mary in our Poetry Club Secret Santa. I had a browse in the Age Concern shop and was able to pick up a second-hand Wham! CD for her at the bargain price of fifty pence. I have no idea whether she likes them or not but it's the thought that counts.

After that, I went to the bookshop to pick up a copy of Liz's book group choice for the month: *Grief is the Thing with Feathers* by Max Porter. It seemed miserly to leave the shop merely with one book and so I also bought an illustrated edition of *A Christ-*

mas Carol, a collection of English Ghost Stories, *The Oxford Book of Christmas Poems* and a biography of James Stewart.

Saturday December 15th

Dylan texted this morning to say that something had come up and he couldn't make it over again today. He wouldn't tell me what the matter was. I wondered whether Sophie might be behind his no-show and considered phoning her but couldn't face another argument.

I lugged my misery around with me for the rest of the day. I lugged a Christmas tree around with me, too, carrying it for three miles before I eventually got it home. Exhausted, I collapsed on the sofa and ate a whole packet of custard creams, then fell into a strange, disturbing dream.

I was on a dancefloor in a nightclub. The music was awful. Balloons fell down from a cage on the ceiling, next to a shining, spinning disco ball. There was a man dancing next to me with bad 1980s hair. He boogied over to me with a balloon between his knees, which he then proceeded to lodge between my own knees, after a series of rather alarming cajolings. I inspected the man more closely and saw that he bore a remarkable resemblance to Samuel Taylor Coleridge. Samuel Taylor Coleridge sporting a mullet.

I looked at my fellow dancers. I was surprised to see William Wordsworth there – and Percy Bysshe Shelley. And Byron. And Keats. They, too, wore their hair short at the front and long at the back. Suddenly, in unison, they clapped their hands and began to act out a sequence of bizarre actions in time with the music: pretending to sleep, waving their hands, hitching a ride, sneezing, going for a walk . . .

I woke up suddenly, my dream interrupted by a knock on the door. It was the Man at Number 29.

'I'm just out delivering Christmas cards,' he said, holding one out in front of me.

'Oh. Thank you!' I said. 'That's very kind of you.'

'Not at all. It was the least I could do. Thanks for all your help with that spot of bother earlier in the year.'

I looked at the envelope. It was addressed to 'The Man at Number 25'.

'Well, thanks to you for all your help, too. I'm Brian,' I said. 'Brian Bilston.'

'Good to meet you, Brian,' he replied. 'My name's Colin. Colin Porlock.'

We shook hands. After he'd gone, I began to write a poem about my peculiar reverie:

> In Agadoo did Kubla Khan
> Push pineapple, shake the tree
> Where Alph, the sacred river, ran,
> Wave your hands, superman!

But that was as far as I could get. It was incomplete, a fragment. I went to bed, unsettled still by my dream and the sounds of its sinister, haunting soundtrack ringing in my ears.

Sunday December 16th

Dave, Martin and Marvin have headed off for the Christmas holidays. Last night's party had clearly taken its toll. They managed a mumbled happy Christmas to me before staggering over to their car and heading off down the street with a jaded parp of the VW Beetle's horn.

I wasn't on good form either, having been unable to sleep through the merrymaking. In the end, I gave up trying and climbed out of bed to go and read some of *Grief is the Thing with Feathers* on the sofa. I looked at the clock: it was 4.30am and I was up with the crows.

Monday December 17th

The shops are full of worried men. I was in one of them on the hunt for a Christmas jumper to wear at tomorrow's Poetry Club lunch. It took me five hours to choose one. I stood in front of the changing room mirror as I tried jumper after jumper, featuring an assortment of knitted elves, reindeer, Christmas trees, mistletoe and snowmen.

I'd hoped it might make me look rather hipsterish, that its wool would hug me with an ironic coolness. But I just looked like an idiot in a tank top with a big Christmas pudding on it.

Tuesday December 18th

I was singing to myself as I walked to the Poetry Club Christmas lunch:

'Last Christmas, I ate a la carte
But the very next day I was ill straightaway.
This year, to save me from tears,

I'm choosing from one of the specials.'

It was the same restaurant that I'd been to last year for my work Christmas lunch. That occasion had not ended well. I made a note to choose my food with caution.

'Once bitten, vegan pie,
Broke my resistance, the microbes multiplied.
Tell me, pastry, do you recognise me?
It's been a year since I have looked at a cranberry.'

I had the Wham! CD with me. I wondered what Secret Santa had brought me. Not another scented candle, I hoped.

'Happy Christmas, I chewed you up and ate you.
Next day by the toilet, I quickly learnt to hate you.
Yes, I know, what a squalid scene,
And if I ate you now, I know you'd floor me again.'

I was the last to arrive and I had no choice but to sit next to Toby Salt, who'd decided to grace us with his presence. He had a 'serendipitous window' in his schedule in between all the interviews and book signings. Mercifully, Liz was sat the other side. She pulled my cracker and I blushed again, thinking of her poem.

I ordered the stuffed peppers. The Secret Santa gifts were handed out by Mary. Mine was book-shaped. I unwrapped it. *This Bridge No Hands Shall Cleave.*

'I wonder who could have bought you that?' said Toby Salt, chuckling.

I didn't admit to him that I already owned a copy.

'Someone who buys their Christmas presents from charity shops, I suppose,' I responded as my food arrived.

'It'll be interesting to see how you get on with it,' he said. 'I know my poetry can be a little too clever for you.'

Luckily for him I had no pistachio shells on hand or he'd have been peppered. I wondered if I should shell him with my peppers instead.

'Not so clever that he couldn't figure out your postcard,' interrupted Liz. 'If it wasn't for Brian, you'd still be sat chained to a letterpress in your underpants.'

I could have hugged her.

Toby Salt glowered. 'I wasn't just in my underpants.'

'That's not what Brian said.'

'Well, we all know how jealous Brian has been of my success,' he said, reaching for the bread sauce. 'He only resents my book because he knows he'll never have one of his own.'

But that's where Toby Salt was wrong.

Wednesday December 19th

....

Eleven Days

In the beginning, there was emptiness
and then He said, 'Let there be white,' and there was white.

On the second day, He said, 'Let there be words to dance upon the white,' but there was still just white.

On the third day, there was white and not much else.

On the fourth day, it was all about the white.

5th = white.

On the sixth day, there were words but they failed to dance

and they were cast asunder and white prevailed once more.

On the seventh day, the words returned and danced upon the white, albeit in a rather tentative fashion as if they were attending their first school disco.

On the eighth day, He said, 'Let there be a plot to make sense of the white and the dancing of the words,' and there was a plot, if only a loose one.

On the ninth day, He said, 'Let there be characters, strongly drawn, to drive the plot, which though it may be a loose one, is all I have to make sense of the white and the dancing of the words,' and there were characters but not of the strongly drawn type.

On the tenth day, He said, 'Let there be love, whatever that means,' and there was love, whatever that meant.

And on the eleventh day, He rested.

....

Dear Diary,

Without you, I don't know how I would have made it through this year. You have been my friend, my confidant, my constant companion. There have been days in which I may not have risen from my bed at all, had it not been for you and the joy of filling up your pages.

But I have a confession to make. And an apology. I am sorry that I tore some of your pages out and burnt them. I was not in my right mind. I had been ashamed of what I had done and wanted to leave no trace of it.

It had all started as a joke. I had never meant it to go so far. We'd just had so much fun reading *A Surgeon in her Stocking* that I had thought I'd try to write a send-up of it. For Dylan. And that's how *A Poet Up Her Chimney* started. But, a few chapters in, I wondered whether there might be money to be made out of this. I was broke. And desperate. It didn't take very long to write. It took me longer to come up with a *nom de plume*; Brian Bilston was never going to cut it as a writer of romance fiction. *Delores Wildflower*, on the other hand, had every chance – and she took it. Delores sent it off to a publisher of romantic fiction, who loved it so much that they offered her an advance for a whole series of titles, provisionally entitled *Poets in Love*.

It would seem that I've made it as a writer, after all.

But none of this could ever justify my rough behaviour towards you, my dear, beloved diary. I hope you can find it in your papery heart to forgive me.

Yours sincerely,

Brian

P.S. I would appreciate it if you could keep this information to yourself.

Thursday December 20th

I squeezed *Grief is the Thing with Feathers* into my coat pocket and headed off to book group. Liz was already there when I arrived and she introduced me to the rest of the group. They seemed like a good bunch and smiled sympathetically when I confessed that I hadn't quite had time to finish reading it.

'Never mind,' one said. 'Life gets so hectic at this time of year, doesn't it? I'm sure you'd have finished it in any other month.' I nodded vigorously and bought some wasabi peas for the table.

'It was good to see you tonight,' said Liz, as we exchanged our goodbyes outside the pub. 'I wasn't sure whether you'd turn up.'

'Oh, you can always rely on me,' I said. 'Happy Christmas.'

She raised an eyebrow, reached across and hugged me before we parted; she, striding off towards her bus stop and I, in search of mine.

Friday December 21st

Traits of the Artist as a Young Anagrammatist

When life gives me *lemons*, I see *melons*;
it sometimes makes me *solemn*, too.
Because when a word *bores* me *sober*,
and starts to *wane*, I shake it up *anew*.

I'm *alerted* to how words are *related*,
how, when *altered*, they might enmesh;
shuffling letters like a pack of cards,
then *dealing* them out, *aligned* afresh.

Faced with a *poser* and on the *ropes*,
I'll make a poem from its *prose*.
An *education* to be *cautioned* against?
It's character building, I suppose.

A *gory orgy* of *words* put to the *sword*:
these are *traits* the *artist* understands,
largely, and in whose *gallery*
the *Ars Magna* of *anagrams* hangs.

I filled in the gaps of the final clue at 31 down, A_T_T_M_Y, and then looked it up in the dictionary:

AUTOTOMY (noun): the casting off of a part of the body by an animal under threat. For example, the tail of a lizard.

It was done! I held it out in front of me to survey my accomplishment and began to wave it around like a chequered flag of victory. I couldn't wait to show Dylan tomorrow. My thoughts turned to how he might help me with the next one. I would teach him the Grand Art of Cryptic Crossword Solving. The two of us sat together, dictionary at our side, decrypting clues, unscrambling anagrams, finding all the answers. We'd finish it in half the time!

And then, suddenly, a vision of the future without him in it came out of nowhere and hit me. I reeled backwards, doubled up with loneliness. I sat back down on the sofa and breathed deeply.

I would give my right arm for him to stay.

Saturday December 22nd

The bell rang and somewhere an angel was getting his wings.

Dylan and his mother were at the door. Sophie took one look at me then burst into tears. I often have that effect on people. I invited her inside with Dylan and made some tea. I arranged some custard creams on a plate. It was one of those occasions.

The police had paid a visit, Sophie said.

I asked her whether one of them possessed the most magnificent beard. She glared at me and I decided to keep quiet from that point on and let her do all the talking.

They'd been making some enquiries into Stuart's charitable

works, they told her. Stuart was out at the time, hosting a Zum-bathon in aid of maimed Bulgarian circus workers.

The police had received an anonymous phone call. The mystery caller claimed that the funds Stuart had been raising from his good deeds had not quite been making it into the bank accounts of his supported charities. What's more, many of these supported charities didn't seem to have any charitable status at all. The following day, in the post, the police received copies of all Stuart's bank statements for the last three years on which a number of rather sizeable deposits had been circled in red with an exclamation mark written next to each one. Also enclosed was a recent leaflet featuring Stuart and advertising a 'Motivatathon'; the list of supposed charities featured on it were also accompanied by exclamation marks.

I noticed the faint traces of a smile on Dylan's lips as Sophie mentioned this.

Stuart didn't return home on the day of the Zumbathon. Nor the next. Sophie sent a series of increasingly frantic and angry messages but heard nothing back, receiving no news of him at all until the police called her to say that they'd intercepted him at Heathrow, attempting to board a flight to Spain. He was wearing one of his motivational T-shirts; it was the one with the phrase 'SOME PEOPLE ARE SO POOR, ALL THEY HAVE IS MONEY!'

I tried very hard to keep my face looking concerned and sympathetic as she told me all this. When she got to the part about never wanting to see Stuart again, I suppressed my laughter with a fit of coughing – and then as she told me that all thoughts of moving were over, I sat on my right hand to stop it from punching the air.

I offered Sophie more tea but she said she had to be getting on. There were a lot of things still to sort out. Out of respect for the gravity of the situation, Dylan and I waited for Sophie to drive off before we began a prolonged bout of whooping and fist-bumping.

I ordered in pizza and we turned the TV on, just in time to catch the end of *It's a Wonderful Life*.

Sunday December 23rd

....

We See Gigs

We see gigs of ambient ska,
Acid jazz and indie guitar.
Blues and Britpop, soul and hip hop
Following yonder stars.

O stars of reggae, stars of punk,
Stars of Belgian neurofunk,
Sublime evenings, sometimes leaving,
Trying not to get too drunk.

Avant-garde industrial rock,
Honky Tonk and bubblegum pop.
Cuban mambo, duelling banjos,
Seventeenth-century baroque.

O stars of country, stars of trance
Stars of new age folk from France,
Find some new kicks, dump the Netflix,
Enter into life's great dance.

....

In December, we have to take a flexible approach to 27th Club.

There are not many gigs to be found on the usual date so we just have to take whatever we can find.

Darren questioned whether a carol service actually counts as a gig but I pointed out to him that it bore all the hallmarks. There was a flamboyant frontman (the vicar), a rowdy crowd (the congregation), alcohol (mulled wine) and a band (choir) who played (sang) all their greatest hits (including 'Silent Night', 'Hark the Herald Angels Sing', and 'We Three Kings') as well as some of more obscure songs ('A Virgin Unspotted' and 'Whence Is That Lovely Fragrance Wafting?') to keep things real for the true aficionados. Like all annoying gig-goers, we sang along in the choruses.

Darren enjoyed it so much that when it was over, he got a book from the merch stand on the back pew. He says he may come back again next Sunday.

Monday December 24th

....

Tense Christmas

I *The Ghost of Christmas Past Perfect Progressive*
    Midnight. Awoken by a ghost.
    I thought I must be raving.
    But then he went and showed me
    how badly *I'd been behaving.*

II *The Ghost of Christmas Present Perfect Simple*
    The next night, a ghost again:
    with a much more recent scene.

More evidence piling up
of how unpleasant *I have been.*

III *The Ghost of Christmas Future Unreal Conditional*
A final late night ghostly vision.
But this one lacked the pain and strife.
I saw if I could be a kinder man,
I would create a better life.

....

I went to Mrs McNulty's house and watched *The Muppet Christmas Carol* with her. She tells me it's her favourite Christmas film, along with *Gremlins* and *The Shining*. Mrs McNulty may be as crazy as a wheel of cranberry-infused Wensleydale but she's not so bad, really.

Christmas can be a difficult time for some, particularly the lonely. I stayed with her to 11pm until she asked me whether I was ever going to leave, hadn't I got a home to be going to?

Tuesday December 25th

The big advantage of spending Christmas Day on your own is that you remain entirely in control of your own agenda: what time to open presents, what to watch on television, what food to eat, when to fall asleep on the sofa. The downside is the relentless gut-wrenching loneliness of it all.

Perhaps it was just as well, then, that Sophie had invited me over to lunch. She'd rather I weren't there, she told me, but Dylan had asked and I could at least help them get through some of the food and drink that she now seemed to have over-catered for. I headed over with my microwaveable nut roast.

For one day, at least, we were a proper family again. We

exchanged presents; I had a new diary notebook from Sophie and Gil Scott-Heron's *Pieces of a Man* on vinyl from Dylan. In return, I gave Sophie a Desk Calendar containing 365 Inspirational Quotes and Dylan got a copy of *Meat is Murder* by The Smiths. Then we ate too much food, argued about what to watch on the television and collapsed on the sofa, happy not to be going anywhere.

Wednesday December 26th

Job Interview with a Cat

Tell me, what is it about this position that interests you?
The warmth, perhaps? The security?
Or the power you must feel by rendering me useless?
Feel free to expand if you wish.

I see you have had experience of similar positions.
Can you talk about a time when you got someone's tongue?
Or were set amongst the pigeons?
Have you ever found yourself in a bag only then to be let out
of it?

Tell me, how would you feel if you had to walk on hot bricks?
What about a tin roof of similar temperature?
With reference to *any* of your past lives,
has curiosity ever killed you?

Finally, where do you see yourself in five years?
In the same position? Or higher up to catch the sunlight?
Or would you like to be where I am now?
Oh, it appears you already are.

Being sociable is exhausting, I find, and it was a relief to find some space for a bit of *me* time. Or to be more accurate, some *cat and me* time. She took up her usual position on my lap and I set to work on the new *Guardian Bumper Christmas Cryptic Crossword*.

It was a promising start: six hours in and I was already two answers to the good. 12 down, *symbiosis*, which *Chambers* defines as 'a mutually beneficial relationship', and 18 across, *catatonic*. The latter was an anagram. The clue was 'Action cat? Not this one.'

Thursday December 27th

I remained on the sofa through the night, so deep was the cat's sleep. She looked so peaceful that I had no mind to disturb her. The morning hours passed in that way, too, but by mid-afternoon I was in need of food and thought it was about time I moved.

It was as I picked her up that I noticed her stiffness – and that what I had mistaken for a lightness of breath was, in fact, an absence of breath. I placed her gently back on the sofa and stroked her, as the winter sun shone softly down upon her fur.

For she loves the sun and the sun loves her.

Mrs McNulty joined me in the garden as I was digging the hole. From beneath her apron, she handed me a hand-sawn wooden box, shaped like a miniature coffin. It was decorated with a series of elaborately carved runic symbols. The inside was lined with red velvet.

She said she had many more boxes back in her house if this one wasn't right. But it was perfect.

I laid the cat down inside it. She looked content. She was dreaming of her next life.

The service was a short one. I read a poem:

'I should like to sleep like a cat,
With all the fur of time . . .'

while Mrs McNulty recited a variety of incantations of her own devising.

'It's over now,' she said.

I shovelled the soil on top and walked back into a house full of emptiness.

Friday December 28th

I Folded Up My Grief

I folded up my Grief,
Laid it gently in a box.
Tied it up with ribbon.
Fixed a sturdy-strong padlock.

In the garden, it was buried
In a hole dug ten feet deep.
But when I went inside,
Grief was still with me.

I confronted it and said –
Grief, I put you in the ground!
Why then are you here with me?
Why follow me around?

Grief said – But I cannot be buried!
For of you I am a part.
You must carry me inside you,
I am chained around your heart.

Coming up for air, I decided to cycle into town to pick up next month's book group selection: *The Third Policeman* by Flann O'Brien. But when I went outside I found my bicycle had been stolen.

I took the bus instead, bought the book, then came straight back.

Saturday December 29th

Tomas rang and he dragged me out for a walk. He could tell something was up and I told him about the cat. I suspected something Wittgensteinian was coming my way and I wasn't disappointed.

'You know, Brian,' he said, 'Wittgenstein once said that "death is not an event in life. We do not live to experience death." '

'But I *have* experienced death. Just not my own yet. And I'm not sure I care for it very much.'

'I don't think many of us do,' he reflected, 'but death is not so easily avoided. Of course, Ludwig had a theory about that, too.'

'I bet he did.'

'He said that if we equate eternity with timelessness, then "eternal life belongs to those who live in the present." '

I thought about this as we walked on. And it occurred to me that, if Wittgenstein was right, the keeping of a diary was itself a form of eternity. For what was a diary if not a record of somebody's life as seen in the present; a journal of daily fragments of the here and now; a collection of tiny pieces of not being dead?

I began to share these ideas with Tomas but he started to shake his head. 'Well, that's not *quite* what Wittgenstein means—'

But I stopped him there. A poet should be allowed a *little* bit of poetic licence.

When I got back home, I called Liz.

Sunday December 30th

In the Betjeman Arms, we were on our third Guinness and second bowl of pistachios.

'This is my favourite time of the year,' said Liz, happily. 'I love the lull of these in-between days.'

'Same here,' I said, taking another gulp. 'Although yesterday I got so old, I felt like I could die.'

'Did it make you want to cry?' she asked, in mock earnestness.

I smiled. As ever, Liz had caught the reference.

'I'll tell you something that *does* make me want to cry. . .' I continued, for here was a topic to which I could warm, '. . . all these retrospectives on the year just gone. Whenever I switch on the TV or open the newspaper: Sports Personality of the Year, Wedding of the Year, Pipe Smoker of the Year . . .'

'Poetry Book of the Year,' said Liz. We shared an enjoyable grimace together.

'Can I ask you something?' I said, apprehensively. 'Why *did* you go and see Toby Salt in Saffron Walden?'

'Oh, I didn't go there to see *him*,' she'd said. 'That was just a coincidence. I went to see Chandrima. Her publisher had invited her to read some poems to promote her new book.'

'Chandrima has a book coming out?' I said, genuinely delighted for her. 'I had no idea. Nor that she was there that weekend.'

'Well, you know Chandrima. She's a quiet one. Her book's coming out in the spring, I think. Anyway,' she said, 'you've not told me what it is about these retrospectives that upsets you so much.'

'I think it's all that looking backwards,' I answered, after a few moments' reflection. 'I'm not sure it actually achieves anything.'

Liz looked at me curiously.

'That doesn't sound like a very Brian thing to say,' she said.

'You're probably right. But maybe I've changed,' I mused. 'Maybe I've got a bit better at being me. Or perhaps nostalgia just isn't as much fun as it used to be.'

Afterwards, I walked Liz to her bus stop. Her bus was already approaching as we got there and I could see her nervousness as she turned around to face me.

'Fancy . . . coming back for a nightcap?' she asked, hesitantly.

It was an interesting question, not least because it caused me to ponder on the etymology of the word 'nightcap' and whether it was coined after the garment of the same name, given that, like alcohol, it had the ability to provide warmth and comfort through the night-time hours, although recent research suggests that alcohol may actually have a detrimental effect upon one's *quality* of sleep, this being dependent, of course, like so many other health-related things, on the *quantity* of alcohol consumed. In other words, there is much truth to be wrung out of the phrase 'all things in moderation' . . .

I don't think Liz could have heard the last bit properly, though, as by that time she had already boarded the bus and was sitting upstairs, staring out bleakly into the cold, winter night, as it pulled away.

So distracted was her gaze that, at first, she didn't notice the man who was busy breaking the human land-speed record by outrunning the bus between its stops, nor hear the wheezes from his chest as he climbed up the staircase to sit down beside her.

Monday December 31st

....

What Goes Around, Comes Around

The world is spinning on its axis;
it never lessens or relaxes.
Through space and time, the planet hurtles
and every day it turns full circle.

It takes one whole year to round the sun.
Yet the revolution's just begun.
And there a simple truth is found:
what goes around, comes around.

Don't ask me why. Don't ask me how.
You'd be dizzy if you got off now.

....

It was only when I got back that I remembered I'd yet to play my Christmas present from Dylan. I took the record out of the bag and inspected it closely. Gil Scott-Heron looked understandably fed up at having to wait so long.

I unpeeled the cellophane and tilted the album to one side. The record slid into my hand. I took it over to the record player and placed it on the turntable. I lifted up the arm and, as the disc began to move, carefully brought the needle down upon its surface, and the revolution began.

A Note about the Poems

A number of poems which appear in the diary have been inspired – loosely, or heavily – by other poems, pop songs, Christmas carols and French grammar books.

1st January: Gil Scott-Heron, *The Revolution Will Not Be Televised* (1971)

5th January: Morrissey, *Everyday is Like Sunday* (1988)

6th January: Wilfred Owen, *Anthem for Doomed Youth* (1917)

7th January: Emily Dickinson, *Because I Could Not Stop For Death* (1890)

11th January: Joyce Kilmer, *Trees* (1913)

23rd January: a tweet by Ian McMillan with the same title and format

2nd February: Philip Larkin, *This Be The Verse* (1971)

19th February: William Carlos Williams, *This Is Just To Say* (1934)

22nd February: The Bee Gees, *Stayin' Alive* (1977)

24th February: Dylan Thomas, *Do Not Go Gentle Into That Good Night* (1947)

27th February: *The Lord's Prayer*

7th March: Stevie Smith, *Not Waving But Drowning* (1957)

8th April: New Testament, Mark Ch. 16

26th April: Kate Bush, *Wuthering Heights* (1978)

27th April: James Brown, *Get Up (I Feel Like Being a Sex Machine)* (1970)

10th May: Carol Ann Duffy, *The World's Wife* (1999)

16th May: Richard Rodgers, *My Favourite Things* (1959)

19th May: Collins Easy Learning *French Grammar and Practice* (2016)

8th June: Adrian Henri, *The New, Fast Automatic Daffodils* (1967)

25th June: John Cage, *4'33"* (1952)

1st July: Edward Thomas, *Adlestrop* (1917)

29th July: R.E.M., *Everybody Hurts* (1992)

2nd August: W.H. Auden, *Funeral Blues (Stop All the Clocks)* (1936)

18th September: William Wordsworth, *I Wandered Lonely As A Cloud* (1807)

25th September: Elizabeth Barrett Browning, *How Do I Love Thee?* (1850)

29th September: Blur, *Parklife* (1994)

6th October: A. A. Milne, *Buckingham Palace* (1924)

11th November: Clive James, *The Book of My Enemy Has Been Remaindered* (1983)

23rd December: John Henry Hopkins, Jnr, *We Three Kings* (1857)

Acknowledgements

As Stuart Mould might say 'Teamwork makes the dream work', and I'd like to thank all those who have helped and supported me throughout the writing of this diary: my agent Jo Unwin, expertly abetted by Milly Reilly, whose wisdom and encouragement helped to save me from myself and this project from relentlessness; Kate Jaeger and Laura Montgomery, who braved earlier versions of the diary and gave me hope that all was not hopeless; the team at Picador, particularly Paul Baggaley, Kish Widyaratna, Camilla Elworthy, Nicholas Blake and Paul Martinovic, who bring such creativity and expertise to the art of publishing; Jon McNaught, whose cover illustrations are nothing short of perfect; Paul and Rachel, whose hospitality turned an unfamiliar place into a home for eighteen months; the twin institutions of my real-life Book Group and 27th Club, the existence of which ensured I'd have to leave the house at least twice a month; my long-suffering family, of course, for putting up with my moody silences and uncomprehending stares into the mid-distance; and the extended family of my Twitter, Facebook and Instagram friends, who have always shown me so much kindness.

Finally, I'm indebted to the enduring genius of Sue Townsend, who showed how a teenage boy from an unremarkable Midlands town might yet dare to dream.